Rig-a-dig-dig

or

Boy Entrant Blues

by

John Mount

This is a work of fiction in the main, although some of the things within did happen. The people involved in the actual events have given me their blessing.
1. Many thanks Danny.
With regard to the Dive Bombers: As far as I can recall there was no such ride in the Barry Island pleasure Park in 1962/63.

Note: The RAF boy entrant scheme ran from the mid-1930s to late 1965 where boys joined the RAF between the ages of 15 to 17 and then underwent training in various occupations (or trades). The accommodation and discipline depicted in this book is, to the best of my recollection, the way it was in 1962/63.

Table of contents:

Part One: Sprogs

Chapter One

I first met Ollie one freezing cold morning back in the January of 1962, in the Cardiff Station buffet. I'd just turned sixteen and was on my way to sign up for the RAF. He came crashing into the room grumbling. "Cold enough to freeze the balls off the proverbial monkey."

He threw his bag under a table,
The woman behind the counter looked up sharply. "None of that language in here thank you!"
He nodded and held up his hand. "Quite right my love." He gave her a beaming smile. "Not nice at all. I apologise." I'm sure she blushed.
He ordered a cheese roll and a tea and sauntered back to the table where he'd thrown his bag.
 He was a little taller than me, about five-eight, and a shock of blond hair hung over his forehead. My first thought was here's a bloke who doesn't have trouble pulling the birds, especially judging by that dazzling smile he'd flashed the woman behind the counter.
After a few minutes he looked over at me and nodded. "You on your way to sign your life away as well?"
He pointed to the brown envelope on the table in front of me and pulled one the same from his pocket. He waved it. "Snap." Then he laughed and came over to join me. He pulled a chair up noisily.
"Ollie," he said holding out his hand. "Ollie Wilson."
 I shook his hand. His grip was firm and confident and getting a close-up look I could see his eyes were a deep blue. His blond hair was swept back into what was known as a Duck's Arse and was heavily greased. This, along with his high cheekbones, gave him a slight look of Elvis. Apart from a few acne spots his skin was smooth and I imagined he didn't shave yet.
I smiled to myself, I had no reason to change my mind; this bloke shouldn't have any trouble getting the girls.
"Mark Draper," I said as we shook hands.
"So, Mark Draper, where are you from?"
"Margate."

"Margate? Wow, happy memories of Margate. Good old Dreamland, eh?" He fished in his bag and pulled out a packet of cigarettes. "London me. Deptford."
He offered me a cigarette. I shook my head.
"No," he said. "I ought to pack it in really. Shan't be able to afford 'em on a Boy Entrants wage for one thing."
He cocked his head to one side. "So, tell me young Draper, are we mental?" He didn't wait for an answer. "You know, signing up like?" He took a long draw on his cigarette and flicked ash to the floor. I slid a tin ash tray over to him.
"stone me," he chuckled. "Mister tidy or what?"
I groaned. "Sorry. Force of habit."
"It's a friggin' big decision."
I shook my head. "Have I missed something here?"
"Sorry, Draper, I was thinking aloud."
"So, what's a big decision.?"
 "Joining up. Big decision."
"Not for me," I told him. "I just want to get away from home."
 He beamed. "That's great, me too. We should get on well, Draper." Then a frown. "Still a big decision all the same."
I was about to remind him my name was Mark when the door opened, and three more boys came in. They put their bags under a corner table and went to the counter.
Ollie nodded in their direction. "More lambs to the slaughter."

   Hearing this Ollie bloke saying he was also getting away from home was just what I needed to hear. He sounded like a regular sort of a bloke, much like me. I'd been

5

dreading finding all the other boys smoking pipes and wearing cravats.

When the train arrived, I was pleased to see that he took it as read that we'd travel together. We found ourselves in a compartment with a chatty boy named Thompson but preferred to be called Tommo and a quiet, shy boy, named Adrian Chadwick. Chadwick was more like the type of lad I expected. No pipe or moustache but he wore brown leather gloves, an expensive looking overcoat and a cravat. He said very little but, when he did, his voice was soft. So much so I found myself having to lean in to catch what he was saying.

After a train journey to Barry we made another short journey to a backwater station called Gileston, where we were met by a tall, heavily built corporal. He stood near the station exit and waited until the whole compliment had left the train, then did a head count. He made a quick note on his clipboard and nodded. "OK lads, I'm Corporal Egan and I'm here to welcome you to sunny Wales, so if you'll just follow me, your carriages await."

Whatever form of transport I had in mind it certainly wasn't a bloody great, canvas covered, lorry.

"Oh, they're joking," a disgruntled voice behind me said as we stared at the waiting transport.

Corporal Egan ushered us on to the three waiting lorries and we set off.

As soon as we got under way the tarpaulin cover began flapping noisily in the wind and within minutes we were all huddled down in our coats trying to escape the biting cold as the convoy rumbled its way towards the camp. It was a journey of no more than a mile or so, but it was enough time to freeze my ears to total numbness.

As I tried to squeeze even further down into my coat I found myself thinking about what Ollie Wilson had said about having doubts. This was enough to give anyone doubts. Didn't we even warrant a bus?

As the lorries lumbered past the main gate and into the camp I got my first glimpse of the Camp.

RAF St. Athan was nestled in bare, windswept countryside in the Vale of Glamorgan. Here before us was what was to be our home for the next year and a half and it didn't look good. Not good at all.

The icy breeze now carried a fine drizzle. I looked around at a Guardroom, a distant line of wooden huts and a flag fluttering above a Parade Square and my heart sank. If first appearances were anything to go by this was one of the most uninviting places I had ever seen, and, under a slate grey sky and a mist of chill rain, it was grim.

The Guardroom door opened and a thin, pale-faced man wearing a large blue greatcoat emerged. The Corporal handed him the clip-board and he squinted over at us through a pair of flimsy looking wire-framed glasses.

"Right lads," he called. "Good afternoon and welcome. I'm Sergeant Watson. Now if you'll all fall in and follow me we'll get you in out of the cold and damp."

Less than half an hour later we were standing at the end of a row of identical drab looking, wooden huts where a large sign read:
Initial Training Squadron
Number 4 School of Technical Training
RAF St Athan.

We were shivering from the cold and clutching a pile of bedding, a pair of working overalls, a pair of black shoes, a beret and a large white china mug.

Not a moment too soon we were ushered into what was to be our new home for the next three months.

If the huts were depressing from the outside, then inside it was even grimmer. Surely it wasn't like this in the brochures they'd mailed to me?

The long, narrow room slept twelve; six on either side and each bed had a small locker one side and narrow wardrobe on the other. In the centre of the room were two small Formica topped tables with four chairs at each. The floor was a dull, shitty brown. Above the door was a large, black wooden box.

Ollie Wilson threw himself down on the bed opposite me and lit a cigarette. Us being billeted together was one crumb of comfort to me. He blew a long plume of smoke into the air and laughed gently to himself.

A tall, ginger haired boy, busily making up his own bed next to Ollie suddenly piped up. "Tha's supposed to be making op bed," he said "Not 'avin' ciggie break."

"Well bugger me!" said Ollie, jumping up and saluting comically. "If I'd known the commanding officer was in the next bed I'd have leapt to it. Sorry Sir."

He crossed to me, chuckling at his own joke. "Hey, Draper," he said. "What language was that geezer speaking?"

I knew exactly what he meant.

"This is worse than I expected," he continued, waving his arm around. "Christ, I thought the building site was depressing, but this? Bloody hell, it's straight out of one of them black-and-white war films. John Mills could walk in any minute now carrying our escape plans." He looked at me and cocked his head to one side. "I bet you're straight from school?"

I nodded.

"Yeah, well, not me. I've had almost a year on a building site. I soddin' well hated it; I just wanted to put a bit of money in the old pocket." He went to the window and flicked his cigarette butt onto the grass outside. "The truth is I couldn't stick it though. Crap way to make a living."

I set about making up my bed.

"And now I've seen this shit hole," he said, looking around the place, "I'm not sure I can see me sticking this either."

I spun round and stared at him. "What, you're backing out already?"

He fished in his pocket for his cigarettes. "I dunno what to think. I don't want to quit, I just didn't expect anything like this." He sighed heavily and came and sat on the end of my freshly made bed.

"Listen, Draper, like we said before, we're here for a reason. I'm like you; I'm not your fucking RAF Johnny. I know sod all about the RAF and I don't much care, I'm only here as a way of escape. I just want something to get me away from living at home. I just didn't expect Alcatraz."

I was a little taken aback when he swore, but then it occurred to me that working on a building site he'd pick it up there.

"You have no idea how pleased I was when you told me that." I said.

He nodded. "Yeah, we're in tune on that one."

9

I nodded. "The thought of going back to living with my shit of a stepfather, Alf, and beer swilling, bullying, older brother, Ray, is enough to make me want to hang on here however bad it is. It's the only bloody way."

He slapped my shoulder and held out his hand. "Put it their partner."

I looked at his hand and hesitated. "Does this mean you get to call me Mark and not Draper?"

"No sweat. Put it there."

We shook hands and, right then and there, the beginning of our friendship was forged. It was a hell of a relief to know I had a kindred spirit.

"I'll tell you something, though," I said, nodding to his unmade bed "The commanding officer over there's quite right. You've got a bed to make."

"Oh, sod that silly twat. There's no hurry? What can they do? They gotta be nice to us 'cause we're still civvies."

Just then a voice from the other end of the hut shouted that he could see the corporal heading back towards the hut. Ollie shrugged and set about making his bed.

The hut was mixture of accents and personalities. There were boys from all over the place: Barnsley, Newcastle, Bristol, Leicester, London and other lesser known places and my head was soon spinning from trying to understand some of the accents. There was a boy from the Isle of Bute who might as well have been from Outer Mongolia. The lad who told Ollie to make his bed was a tall, ginger lad called Andy Braithwaite. He was from Bradford and at first, I honestly thought he was joking his accent was so strange. He came up to my bed and said, "'As tha nearly done wi' broom?"

I had no idea what he meant until he pointed to the broom I was using.

.

The day after was signing up day. The last chance to pack up and go home for free. After that it cost twenty quid and twenty quid was something I didn't have.
Ollie and me made our way to the hut where the deadly deed was taking place. One of the lads from our room, a big lad called Geordie, tagged on beside us.
"I can't believe we're about to sign nine years of our life away," said Ollie. "I tell ya, we're fuckin' mad."
"You can still change your mind. It's not too late," Geordie reminded him.
I slapped Ollie on the back. "Not us, eh mate?"
He shrugged. "I still say we're nuts."

We signed away nine years of our lives that morning. Nine bleedin' years! Walking back afterwards it occurred to me that nine years was over half my current lifetime.
That afternoon, as if to remind us we were no longer civilians, we were marched to the barber's and given our first taste of a short-back-and-sides haircut. The barber was a good humoured civilian with a heavy sing-song Welsh accent. As I sat in the chair I ran my fingers through my hair and sighed. "Farewell trusty locks."
The barber shook his head. "The rule is: what goes under your hat is yours and what doesn't is mine. If you want to keep that then it's yours." And with that he ran the clippers quickly round the back-and-sides. I understood why freshly shorn sheep look so pissed off.

The following morning, we discovered the reason for the large box above the door when, at six-thirty, a voice crackled out of the speaker informing us that it was reveille, followed immediately by the sound of someone coming along the corridor hammering on a metal drum of some kind.

The huts were linked by a long corridor and the din, coming from the far end was making its way along the corridor toward us. The racket eventually reached us, and the door flew open.

The room flooded with light.

Boys spewed from their beds and staggered bewilderedly around like zombies in a bad horror film, eyes squinting against the intrusive light.

A corporal stood in the doorway holding a dustbin lid and a metal rod. "Good morning boys," he boomed, grinning. "I'm Corporal Egan and this is your early morning wake up call." The grin disappeared, and he strode into the room.

"Right you shower, out of them smelly pits! Hands off cocks, on with socks! Come on, come on! Let's be having you!"

He stood looking around the room at the startled beings around him. "So, here we are," he said. "A nice shiny, new clutch of Boy Entrants."

He tapped the side of his leg with the iron bar as he spoke. "You have a lot to learn lads, and we expect you to learn very quickly. There is no room for skivers or shirkers and no room for schoolboys. You are about to become young airmen."

He gazed around the room nodding. "Right! Your first lesson." He shouted down the room. "ATTENTION!"

We all stood stiffly upright, arms to our sides and eyes to the front.

"From now on," he bawled, "at any time me, or one of the other NCO's, enter the hut, the first person to spot us will call out loud and clear: 'NCO present'. Have you got that?"

He paced up and down the room glaring with menace. He halted in front of Ollie's bed.

"You boy," he barked. "Name!"

"Wilson, Corporal."

"Right, Boy Entrant Wilson, I've just this second opened the door. What are you going to do, lad?"

Ollie looked at him blankly. "Corporal?"

"For heaven's sake Wilson are you stupid or just still asleep? What have I just been saying?"

Ollie twigged and called out, "NCO present!"

"No, no. Shout it out, lad! Shout it loud. The boy at the end can't hear you. Good lord lad, I'm stood here a foot away and even I can't hear you."

Ollie threw his head back and bellowed: "NCO PRESENT!"

"Better, lad, better. Now, when you hear this called out you will stop what you're doing and stand to attention. Is that understood?"

"Yes, Corporal," we all replied.

"I can't hear you again; IS THAT UNDERSTOOD?"

"YES, CORPORAL!" we shouted back.

He nodded and smiled. "Good." And with that he turned on his heel and was. Gone.

Ollie looked over at me. "Our corporal seems like a right nice bloke!"

I nodded. "Yeah. The embodiment of charm."

It wasn't long before Bonner, a brash and pushy lad from Belfast made it clear to us all he was doing things his way and his way only and there was no one going to stop him.

He was a powerful looking boy; not tall, no more than five-ten maybe – just powerful. His black hair was cropped short in a flat-top style a bit like the American GIs, and his square chin already, at the age of seventeen, showed signs of a five-o'-clock shadow.

He exuded menace and he frightened the shite out of me.

Every morning we were expected to make our beds and sweep our piece of floor space before heading for breakfast. There were two brooms in the room and, as we stumbled out of bed, we would call out our place in the queue for the use of one of the brooms. It was this stupid little ritual that showed us what we could expect from Bonner. He made it very clear that he felt himself above this menial process and simply grabbed whichever broom was nearest whenever he deemed himself ready.

At first no-one challenged him; we were all too scared. I'd never considered myself a coward, never had much bother at school or anything, but living with Bonner was a worrying prospect. I had no idea how I would react if he picked on me. He'd already threatened a couple of the other boys over almost nothing. He seemed intent on making himself public enemy number one. I reckoned the only one likely to stand up to him was Geordie. Geordie was the best part of six foot and had the physique of a rugby player. His black hair was thick and unruly, and he plastered it down with hair oil. But it wasn't him who challenged Bonner.

The morning Bonner took the broom from the end of Ollie's bed no-one took any notice; after all, it was expected that he would help himself to the broom as soon as he was ready. Why should this day be any different? But then slowly I became aware of the way Ollie was staring at Bonner as the big lad began sweeping around his bed. His jaw was clamped tight and his eyes bore into Bonner's back.

I remember thinking, 'leave it alone, Ollie; he'll kill you'.

But then Ollie spoke. "Listen, Bonner, there's a queue for that broom as you fuckin' well know."

Bonner paused from his sweeping. "And?"

"So, quit being such an awkward twat and hand me the bloody broom."

Jim Bonner grinned. "Jaysus, Wilson, if you aren't pushing yer luck here." He turned back to his sweeping.

Ollie walked over to Bonner and held out his hand. "Broom please, Jim."

"Fok me! Piss off, will yis?"

Ollie stood holding his hand out. "Jim, I was using that broom and I'd like it back, please." His voice was cool and steady and by now the whole room was looking on in silence.

"Yous'll get it when I'm done, okay?"

Ollie stood his ground. "Now, please, Jim."

Bonner leant on the broom, using it like a crutch, and pushed his face into Ollie's. "If ya don't get out of my face in the next few seconds I'll down ya. D'ya understand?"

The speed at which things happened was amazing. Ollie kicked the broom out from under Bonner's arm and before the lad had time to react Ollie's fist shot low into his stomach, once, twice, like a steam powered piston. A loud rush of air left the Irish lad's body and he bent double. As

15

his head came forward Ollie's elbow cracked into his cheek.

Ollie knelt and grabbed his face roughly in his hand. "You fuckin' well listen to me," he hissed, banging Bonner's head back down on the floor. "You may well see yourself as the big hard man here, Bonner, but it ain't gonna work. We've got eighteen months living together and we all know the rules and we all have to follow them, even you, so quit pissing around!"

But Bonner couldn't have answered even if he wanted to. As Ollie walked away rubbing his elbow Bonner was still fighting for breath and already a swelling was showing under one eye.

Chapter Two

The weather remained cold and grey and we were soon introduced to 'bull'. Bull, or bullshit to give it its full title, was our slang for cleaning. We cleaned the hut windows inside and out, we polished the brass fittings and we polished the shitty brown lino to a mirror finish. Polishing the lino was known as bumpering. The bumper being a heavy iron, mop like instrument, that we took turns in shoving round the room. Once we achieved the deep shine we were no longer allowed to enter the room wearing boots or shoes. The saying was: if it stands still polish it, if it moves salute it.

After a few days our uniforms arrived.

I was horrified at how rough the material was. It was like wearing scouring pads against the skin. It was so bad I very soon found myself pleased to wear the ridiculously long RAF issue underpants with legs that reached almost to the knee. At first, we all laughed at them, swearing that we'd never be seen dead wearing something like that. But, as soon as we experienced the roughness of the trousers we were quick to change our minds.

Our days were split between square bashing and classroom. Classroom being general education and things like 'the theory of flight' and 'RAF history'.

The lad we'd travelled with on the train, Chadwick, the one who had been dressed like he belonged in the RAF that first day, had really begun to interest me. He was a total loner. I thought it must be awful to be friendless even if it seemed to be the way he wanted it, and I made it my mission to say hello whenever I could.

Then, one morning, I was struggling to get my beret to look right.

It was proving to be a most awkward thing. I stood in front of full- length mirror outside the storeroom pulling it this way and then the other, but it just stuck out like something from a Norman Wisdom film.

Just then a hand appeared in the mirror and pulled it hard over my ear. "Here, let me help you."

I looked in the mirror to see Adrian Chadwick.

"You're trying to put it on square," he smiled, "whereas it actually needs to tilt towards your ear." He tugged it into place. "There, like that."

He was right. It actually looked something like right.

"Cheers, Ade; you're a star."

"Anytime," he said, and disappeared into the storeroom at the end of the hut.

I had never met anyone so shy. If you spoke to him he invariably blushed. He was medium height and build but his face was veering towards chubby and his cheeks looked as if he scrubbed them every morning.

He was always disappearing into the storeroom and this time I followed him in. I found him sorting through some books in his suitcase.

He looked up as I entered. "I was just looking for something fresh to read," he said, sounding strangely apologetic.

"Yeah, so I see."

"Do you read much, Mark?"

"Oh, bloody hell yeah," I said. "All the time."

"That's great. Maybe we could exchange?"

I nodded. "Yeah, okay, excellent idea."

I picked through a few of his titles. Apart from Dickens I'd never heard of them.

He watched me with a smile on his face. "Not your cup of tea?"

I shook my head. "Nah, I'll stick to my James Bond and Hank Janson."

"Good Lord, Mark, are you serious?"

"What?"

Sorry, that was a bit rude of me."

With that he rummaged through his case. "I've got just the thing for you. He handed me a book.

"Brighton Rock by Graham Greene?" I frowned at him. "And you reckon I'll like this?"

He nodded, "You'll absolutely love it."

"Okay, I'll give it a go."

I was about to leave but then turned back. "Adrian. Can I ask you something?"

"Sure thing, fire away."

"You seem an okay kind of bloke, why are you keeping to yourself to yourself?"

He sighed heavily. "You'll hate me."

I was intrigued. "Try me."

He stood. "I never expected to find myself billeted with so many ...." he thought for a minute. "Well, how can I put it? He pondered again. "Such a rough bunch."

I laughed. "I'm not laughing at you," I quickly explained. "It's just that I thought the same when I met you. Only in reverse. I thought I'd stand out like a ballet dancers cod piece. Loads of cigarette holders and posh accents."

"Ah, I see," he said. "And now I've been put in the snobby RAF bin and I've put you in with the rough bunch." He smiled and stood up. "It just shows how wrong we can be about people."

Then, to my surprise, he reached out and brushed my cheek with his fingers and then left the room.

That evening I lay on my bed and smiled to myself. I was winning; our conversation in the storeroom was by far the longest I'd had with him since we arrived.

But then there was the bit with my cheek. What the hell was that about? I could still feel his fingers on my cheek.

The following morning, we awoke to a winter wonderland. Having done the morning tasks and breakfasted, we lined up on the parade ground for the usual morning drill. The snow swirled around until, within minutes, we resembled a squadron of snowmen. The short-back-and-sides haircut

19

had removed any protection from the wind and my neck was soon painfully chafed.

Sergeant Watson shook the snow from his greatcoat. "This is in for a while by the look of lads, so it'll have to be plan B this morning." And we were quickly marched to a large, empty aircraft hangar.

As we lined up inside we heard marching feet outside. A squad of boys wheeled past the open doors.

"It's the senior entry," Someone whispered, and we all looked out as the squad filed past.

The boy out in front was wearing sergeant's stripes on his arm and, seeing us watching, called out at the top of his voice: "Rig-a-dig-dig!"

The response from his squad was a full-throated roar: "Oy-oy-oy!"

"Rig-a-dig-dig!" The boy sergeant called again.

"Oy-oy-oy!"

"Rig!"

"Oy!"

"Dig!"

"Oy!"

"Rig-a-dig-dig!"

"Oy-oy-oy!"

They rounded the chant off with a huge shout FORTY-FIRST!"

Sergeant Watson smiled. "See that lads? What you saw and heard there was pride; pride in their marching, pride in their entry and pride in their uniform. You don't have it yet; not by a long way." His smile disappeared. "But you will have. I'm here to make sure of that. In a few weeks from now that will be you. And woe betide anyone here who lets this entry down." He called us to attention. "You're the forty-fifth. Be proud of that."

20

As we set off marching again the Sergeant took us completely by surprise by calling out: "Rig-a-dig-dig." There was silence.

He called it out again, louder. A few voices called back: "Oy-oy-oy."

By the last line we were all calling out as loud as we could, and we finished with a rousing: "FORTY-FITH."

The chat with Chadwick in the storeroom seemed to lift him completely. He would quite happily come and sit on my bed for a chat. I felt quite chuffed. But then things changed.

During a lecture we were crowded round the instructor's desk watching a rifle being dismantled and Chadwick reached behind and squeezed my crotch.

I knocked his hand away and prodded him in the back. He turned and gave me a mischievous grin.

A few minutes later his hand came looking for me again. I pushed it aside and moved.

Come break time we went out to the NAAFI van for a snack and I took him to one side. "What the hell are you doing?"

He laughed. "Don't get in a state, Mark. It's only a bit of fun."

I looked quickly around. "It's not fun if someone sees us."

He squeezed my arm. "But they didn't, did they?"

"No, but that's not the point." I was a bit annoyed at his nonchalant dismissal but pleased it was just a bit of fun. I smiled. "Just don't do it again."

Over the next couple of days, it seemed he'd taken it on board. We discussed films we liked, TV, music and anything that cropped up and all the time he kept his hands to himself. I felt more relaxed.

Ollie and me were playing darts one evening when, out of the blue he asked me how I was getting along with Chadwick.

I stopped in mid throw. "What?"

"I just asked how...."

"Yeah, yeah. I know what you said," I interrupted. "I asked Why?"

He shrugged. "Just curious. He seems to have taken to you, that's all."

I was sure he knew something. Had he seen us? Had someone else seen us and told him about it?

"There has to be a reason why."

He went to the oche. "Not at all. I simply wondered." He concentrated on his dart throwing.

"Ollie, there is no way you...."

"Hey," he said chalking up his score. "Subject closed, okay. Your throw."

It was an hour of sweeping that brought it all to a head. To my amazement I failed a kit inspection with dirty buttons. I was really pissed off, especially when Ollie found it funny. There was nothing wrong with the buttons to my mind. "I honestly believe they just wanted someone to do the sweeping or cleaning somewhere. I was just the lucky one."

Ollie laughed. "It wouldn't surprise me."

Luckily my fatigues amounted to simply sweeping the classroom floor the following evening.

It was a piece of cake.

I reported to the duty officer who just said he would be back in an hour and I should do whatever it was I was supposed to do. He clearly didn't give a toss.

I slipped off my tunic, rolled up my sleeves and set about sweeping.

In less than twenty minutes I was almost finished so I sat at one of the desks and slipped my book out of my bag.

I had only read a couple of pages when I heard someone coming. I quickly put away my book and carried on with my work.

The door opened and in walked Chadwick.

"Adrian," I said frowning. "What the friggin' hell are you doing?"

He smiled. "Come to chat with my friend Mark."

"Well, you can't. This is out of bounds. I suggest you leg it before the duty officer comes back."

"I'll risk it," he replied, strolling into the room.

As he walked towards me it occurred to me that he really was coming out of his shell these past few days. Far more confident and relaxed.

"Adrian don't be daft." I hissed. If you get caught, you'll be on a charge."

"Just a bit of a chat," he pulled a chair up and sat down. "But first a question. Have you spoken to your pal Wilson about us?"

"Don't be a prat. Course not. Besides there's nothing to talk about. Nothing happened. What made you ask that?"

He shrugged. "He just seems to be giving me strange looks."

I laughed. "You're paranoid."

"Maybe, but we don't want to get tongues wagging." He pulled his chair nearer. "You were correct about me being silly in the classroom. Sorry."

I grunted. "Well, yeah, glad you realise it."

He reached over a touched my knee. "We're safe here."

My heart sank. Surely, he wasn't going to try again?

"Adrian don't even think about it."

He ignored me. His hand moved smartly from my knee to my crotch.

I stood up quickly, sending my chair spinning backwards. "I don't believe you. Not again?"

But he looked surprised. "Why? You were okay with it in the classroom."

I shook my head. "No way!"

He became flustered. "But you... I mean... I don't understand. You were laughing and... "His voice petered out.

"I was okay with the classroom because you made it out to be a joke thing."

"That's okay. We can keep it a fun thing," he said, suddenly brightening up. "That's fine, anything you want," and he reached out for me again.

No Adrian!" I snapped. "Pack it in! Not a fun thing or any other thing, I'm not interested. You've got the wrong guy."

He looked stunned. "But," his cheeks flamed. "I honestly thought..." he went silent.

I sighed. "I'm sorry Adrian, it's just not my thing."

"No," he said quietly. "I'm the one saying sorry." He rubbed his forehead. "I really am sorry." He looked like a child who had just been severely scolded. "I don't know what to say." He shook his head. "I honestly believed you were okay with it. You've been so easy to talk with and, in the storeroom, it was you who came to me. I loved that.

You made me feel special. Now I feel such a fool. I think I'll go now." He ran his fingers through his hair. "Yes, you're right; I shouldn't even be here."

I was amazed at the speed he'd changed. He looked bewildered and lost and I found myself feeling a bit guilty He walked to the door and then stopped. I thought I saw a tear on his cheek. "Can we still be friends?" he asked, his voice little more than a whisper.

He sounded so pathetic I nearly started crying. "Course. I'd like that," I replied.

He nodded then turned to leave.

"Oh, Adrian," I called. I pulled my book from my bag and held it up. "I'm loving Brighton Rock."

He smiled, wiped away a tear and nodded. "I'm so pleased."

Then he was gone, leaving me to ponder over what had just taken place.

Chapter Three

Early March we were told we had a bit of freedom coming. Okay, it was only a seventy-two-hour pass, but it was time away from all the square bashing and bullshit.

The day the news arrived Ollie came bouncing into the drying room where I was ironing a shirt. "Way ta go, eh Draper? A few days away from here. Can't be bad, eh?"

I grunted and carried on ironing.

"Oh right," he said. "We're still in that mood. Bloody hell Draper, was it something I said or something I did? You were sulky all day yesterday".

I banged the iron down. "No, not something you said; something you didn't say."

Ollie threw his arms in the air. "Stone me, what's that supposed to mean?"

I prodded him in the chest. "Some best mate you are! You bloody well knew about Chadwick and said bugger all."

He grinned. "So that's what got you all hot under the collar?" The grin got even wider, "Ah, right, I see. You've been indulging in sexual activity of a …."

"Woah," I interrupted. "Just don't say it."

He put his arm around me and kissed me on the cheek. "Fear not, young Draper, your secret is safe with me."

I tried to stay angry but failed miserably. "It's not funny," I said, unable to keep a straight face. "You should have told me."

"How am I supposed to tell you that. I didn't know he was a shirt lifter."

"Oh, yeah? Then what was all that stuff when where playing darts?"

"I didn't actually *know,* he was that way," he drawled. "I just had a gut feeling."

He shut the door quietly and hitched himself up onto a draining board. "Right, Draper," he said in a hushed voice. "Let's have it. All the details. What happened?"

I told him everything and when I'd finished he ruffled my hair playfully. "Excellent. Sounds to me like you handled it brilliantly."

"Okay, but I still say you should have warned me about your suspicions."

"Fair enough," he slipped down from drained board. "Now let's start getting ready for this leave and you can tell me about this strange sexual preference of yours," he laughed. "You've kept this quiet."

All I could think of as we got ready for leave was seeing my pal Lenny again and being back in Margate.

Margate was great place to grow up; or, I suppose, to be more honest, a great place to stay a kid.

When we had money, me and Lenny, would go to Dreamland amusement park. One of our favourite pastimes was standing by The Sphinx. If you knew the best place to stand the views were fantastic. As the unsuspecting girls walked across the bridge from one side of the ride to the other a jet of air would belch up from below and lift the skirts up high revealing stocking tops and, with a bit of luck, that creamy white bit of no-man's-land. And me and Lenny knew the best place to stand.

In the evenings the place would be alive with Rock 'n' Roll music blaring and lights flashing. The noise and smells weaved a kind of a magical spell that drew me in every time I went there: girls' screams mingled with the music as the big dipper plunged down the rickety, wooden track and roared up the other side. The sweet smell of candy floss and toffee apples one minute was replaced with the pungent whiff of onions frying on the hot-dog stand the next. The place was electric, and never failed to suck me right in.

More often than not we were too broke to go on the rides but somehow just being there was good enough.

And now I was going for a brief visit and I couldn't wait. Dreamland probably wouldn't be open but me and Lenny had plenty of catching up to do.

On the train from Cardiff to London Ollie and me shared a compartment with Colin Masters, a tall, quiet, likeable guy from Dover and Jim Bonner who was going to stay with relatives in Maidstone. It seemed he considered the travelling time to Belfast enough to put him off.

"Didn't anybody tell you?" Colin Masters asked. "The Irish lads were given an extra travelling day if they wanted?"

Bonner nodded. "Yeah, but I'm not that bothered about going home." He gazed out the window dreamily. "No fockin' way."

I smiled; it would seem another soul glad to be away from home.

We travelled in our best uniforms but the minute I got home I was changed into a pair of jeans, a thick woollen jumper, my bum-freezer coat and my winkle picker shoes.

It was early afternoon but the dark of a winter's day was already moving in.

I made my way to the sea front. The beach was deserted except for a man walking his dog along the shore line. I ducked under the railings and jumped down onto the damp sand.

I just walked. Going nowhere in particular, just walking. I began replaying the last few weeks. I compared the RAF that I'd imagined to the stark reality of the way it was. It was going to be a long eighteen months. I smiled at the memory of seeing the huts for the first time, they really were a slap in the face.

I thought about Ollie with his mates in Deptford, wondering what sort of life he led away from me. My thoughts inevitably turned to Chadwick and all that entailed, and I realised what a twerp I'd been.

I walked, with no idea of time, until I realised it was dark. I set off back, heading for the promenade steps.

Then I stopped and, without even thinking about it, I threw my head back and yelled out at the top of my voice: "RIG-A-DIG-DIG!"

And I could have sworn a reply of "Oy-oy-oy," floated back to me from out at sea. I laughed and set off for home for a bit of tea.

I'd written to Lenny that I was going to be home Friday, and we arranged a meeting that evening in The Pelosis coffee lounge.

He was already sat nursing a coke when I got to the café. He looked up as I entered, and I couldn't believe the change in him in such a short time. His wiry, brown hair was parted in the middle and very neat, and this on a guy who always had an unruly mane falling over his eyes. He wore a pale-yellow shirt under a light grey waistcoat and hanging over the back of his chair was a very nice-looking cashmere jacket.

I was still taking it all in when he laughed. "Bloody hell my mate, do you really have to have a haircut like that?"

I ignored him and ordered a coffee. The young lass behind the counter passed me my coffee and smiled. "I bet that's cold."

I thought she was referring to the coffee but then I realised she was looking at my hair.

Living in a camp where everyone had identical short-back-and-sides it wasn't something you thought about. Now, it was obvious. It was like some kind of badge for all to see.

Lenny was still staring at it as I sat down.

'Alright, don't make a big deal of it. Anyway, talking of haircuts, what's going on there then?"

"Eh?"

I pointed to his hair. "The Barnet, mate?"

He smiled. "Like it?"

I shrugged. "It's different, I'll say that."

"It's all the thing in the smoke."

"London?" I said. "What's going on there then? Hardly on your doorstep."

"I go up almost every weekend. Kip over at me mate's gaff in Bermondsey."

He tugged his shirt collar. "Just clock the threads. We go shopping at all the best clothes shops and in the evening it's off to a club for a bit of dancing."

As he went on detailing his life style I realised we were already different people. He was still my mate, but he was a working man now and I was still a schoolboy. I lived

looking forward to graduation day over sixteen months away and he lived looking forward to the next weekend.
I had just enough money to go the camp cinema once a week and buy essentials like toothpaste and polish and he could go shopping for clothes every weekend.
We chatted on for a bit, but I had no intention of telling him about our wooden huts and square bashing.
When we parted I was left feeling a little confused. Was I envious of Lenny's life? Yes, I suppose I was.
Had I made a mistake? Was the RAF life really for me? I wasn't sure now, but then again, had I ever been *really* sure?
Although I was not in any kind of hurry to go back to camp I was actually looking forward to seeing Ollie.

Saturday it turned somewhat milder. Maybe we'd turned the corner and spring was not so far away after all.
Ray was at home, so I grabbed my coat and guitar and went into the front garden. I perched on the front garden wall and sat quietly strumming. I'd sung a bit of Skiffle before joining-up, just at the Church Hall youth club and at the summer fete. Sitting on the low garden wall I ran through the songs I knew, in truth I was bored. Margate in the winter is just another cold and empty town.

After a while I became aware of a young girl standing over the road watching me. I stopped playing.
"Is that it?" she called.
"Is that what?" I called back,
She checked for traffic and crossed over.
She was quite nice looking although her mousy brown hair was a mess. She stood studying me for a while and then said. "Hi there."

"Hi to you." I said back to her.

It felt like she was waiting for me to say something but then she cocked her head to one side. "You don't remember me, do you?"

But I did remember her. Not at first maybe but, oh yes, it was at the local youth club less than a year ago and our skiffle band were playing there.

I remembered it very well because we went outside and had a really good snogging session.

I heard later from a friend of mine that she was known to go a lot further than just a snog.

"How could I forget you? It was a great night." I said.

She laughed gently. "I seem to remember you were a great kisser."

"Yeah, well, as I see it, it takes two to tango."

She wiped the wall with her glove and sat down. I suddenly remembered her name, Denise. Denise Holt.

She was a year below me in school which meant she had to be no more than fifteen. We chatted for a while and then she said, "you ought to pop over sometime this week I've got some great records."

"Oh, shite, I can't," I said with genuine regret. "I'm only on a short leave."

"How short?"

"Short, short, I said. Shrugging. "I go back Monday."

She thought about that for a minute. "Well, okay, what about tomorrow?"

I tried to sound nonchalant when, in reality, my stomach was doing somersaults. "Tomorrow? Mm, I think that should be ok."

Was this an invite for more than just listening to her records? If my mate Steve wasn't bullshitting me, it could well be.

She stood up and brushed her skirt. "Right then, tomorrow. My mum leaves around nine so call it nine-thirty to be sure?"

I nodded. "Okay, nine-thirty sounds fine.

I watched her walk away. "Fingers crossed" I said to myself.

My older brother, Ray, and me shared a bedroom and he had to be up at seven to meet his mates to go shooting. Ray being up at seven meant me up at seven; or at least awake. The last thing he would do before leaving the room was to give my bed a good kick. He found it funny.

 I'd normally managed to go back to sleep but not this morning. No, there was no way I could sleep now I'd started thinking about Denise.

I waited until I heard Ray closing the back door, slipped out of bed, opened the wardrobe and started going through his pockets.

"Come on, come on," I said under my breath. "Don't let me down."

He had three suits and it wasn't until the last pocket of the third suit that I found my prize. "Yes. Good old Ray."

I stared at the rubber Johnny in my hand and smiled, judging by the state of this packet Ray's love life wasn't up to much. He must have been carrying around for months.

The lubricant had started to leak out and I didn't want to make a mess of my pocket, so I wrapped it up in a bit of toilet paper and headed downstairs for some breakfast.

My mum was in the kitchen pouring herself a cup of tea. "Thought I heard you moving about," she said. "Bit early for you isn't it?"

I shrugged. "Just awake I suppose." I looked out the window. "Where's Alf?"

"He's gone in to work."

"What on a Sunday?"

"If there's a bit of overtime going he'll have it."

I popped a couple of slices of bread under the grill.

"I suppose it's being used to all these early mornings," she said, blowing on her tea.

I frowned "Eh?"

"You. Getting up so early. I expect you've got in the habit by now."

I smiled. "Oh yeah. I expect so."

"What do you have for breakfast in the Airforce?

"Almost anything really," I said. "Sometimes I have egg and bacon another morning corn flakes."

I took my toast to the table and started buttering it.

"It sounds nice. I expect you love it. More luxurious than here." She sipped her tea. "I bet you can't wait to get back."

I smiled. "More luxurious than this? I dunno about that, mum, but I'd much rather be here."

"Here with your dear old mum, eh?"

"Of course."

She gave a whimsical smile. "That's nice. I miss you being here."

I frowned. She looked sad. It had never occurred to me that with Ray and Alf out of the house from early morning to early evening, and me gone, she would have breakfast and lunch alone.

We chatted while I had my toast and tea and I was surprised how much sadness there was in her voice. I felt sorry for her.

I washed the last of my toast with my tea and went upstairs to clean my teeth. When I came down she was happily singing along with a Max Bygraves song on the radio. I kissed her on the cheek.

It was half-past-nine.

Denise opened the door, looked around for a second and then ushered me in.

The record player was upstairs in her bedroom and I followed her up. The bedroom was huge and there didn't seem to be anything she hadn't got.

There were fitted wardrobes all along one wall and a dressing table and mirror on the other. She had a double bed with a bedside table either side. One table held a telephone and on the other was an auto change record player.

I sat down on the chair at the dressing table.

"Stone me, Denise," I said. "Is this all yours?"

"Well of course it is,' she said laughing. "Who else is there?" She was sifting through a box of records. "What would you like?"

"I'm not fussed. Have you got any…" I was about to say Shadows when she gave a strange squeak and slipped a record out from its sleeve. "Ooh, I love this one." She loaded it onto the spindle and pressed the play button. The Everly Brothers 'Dream' floated into the room. She held out her arms. 'Dance?"

I went over to her, but she gave a frustrated sighed and turned me round. "Don't be silly. You can't dance with your coat on."

35

I slipped out of my coat and joined her.

We shuffled slowly round the room for a minute or so and then she whispered. "Kiss me."

I pulled her to me and put my lips to hers and we kissed as we slowly circled the room. Then suddenly she opened her mouth and pushed her tongue into my mouth. At first I was shocked, but I quickly joined in and it was wonderful.

The record finished and she broke away from me and went to the record player. She filled the spindle to the top. A record dropped noisily onto the turntable and the music began.

Denise sat on the bed and waved me over, "Sit here, "she purred, and I didn't need a second invite. I don't know how long we kissed but it was heaven. After a while I chanced my arm and touched her breast. She kissed me even harder. I figured that was a good sign and slid my hand inside her blouse. For a moment she held me and then pulled away. I thought I'd blown it.

I couldn't believe it when she slid her blouse over her head and released her bra. She lay back and smiled, I'd never touched a naked breast before. It was so soft and smooth I almost stopped breathing. I squeezed them gently and she pulled me to her tightly. I wanted to look at her breasts again, but she was holding me too close. We began kissing again and she was moaning gently and pulling my hair. Well, at least the bit still long enough to grab.

After a while I felt confident enough to slide my hand up her skirt. This was new territory for me and I was aware of my hand trembling as I slid up the inside of her thigh. She made no effort to stop me. I reached her panties and she was soaking wet.

I had no idea what to do and it was a shaky hand that pushed aside the wet garment.

Whatever I *was* doing she seemed to be enjoying it, her breath was coming in short moans and groans.

Then she did something that took me to another place; she slid her hand inside my trousers and held my cock. She squeezed gently, and I felt a shock wave shoot through body.

I pushed her hand away and quickly undid my trousers and freed myself. I realised that without intending it I had removed my pants as well.

Her hand returned, and she stroked me gently. "Have you got anything?" She asked.

I jumped from the bed and rummaged in my coat pocket and, having found the leaking packet, jumped back onto the bed.

I lay next to her and tried to fit it. The bloody thing wouldn't go on. Whatever I tried it refused to slide down. "Let me," she whispered.

She took it from me and turned it over. I felt such a fool. She smiled at me and began to slowly roll the cool rubber down onto my hot, swollen cock.

She slid it all the way down and began slowly rubbing me as she did and suddenly I realised I was in trouble. Big trouble.

I was throbbing and twitching completely out of control and I could only look down in horror and watch as the little bulb at the end began to slowly fill.

I glanced up at Denise and saw that she was staring at it as well.

She giggled. "Oh dear, that was a surprise. I hope you've got another one?"

As my cheeks flared I shook my head. "I'm sorry."

I was about to say that this has never happened before but then thought better of it; she was clearly so experienced she must know this was my first time.

She giggled again, and I simply wanted a big hole to open up for me.

"Can you get another one?"

"I dunno. I suppose I could nip to the barber's shop."

She looked at me and sighed. "On a Sunday?"

I was devastated. The moment was gone, and I'd totally blown it.

"What about Monday?" She asked, quickly dressing.

"I can't," I reminded her grumpily "I'm going back to camp Monday, remember?"

I watched her fasten her bra and took a last look at those wonderful breasts.

"Bugger, bugger, bugger!" I groaned. "What a bloody twerp."

Chapter Four

Monday evening, back in the hut, was pandemonium with
everyone telling their stories at the same time – or so it
seemed, and there were plenty of stories to be told.
I couldn't make up my mind about what to tell Ollie. I was
bursting to tell him about my amazing time with Denise,
but not so sure about the embarrassing end. Knowing
Ollie, he'd laugh his socks off and then, I dare say, it
would be all round the hut.

We were sat on his bed and I was half listening to his tales
about his weekend. I say *half* listening because, in truth, I
was working out how much I needed to modify my story.
Surely a little white lie wouldn't hurt?
"Anyway," Ollie said, having finished his tales. "How was
your time back in good old Margate,
I told him about my meeting up with Lenny and the about
the Mod thing and his clothes. Ollie snorted, "Sounds like
your mate's got more money than sense."
 I told him briefly about my guitar and about how I used to
sing skiffle in the local youth club. "It's in the storeroom, I
brought it back with me," I said. "D'ya wanna shuffty?"
Ollie shook his head. "Later."
"It was that guitar that got me chatting to Denise." I told
him.
Then I told him about Denise and the invite to her massive
bedroom and how I'd felt when I saw her naked breasts
and how I squeezed them.

Then I got near the end and tried putting off the finale.

"So, there we were snoggin' and what have you, you know, me playing with her down stairs bits and her rubbing me, it was amazing."

"Bloody Nora, Draper," he said and punched my shoulder playfully. "You lost your cherry. Brilliant mate."

I shook my head. "Well, No. Not exactly."

"No? You mean you didn't do it?"

"As I said; not exactly."

His eyebrows suddenly shot up. "Don't tell me. Let me guess." He grinned. "Her mum came home and caught you in bed with her poor little daughter, pants down and bare arse whipping up and down like a fiddler's elbow?"

I laughed. "No. Now just shut up and I'll tell you." I felt my face begin to redden. "You'd better not take the piss."

He sat listening, straight-faced as I related the story of the embarrassing ending.

"Is that it?" he said frowning. "

"I thought you'd laugh and take the Michael."

"Come off it. I'm your best mate." He stood up and slapped my back. "As if I'd laugh at you for that."

I nodded. "Cheers Ollie."

He grabbed his washing kit from his locker. "Off for a bath."

He turned and walked away. As I watched him saunter off I saw his shoulders bouncing up and down and I realised he was laughing. The bastard was laughing! Then he let out an almighty roar and left the hut laughing his head off.

I groaned. That settles it I thought, it'll be all over the hut by breakfast. Some bloody mate he is.

Nobody noticed Chadwick was missing until bed time. Big Geordie had the bed next to Chadwick and when he returned from the washroom around half nine he looked around the room and then in the storeroom and came back into the room frowning. "Anyone seen Chadwick?"

Silence.

Then Andy Braithwaite, the red-haired lad with the thick Yorkshire accent who had told Ollie to make his bed on the first day, called down the room. "Do you not remember, Geordie? He's been chosen as our Leading Boy. He'll be in his cosy little room."

Geordie looked at the empty bed. "Ah, right, okay. D'ya now what? I'll miss having old twinkle toes. He was such fun."

A ripple of laughter ran around the room and Braithwaite called back. "Whereas I bet he won't miss tha snoring and smelly farts all night."

But when Chadwick never appeared for breakfast next morning, it was the talk of the mess hall.

That morning as we were being dismissed from Corporal Egan's square-bashing period a voice from somewhere behind me shouted out: 'Excuse me Corporal. We were all wondering where Chadwick was?"

The NCO smiled. "Are we missing our young friend then?"

That was met with laughter.

"All right quieten down you lot. I expect he'll be back later today."

And that was that.

But, come lunchtime, when we returned from drill, we all knew different.

Chadwick's bed was made and there was a beret on it. And it wasn't Chadwick's. As we all stood like lemons, looking and wondering, the door open and in came a boy we'd never seen before. He retrieved the beret from the bed. "All right lads?" He chirped, adjusting his beret. "I'm Monkey. Your new roommate." He grinned, "ready for lunch?"

It turned out his name was Montague Keys, but he hated it so much he'd taken to calling himself Monkey, and it suited him.

He was a five-foot bugger-all bundle of nervous energy. His chiselled features gave him a weaselly look with a sharp nose and high cheekbones. He wasn't ugly more comical.

Within minutes of him joining us at our table for lunch it was as if he'd always been there.

Monkey had been in the intake above us but had to have an operation and it was a long recovery, so he had to move down to us in order to get back on track. "I've still been going to classes with the lads in my entry, but it was just a case of treading water until they could find a place for me with you lot."

He was happy to answer all the questions that came his way. I think he enjoyed being the centre of attention.

He insisted he didn't know anything about Chadwick. "To be honest with you lads I've never even heard the name before." He looked round the table at all the doubting faces. "Straight up lads cross me heart and whatever else you want."

By this time, we all seemed to be drifting into our own little cliques. All, that is except Bonner and Monkey.

Bonner remained a loner. The episode with the broom had had little or no effect on him. Monkey, on the other hand, straight away made it clear he just wanted to be everybody's friend.

It was early the following week that the news reached us. We now had a new Leading Boy, Colin Masters, the, tall quietly spoken lad from Dover and it was he who told me and Ollie about Chadwick.

We were reading the duty roster when Masters' head popped out of his room.

"Hey, lads, don't tell anyone I told you this okay?" he said in a hushed voice."

We both nodded. "Only, I know you were a pal of his, Mark."

I stared at him. "Who?"

"Chadwick."

"Chadwick?"

"Yeah, it looks like he was caught misbehaving with another lad on the train. He's been booted out."

My heart sank. "Oh no, the silly sod. Who was the other lad?"

Colin master's shrugged. "That's all I know. Honest. I don't even know for sure that I heard right."

"Who told you?" Ollie asked.

Masters shook his head, "actually nobody. When I was called into the NCO's hut to get my leading boy lanyard I overheard Sergeant Watson on the phone. That's why I said I'd appreciate it if you keep it to ourselves for now."

He disappeared back into his room.

That evening I read the last few pages of Brighton Rock. Chadwick had been right; I loved it. I put it away in my bedside locker and thought 'well it's mine now I suppose. I can't give it back'. It would be my souvenir. I was going to miss him despite our little upset. All I could see in my head was him standing in the doorway wiping away a tear. "Poor old sod," I said under my breath."

At last the winter was giving way to milder days. Most evenings when all our duties were done and dusted I went down the corridor to the drying room with my guitar. Playing in the hut was not welcomed and the drying room had much better acoustics.
The drying room was more an ironing room than a drying room. It was shared by all the huts in our line and each room had its own iron.
I was quite happy sat playing while boys ironed trousers or shirts. Occasionally someone would come in just to listen and at times we'd even get a sing song going.

I was singing one of my skiffle songs one evening when a lad I'd seen before, but never spoken to, came and stood, arms folded, and watched me. Something about the way he studied my playing told me he was somewhat unimpressed.
He watched as I finished my song and smirked. "Every time I pass this room you're playing the same songs."
"So?" I said gruffly. "It's just stuff I like playing. You don't have to listen."
He shrugged. "Okay." Then he turned and left.
I shook my head. What a strange bloke.

Less than ten minutes later he returned carrying a somewhat battered guitar.

He sat himself next to me. "Lonnie Donegan pinched all that stuff."

I frowned. "What?"

"Yeah," he said, tuning his guitar "He calls it Skiffle but it's American folk music with a bit of Bluegrass thrown in for good measure." He cocked his head to one side. "I bet you don't know where the word Skiffle actually comes from?"

I mimed a long, gaping, yawn, but it seemed he had a rather thick skin because my sarcasm was simply ignored. "Skiffle Parties were thrown to get money to help a neighbour pay the rent in the very poor neighbourhoods in the southern states."

I yawned again, and this time he smiled. "Okay, I get the point. Sorry."

I grunted. "Well thanks for the lesson anyway. Is it okay if I carry on now?"

He strummed a chord. "I didn't mean to bore you," he said, "but music is my passion, from The Shadows to Chuck Berry and from Elvis to Peggy Lee."

I nodded. "Good for you, but if you remember, before you took over I was enjoying myself playing silly skiffle songs. Is it okay to carry on now?"

"Look," he said. "We seem to be getting off on the wrong foot here. "My fault entirely." He offered me his hand. "I'm Tony. Tony Charles but everyone calls me Chas."

I shook his hand. "Mark Draper."

He was lean and wiry, and his sandy coloured hair was soft and combed in a neat quiff. He was obviously quite passionate about his music and clearly not going to be put off by my disinterest.

"Do you know this one?" he asked and started playing his guitar. I sat mesmerised as he played, using his fingers and thumb to pick out the melody notes I didn't know it at all and I shook my head. "No idea."

"It's by an American Country guitarist," he said.

I asked him where he'd learned that fingerpicking style, but he just started playing another song.

He played a couple more songs and then took his guitar off. "Right, that's it, gotta go, letters to write." He took a cloth from his pocket and ran it up and down the strings. I laughed. "Is it worth it? It's about ready for the scrapyard." He laughed. "Ya cheeky sod, I made this with my own fair hands. It's a work of art."

"I'm just jealous because I can't play like that," I said.

He paused in the doorway. "Sorry if I ruined your sing-song. I get carried away at times. We could get together now and again if you like."

I nodded. "Okay by me.'

Life trundled along, each day much like the day before. We seemed to be over the squabbling stage and even happy to work as a team. Even Bonner seemed to make an effort.

I met up with Chas whenever I could, and he drew a page of chords for me to learn. I would need to get learning quickly, he was miles better than me.

Yes, things were improving and when we were told we were to be granted permission to go off camp the coming weekend we were over the moon.

It was to be a short moment of freedom, starting Saturday lunch straight after classes and finishing no later than nine. I'd decided I'd take a walk locally to the village of Llantwit Major, a couple of miles away.

There was one little snag. On the Thursday before the weekend passes were to be handed out we were told we were to have a full kit and room inspection on the Friday and anyone failing, for whatever reason, would not be given a pass.

Masters, the Leading Boy, pinned the notice on the board and called down the room. "I suggest we get up at six and make sure we all get it right. You'll each inspect the finished kit of the next bed down. We'll be leaving nothing to chance."

"Six?" grunted Bonner. "Feckin' hell man, half-six is bad enough. How long does yous all need to do a kit layout?" He looked around the room. It was clear by the looks coming his way he was a lone voice. He shook his head and gave a disgruntled sigh. "Okay, okay. Up at six we are."

Masters gave a satisfied smile and went back to his room.

By half-six we were all about done. We agreed to get breakfast and then inspect each other's lay out. The inspection was around eight, depending which end of the corridor they started, and we were breakfasted and washed, and all finished by seven-thirty. It went like clockwork. We waited.

Then someone saw them approaching. "They're starting at the other end."

We were ready.

But not for a raid.

The door to our hut flew open and half a dozen Senior Entry boys rushed in. Before we had time to do anything about it four of them were running down the newly buffered floor, wrecking the kit lay-outs as they passed and the two tail end Charlie's were throwing stuff at the windows.

Then they were gone.

There was a stunned silence. "Oh shit!" Geordie shouted." Bastards. The lousy fuckin' bastards."

But there was nothing else to be said. The room was awash with panic as we struggled in vain to get the kit repaired. It was never going to be.

Friday evening Masters came in carrying a paper bag. "Listen lads." He called. "The whole room failed the inspection, so, no surprise there."

A disgruntled mumbling filled the room.

"Hold on, hold on. Before you get too pissed off there's a bit of good news." He smiled. "Well for most of us."

"Come on," I said, "don't stand there smiling, spit it out."

'Sergeant Watson says it's unfair to punish everyone. Between you and me I think the inspection team had a good idea what had happened. Anyhow, whatever his reason, he says only two of us will have to stay here on Saturday and clean the windows and bumper the floor." He held up the paper bag. "Hence the bag. We're all in there and we just need two names drawn out." He shook the bag. "Who wants to do the deadly deed?"

Tommo Thompson piped up. "Give it here. I'll do it." He drew a slip of paper and read out, "Geordie Mason." Geordie moaned. "Shit' I've just ironed my trousers specially."

Tommo dipped into the bag again. He glanced at the slip of paper then over at me. He grinned. "Mark Draper."

"You don't have to look so pleased ya twat," I said snatching the paper slip from him. I glanced at my name and screwed it up.

I tried to look on the bright side. Cleaning the windows and floors wouldn't take long.
We watched as one after the other the lucky ones left the huts for their Saturday afternoon break. When they'd all gone Geordie smiled at me. "Pie?"
Nearly all the lads had food sent from home. My mum always sent me home made fruit cake every couple of weeks or so. Geordie's mum had made him a rather tasty looking beef pie.
"As soon as we get this cleaning done we can have a game of cards and a bit of pie," he suggested. "Not a bad way to spend the afternoon,

And, sure enough, we made short work of the cleaning and I got the cards and Geordie fetched the pie.
"Can you manage half?" He said putting the pie on the table. "It's a big un."
He wasn't joking. "That's what I call a pie," I laughed. "Pity it's not hot."
He nodded and shuffled the cards. He was about to deal when he suddenly had a brain wave. "You like your pie hot my friend? Then hot pie you shall have."
He disappeared into the storeroom and seconds later he re appeared holding the iron. "Ta-daaa," he sang. "A pie heater."
It took ages for the pie to get anything like hot on the iron; In truth it was hardly that hot when, eventually, he cut it in half.
Not hot but very tasty and packed with beef.

49

I thought no more of it until the following week Bonner received a parcel. He ripped open the brown paper package to reveal a pair of pale blue trousers. He held them up and inspected them.

"New kecks Jim?" asked Monkey. "Very smart."

Bonner shook his head. "My best trousers. Got them sent from home." He eyed them with pride.

"Why didn't you bring them back off leave?" Ollie called.

Bonner screwed the packaging up and stuffed it in the bin. "I didn't go home."

"Ollie held up his hand. "Yeah, of course. I remember."

Bonner shook the trousers. "In need of a quick ironing," he said.

With that, he got the iron from the storeroom and made his way to the drying room.

A roar echoed through the corridor and seconds later Bonner made his entrance. The door flew open and he stood holding his trousers which now had a long, greasy mark down one side.

"Who the feckin' hell used the iron last?" he bellowed, looking round the room.

"I'm gonna kill some bastard in this room!"

He stormed into the room, eyes glaring and face reddening. "Come on. Who was it?"

"Steady down here Jim." Masters had emerged from his room. "What's this all about?"

Bonner swung around and pushed the trousers in the Leading Boy's face. "This here is what it's all about?"

Masters pushed the trousers away gently, looking a bit like he wished he'd stayed in his room. "Okay, Jim," he said softly. "I can see why you're upset, but …"

"But fock all," roared the big Irishman. "Some little shite is gonna pay for this."

I then made a big mistake. I looked over at Geordie.

He was straining like mad to keep a straight face.

He caught my eye and shook his head as if to say I can't hang on. I'm going to laugh, I know I am.

I knew I had to look away, if I didn't I'd join him. But looking away didn't work because in my mind's eye I could still see him. He was going to drop us right in it.

Eventually, I took a deep breath and looked over to him. He was pretending to dry his face on a towel, Jamming a handful into his mouth. This was even more dangerous than before because he looked hilarious.

I glared at him and mouthed "NO."

Bonner was stomping along the room towards hid bed but suddenly stopped dead and turned to face me. He'd seen me.

"What's up with you Draper?"

I felt my stomach lurch. In two strides he was standing so near I could feel his breath on my face.

"Nothing. Why?"

"You were saying something to someone." He looked across the room. "Mason, I think."

Geordie wasn't laughing any more. "What are you two hiding?" Bonner said, calming down a fraction. He looked over at Geordie then back at me. I wasn't sure what to say.

"I asked yous a question." He poked me in the chest. "Are you deaf?"

"For fuck's sake, Jim, I'm telling ya," I hoped my voice wasn't sounding too shaky. "Nothing."

"Someone's put oil or grease on the iron and it's ruined my best trousers. I don't care if we're stood here all feckin' night, someone's gonna tell me who did it, and you

Draper, *you* are fucking well up to something, I bloody know it and if you don't want to lose your teeth any moment now I suggest yous tell me what!"

I tried to swallow but my throat had turned to sand paper. I wanted to sit down but daren't move. This could get out of hand.

Geordie let out a heavy sigh and came across to my bed space. "Give me the friggin' trousers Jim." He took the trousers from Bonner. "It was my fault, so if you've got to smack somebody then it's me." His voice was calm and resigned. "I did it, but I didn't know I'd done it. Sorry mate." He rolled the trousers up and put them under his arm. "I'll get 'em cleaned. For you. Okay"

To my utter amazement the big Irishman calmed right down. Geordie had somehow taken the sting out of the situation.

He grunted. "Fair enough, but if they don't come clean? What then?"

Geordie smiled, "you can take it out on my body."

"Oh, don't worry about that," Bonner said, the menace returning, "I will."

One evening I was sat in the storeroom strumming my way through a couple of new chords when Ollie poked his head round the door. "Me, Monkey and Geordie are off for a game of snooker. You coming?"

"Yeah, course."

"Good lad." He nodded. "Grab yer jacket."

"Will do," I replied. "Just give me a couple minutes and and…"

"For fuck's sake, Draper," Ollie snapped. "You spend so much time with that fuckin' guitar you're becoming a boring twat." He turned to go.

That really stung. I jumped up. "Woah! hang on, Ollie. Give me a minute to put this away."

Ollie just grunted.

I emerged from the storeroom and all three were ready to go. They gave me a round of mock applause.

"Come on, Draper, shake a leg or we won't get a table."

I fell in beside Ollie as we marched to the games room.

"Ollie is there any chance you might call me Mark"

'F'fuck's sake why?"

"I thought that's obvious. It's my piggin' name!"

He looked at me and frowned. "So's Draper."

I groaned. "I suppose so."

The NAAFI was unusually quiet, and we soon got a table. Me and Ollie had challenged the other two and I was just getting into position to take my shot when Ollie spoke.

"Ah, bollocks Ollie," I moaned. "You put me off my shot. I could've potted that green."

"Rubbish. You'd never have potted that in a month of Sundays."

I chalked my cue. "What was you saying?"

"I was asking what you and this Chas bloke are cooking up that takes up so much of your time?"

"Bloody hell, Ollie, you really have got a bee in your bonnet about this, haven't you?" I said tetchily. "I hardly know the bloke."

"So, what's with all this practicing?"

I sighed. "It's simply that he suggested we got together, and I said okay but I can't play well enough to join in with him."

Geordie bent to take his shot. "So, what are you going to do?" He took his shot and the red shot into a corner pocket and he called out, "blue," and moved round the table to get on to his next shot. Then he paused to chalk his cue. "You two gonna start a group or something?"

I laughed. "I don't think so somehow."

But it was something that had crossed my mind.

Chapter Five

That night, after lights-out I got to thinking. What if Chas was indeed contemplating getting a group together and I was the first person he'd found? I mulled it over for a while. Surely, I wasn't anywhere near his standard? There must be a better guitarist here somewhere. I was trying hard to get a few more chords under my belt, but nothing to shout about. And did I want to be in a band anyway? I decided Chas would say something, if there was indeed anything to say, when he was ready. I'd wait and see. I didn't wait long.

Two nights later I was in the drying room and I'd just started playing when Chas arrived accompanied by a big-set lad carrying a thin, black, cheap looking, bass guitar. I wondered if it was home-made like Chas's

He wasn't that tall: five-ten, maybe a bit taller and he wasn't fat. He was just a big lad. His name was Dave Wanderley, but he insisted I called him Jumbo. "Everyone calls me that,' he said grinning.

"Why?" I asked, straight faced.

He was just going to explain when he saw me beginning to smile."

He laughed. It was a booming laugh that echoed round the empty Drying Room. It was the laugh I imagined Santa Clause would have. "Right," he said. "Very funny. Had me there for a second."

Chas hitched himself up onto the giant ironing boards. "What do you want to try?"

I shrugged and turned to Jumbo. He turned to Chas. "What sort of stuff are you thinking of?"

Chas strummed a chord. "D'ya wanna try Walk Don't Run?"

Jumbo nodded. "Okay with me."

Chas looked at me. "C, A-minor, F and G."

He might as well have asked me to tap dance while juggling four oranges and whistling God Save The Queen. "Okay, not a problem," Chas said. "Plenty more to try."

Three or four more titles were suggested none of which I could play. Jumbo was just about to try another, but I held my hand up. "No more, lads. To be honest this is exactly as imagined it. I'm still learning. I'm not a three-chord trick merchant any more but I'm still a wee way from playing in a group."

There was a silence.

Then the door opened, and a curly haired, boy barged in. "Ah, I heard you were here."

"Paul?" Chas said looking surprised to see this newcomer. "I thought you weren't interested?"

"No, I said I've not got my guitar here. I'm still interested."

Chas pointed to me and Jumbo and made introductions. "This is Paul from my hut."

"Hi." Paul nodded to us. "How's it going?"

"Paul's a rhythm guitarist," Chas explained.

"Yeah, I'm bringing my guitar back after our next leave and then Chas said you'd be okay with me joining in."

I gave a short laugh. "Here, mate," I said, offering him my guitar. "Use mine 'Cause I'm not." I handed him the guitar. "Just bring it to hut N4 when you've finished." I said as I walked away resigning myself to the fact that I wasn't good enough to be part of any plans for a group.

The following week we were scheduled to go to the rifle range. I was gobsmacked. "Rifle range?" I groaned staring at the notice board. "We aren't going to need to know how to fire a bloody rifle f'fucksake!"

"I quite fancy it, Ollie said.

"Aye, make a nice change." Said Geordie. "Something different."

I seemed to be the only one in our hut that was disgruntled. There was a fair bit of excitement at the idea

The morning on the rifle range we found ourselves under new drill NCO's. Corporal Evans, a powerful looking man with a military 'tash and booming voice and a pale faced Sergeant with a nervous twitch in his right eye. He was Sergeant Sharpe. He walked in the room and proceeded to amble to the far end, looking carefully at each boy as he passed. Then he turned and came back down the room looking at the boys on the other side. He did this in to complete silence; Just the sound of his boots on the lino floor.

"Right," he said when he'd completed his tour. "I'm Sergeant Sharpe and this is Corporal Evans. We will be nursing you through the rest of your stay here in ITS and on into your time on the Wings. For those of you who don't know what I mean by the Wings, that's where you will move to when you graduate from ITS."

He tapped his wooden pace stick against his leg and then marched quickly over to Monkey. "Name?"

Monkey came smartly to attention. "Boy Entrant Keys, Sergeant."

Sergeant Sharpe waved him away. "Stand easy Keys." He looked at Monkey for a few came moments and then nodded. "Boy Entrant Keys, you look familiar. Why is that?"

Monkey explained, and the Sergeant allowed himself a satisfied smile. "I pride myself I rarely forget a face."

We were marched to the parade square by Corporal Evans and given the order to stand at ease. After what seemed ages, a three-ton lorry arrived on the square and Sergeant Sharpe jumped down from the cab. We were called to attention.

"Right you lot. This morning we're going to take our life in our hands and let you loose with a rifle. We're going on the firing range."

57

"Why the bloody hell do we want to fire a rifle," I whispered to Tommo standing next to me.

"YOU THERE!" The sergeant boomed. I suddenly realised he was pointing at me. "Name?"

"Boy Entrant Draper, Sergeant." I swallowed hard, but my throat was drying rapidly. He was coming straight for me.

"Right. Boy Entrant Draper," he snapped, standing right in front of me, "What's so important it can't wait?"

"Nothing Sergeant," I croaked. "I was just surprised we're going to fire rifles."

"And how are you going to defend your country if you can't shoot straight?"

Several ideas sprung to mind, but I simply nodded. "I suppose so Sergeant."

"Corporal. Notebook. Draper."

Corporal Evans scribbled something in his notebook.

We boarded the lorry rumbled off and we all sat in silence. I was wondering why my name was in the Corporal's notebook?

After a short drive we arrived at the rifle range.

Sergeant Sharpe gave us a talk on the Lee Enfield 303 bolt action rifle and then a demonstration on how to hold it, load it, operate the bolt and fire it. Once he was satisfied we'd all understood he turned to Corporal Evans.

"Reminder please Corporal."

Out from Corporal Evans's pocket came the notebook.

"Demonstration," he said flipping open the book. "Draper, Sergeant."

"Out here Draper," he called.

I marched out to the front.

He pointed to the six, long, mattress like mats. "Now we've established you're ready to defend your country, perhaps you'd give us all a demonstration of how to safely use a rifle."

I stood like a fart in a trance. What was he wanting? Where do I start.

"Come on Draper. We're all waiting. Prone position if you please."

I laid on the mat,

I picked up the rifle and loaded the ten rounds of live ammo the way he'd shown us. The gun was heavier than I expected.

"In your own time Draper. Ten rounds at the target in front of you."

I squeezed off the first round. Two things happened. First, the noise was so ear shattering my eyes started watering. Second thing was the pain in my shoulder. Corporal Sharpe was knelt beside me. "Hold it tighter. Right in to the shoulder."

He was right, the next shot kicked like a mule, but I didn't get the pain like before. By the time I'd reached my fourth shot my eyes were running so badly I was firing blind and hoping I was somewhere near to hitting the target and I was about a foot further back from where I started.

When all were done the NCOs collected up the targets as we were given a smoke break.

After about five minutes we were called back. "Some good shooting and some not so good and, would you believe it," the sergeant looked straight at me. "I'm pleased to say we actually have a marksman here today. Congratulations Draper."

I waited for the punchline. They were going to make me look a fool somehow, I just knew it. But the Sergeant came over and shook my hand. "Well done Draper. Now you'll have to get you needle and cotton out." He handed me a marksman badge. "Get sewing."

I smiled and thanked him but all I could think was how ironic; the one person who didn't want to shoot a bloody rifle was the one person to get a badge.

I was pissed off. When the idea of being in the group first came up I was not bothered about it. I'd even admitted I wasn't good enough yet. But now, now that this bloody Paul had shown up, I felt hurt and angry. After I'd left the Drying Room I'd listened at the door. My heart had sunk. Paul was really good.

"I know I'm out of order here, Ollie," I moaned, as we made our way to breakfast. "But I can't stop thinking about it."

"So, what you're saying is you didn't want to be in the group, but now you can't be in the group you're angry because you're not in the group?"

I nodded. "That about sums it up."

"Luckily for you, Draper, you have Ollie Wilson as a best friend."

"What's that supposed to mean?"

"I have the answer."

"Oh, yeah. What?"

"Become the singer."

He held the Mess Hall door opened for me. "Nice try, Ollie, but it's an instrumentals band."

We took our trays to an empty table and sat down. Ollie began buttering his toast. "That just leaves... "He trailed off.

"What?" I asked impatiently.

He grinned. "Ta-da-daaa." He did a drum roll on the table. "Be the drummer."

"Oh, bloody funny. I can't play the sodding drums."
Ollie shrugged. "Get learning, it can't be that difficult."
I shook my head and smiled. "That's so stupid it's almost brilliant."

It funny how things turn out. Ollie's idea seemed excellent one minute and downright bloody stupid the next. So, when I eventually decided to investigate this drumming idea, you can imagine how I felt when Chas announced they'd found a drummer.
We were on Sports Afternoon and making our way to the sports field when he dropped the bombshell.
"When? Who?" I spluttered. "I mean how did this happen?"
"His names Red and he's Senior Entry. He's in the camp brass band and he uses the Band Hut to practice. He has the use of the drum kit."
"Great news," I said, trying not to look too disappointed.
"Yeah, great isn't it? But it gets better. He gets us permission to use the amp they've got in the hut."
"Amazing," I said. "Really fallen on ya feet there."
Do you want the best bit?"
"There's more?"
He nodded, and his face lit up. "We're doing four numbers during the band's break at the dance."

When we parted company, I was pissed off all over again.
Maybe I really did want to be a drummer. It was almost as if I was back in childhood and I wanted the toys my brother was playing with until I got them and then I wanted whatever he was playing with next.
I set off jogging round the running track my head spinning.
I hadn't gone far before I stopped running. Something

dawned on me. This Red bloke was senior entry. They were graduating before long. I smiled to myself. "Bye, bye Red the drummer and hello Mark the drummer." I set off running again only this time there was a spring in my step. I said it out loud: "Mark the drummer." It sounded right. I felt sure I could do it and I felt sure that this time my head was straight. "Yes," I said to myself. "Mark the drummer sounded great."

So, there it was. No chopping and changing my mind this time. My mind was set. But, I thought, where do I start?

"Will you come with me, Ollie?" I'd decided to talk to this Red guy. I wasn't sure what I was going to say but I knew I had to do something.

Ollie was cleaning his teeth. I stood behind him talking to him in the mirror. "Why," he asked, spitting a mouthful of toothpaste into the sink.

I shrugged. "I dunno. Just thought you might, that's all." I turned away. "Never mind. I'll catch up with you later."

"Don't sulk."

"I'm not."

He flicked me with the corner of his towel. "Your sulking and trying to make me feel guilty. Well it ain't working. I'm playing dominoes with Tommo. Meet us in the NAAFI when you get back." He grinned. "Now, fuck off."

I was more than a little nervous by the time I reached the hut. Looking through the window I could see The Band Hut was mainly Senior Entry boys. I went around to the door.

A sign outside read: 'Band practice 19:00 hrs to 20:00 hrs.' I checked my watch. Almost half an hour left but there was no playing at the moment. I went in.

"Hey, you. Sprog," a Corporal Boy shouted. "Out!"

I remained in the doorway.

"Okay, So, you want to stay do you?"

"I'm just looking for…."

"Stop!" Shouted the Corporal Boy. "I don't want to hear another sound from you until you've passed through the initiation." There was a cheer from the others.

He waved me in.

I was shitting myself as I walked over to him. If only I'd insisted on Ollie coming with me.

"Right sprog. You've decided to enter the Temple of Band. Let the ceremony begin."

I shuddered, not knowing what to expect.

"Close your eyes. Dawson, if you would be so kind."

Someone came behind me and undid my trousers. A cheer went up as they slid to the floor.

The Corporal Boy put his hands on my shoulders. "On you're knees sprog."

I knelt before him.

"I'm about to put something in your mouth. You will not flinch. Understand?"

I nodded. There was a long silence. Then a strange moan began, quietly at first and then very gradually it got louder. After a while the room was echoing with this strange moan. It was like something from one of my Dennis Wheatley books. Then I felt something touch my lips and the humming stopped dead. I didn't flinch as the object slid in my mouth. I recognised it as a reed instrument; a clarinet or something.

"Now stand!" Ordered the Corporal Boy.

I stood.

"Blow."

I blew. A horrible squeaky noise came out."

"Failed!" He yelled. "The sprog has failed.",
Suddenly my underpants were whipped down and a shock
of cold water hit my crotch. This was greeted by a loud
cheer. I opened my eyes.
"You failed, Sprog. Leave the building, please."
I stared at him. "I'm sorry, Corporal, but I passed. I never
flinched." I don't know where this sudden bravado came
from, but I found myself stood, exposed and wet and not
caring. "I passed. I never flinched." I insisted. Several
boys clapped.
"What do you want?"
"I'm looking for Red."
"That's me." A tall, skinny boy holding a trumpet held up
his hand. "Who's asking?" Just one look explained his
name, his mess of hair was bright red.
"I'd like a word." I said.
"I'm listening."
"Alone."
He blew a spray of condensation from his trumpet. "Just
say what you have to say. You're holding up the band
rehearsal."
"You're playing drums for Chas's group at the dance, I
believe."
"Now tell me something I don't know."
I suddenly realised I was standing half naked. I removed
my sopping wet underpants and wrung them out. Then I
pulled my trousers up. They were also rather wet. "I want
to learn to play the drums."
"So, what's it to me?"
"Well, I was hoping you might get me started."
"I graduate soon and we're well busy 'till then."
I nodded. "I know."

'So, you expect me to teach you in a couple of lessons?"
There was a bit of laughter at this.
I shrugged. "Not teach me. Get me started."
To my amazement he didn't laugh or tell me not to be
stupid. He just nodded. "I'll be here after band practice."
I smiled. "I would wait but I need to nip back and get some
dry togs. I'll be straight back."

.

He was really helpful. He said the very first thing I'd need
is a set of drumsticks. Then he talked to me about getting
started and the first things I'd need to learn. He showed me
each thing on his drum kit.
"Most important things to bear in mind," he said when
he'd finished. "First: practise, practise, practise. Second,
practise some more. And third, believe. No matter how
long it takes to master the pattern you're working on, stick
with it. Just remember to believe you can get it and you
will."
 I was looking forward to watching him at the dance.

Chapter Six

The gap between signing up and our first bit of leave
seemed a lifetime, but the end of term leave was on us
almost without warning.

We sat the end of term exam and to my surprise it was a complete breeze. I honestly think it would have been harder to fail than to pass.

Our pay during the ITS weeks had been minimal to say the least. When boot polish or toothpaste or any of life's essentials came along it was especially difficult. The upside was the remainder of our wages, or should I say, the bulk of our wages, was saved for us and released to us when we were going on leave.

I was going home for a fortnight which meant a wallet full of cash.

Ollie and me had decided to get together for the day during the two weeks but left it open. "There's no point in getting together on a day when it's pissing down or blowing a gale," he said, and I had to agree with that. He was on the phone and I had a phone booth almost outside my front door, so I said I'd phone him.

The journey home was uneventful, and I slept through a big chunk of it. When I woke, rather than feeling refreshed, I felt stale and weary. Maybe I needed this leave more than I realised.

The weather was very deceptive. The first morning of leave the sun was shining in a clear blue sky, but the breeze coming from the sea was bitter. I was up early and out walking by eight-thirty. I had no intention of getting up so early, but big brother Ray couldn't resist his little bit of fun.

 He'd already given me a hard time at the tea table the night before.

His target was my hair. He thought it hilariously amusing to rub his arm vigorously over the stubble at the back of my head. Then, this morning, just as I was hoping for the luxury of a nice lie in, his idea of fun was to grab my mattress and tip me out of bed.

Ray was a hard man and I had no intention of taking him on no matter what he did. He was a farmhand and worked long hours in all weathers. All the heavy lifting had left him with a body builder's physique. I don't know what the pay was like, but he certainly earned it. I know I couldn't do it. But that didn't stop him being a complete arsehole.

I turned up the hill and round towards Cliftonville high street. There was a shop there I wanted to check out. The breeze had tuned my ears numb and it reminded me of our transport up to camp on the first day. I smiled to myself, thinking about all I'd been through in the first three months.

I arrived at the music shop and was looking at the guitars in the window when a hand grabbed my shoulder. "Mark Draper, as I live and breath."

I didn't need to look. "Ricky Windsor."

I turned and faced the six-feet-four mountain. "Bloody hell Ricky, you're still growing!"

He shook his head. "Nah, just put on a bit of weight, that's all." He looked at my hair. "I see you joined up then. You said you might."

"Yeah, well, there ya go. So, what about you? What are you up to these days?"

He pointed to the shop. "Ta-daaa. You're looking at my domain."

"Eh?"

"I'm the assistant manager."

He gave me a tour of the shop and we chatted for a while and I suggested he might like to join me and Lenny in the pub in the week.

He nodded. "Yeah, might just do that."

I went to leave and stopped at the door. "Oh, by the way. I almost forgot," I said. How much is a drum kit?"

He shrugged. Anything from fifty quid to a hundred and fifty."

I grimaced. "Oh, right. Got any drumsticks?"

That evening Ray surprised everyone by arriving home from work on a motorbike. He parked it in the back yard up against the house and walked in grinning.

Mum peered out the window. "Who's that belong to?"

His grin got bigger. "Me. I just bought it off Walter Cartwright on the farm."

"What do you want that for?" asked mum.

"It's a damn site better than biking to work."

I stood next to my mum and gazed out at a Royal Enfield motorbike. "What's that? A two-fifty?"

"Correct bruv. It's knockin' on a bit but she goes like a dream." He put his arm round my shoulder. "If you're a very good boy I might even take you for a spin."

Mum shook her head. "Horrible things," she mumbled. "Nothing but death traps."

Saturday morning, I decided to call on Denise. She told me her mother worked on Saturdays but as I neared her garden gate I saw her mum shaking a duster from an upstairs window.

I was completely thrown. If she was home I had no chance. I had no choice but to try again in the week. No Denise was too much to contemplate.

I left it until Tuesday and tried again. I walked past, glancing at the window, to see if her mum was there but couldn't see anyone.

I walked past the house a couple more times in the hope she might see me but with no joy. If she only knew how much courage it had taken for me to eventually go into the local barbershop and ask for a packet of Durex she'd make the effort to show.

After parading up and down the street for a lot longer than I should, I decided the only way to find out was to knock. As I walked up the path I sensed I was being watched.

I knocked on the front door and her mum answered.

"Yes?"

I smiled, trying to remember how Ollie smiled at the woman in the Cardiff buffet. "Hi," I said cheerfully. "Is Denise in?"

She frowned. "I know you, don't I?"

I was thrown. "Pardon?"

"You're Doreen Andrews boy."

I nodded. "Yes, Mark Draper. I was hoping to talk to Denise. Is she in?"

She shook her head. "I'm afraid not. She's staying at her gran's in Maidstone."

"When will she be back?"

She shot me a rather suspicious look. "Why?"

I searched my brain for a reason. "Erm, well, she promised to lend me some records."

"Well, I'm sorry, she's working there for a while. I can't say when she'll be back. Sorry." She glanced up and down the street. "I'll tell her you called."

The door shut and that was that.

That following evening, I met Lenny in the Dog and Duck pub. He assured me it was a place where we could get served. He arrived wearing a very snazzy dark blue, pinstripe, Italian suit. Instead of a tie he wore a cravat. I buried my face in my hands and groaned.

His grin went from ear to ear. "What's up?"

I looked up. "What the friggin' hell are you wearing"

"Smart eh?"

"Okay, yes, smart. I admit it's smart but… Well it's not ya normal pub gear is it?"

He laughed and sat down. "Nah, course it's not, it's my Saturday night dancing gear. I just thought you might like a shuffty at what the well-dressed Mod is wearing."

"Maybe, but it's a bit embarrassing. F'chrissake don't stand up and play darts."

We chose a table in the corner and sat down. I told him about Ricky hoping to join us later and he seemed pleased. "I ain't seen Ricky since school." He lit a cigarette. "Right, now we've done admiring the threads, tell me about RAF life, you never said much about it last time we met."

I told him about the huts and the early mornings and I related the tale of Bonner and the broom. I even told him about Chadwick.

But when I told him all about Denise and how for some reason she was at her gran's house just when I was hoping for my leg over he smiled a knowing smile.

"What?" I said.

"I hate to piss on your parade, Mark, but I already knew. It's the worst kept secret in the world."

"What? About me and Denise?"

"No ya daft prat. About Denise going away."

He drained his glass and pushed his empty glass my way. "Your round I believe."

"Yeah, no problem" I said quickly. "But what about Denise Holt?"

He leant over the table. "Do you know a bloke called Bradley Aims?"

I shook my head.

"No matter. Well, it seems he's been shagging her since she was fourteen. He's twenty bloody three, would you believe?"

I sat back in my seat. "Bloody hell."

"Hold on, my son, best is yet to come."

"I hope your not gonna say what I think you're gonna say."

Lenny grinned. "Which is?"

"He's got her up the duff?"

He was loving this. "Bingo! Give the man a teddy bear."

I stared at him. "You mean not only did I nearly shag a pregnant bird, I didn't need a bloody johnny after all."

He nodded wildly. "Ya just gotta laugh."

I didn't.

I went to bar and bought two pints. I was hoping Ricky might arrive as I was getting served but there was no sign of him as yet.

I put the beers on the table and sat down. "Right then? What's new with you?"

"Me? He smiled. "Just ask me who's got a bird, then?"

"Err, let me think. No, I can't think for the life of me."

"Twat," he said, smiling.

"Sorry, I couldn't resist it." I took a swig of my beer. "Anyone I know?"

He shook his head. "No, she's from Herne Bay. We met at a Mod dance in London."

"You and your bloody Mod thing. Are you the only one in existence 'because I've never heard of it apart from you?"

"Hey, listen pal, the Mods are coming. Yes, its a London thing originally but it's growing fast. Just you watch."

"Fair enough, Lenny, but what is it? What is a Mod?"

"It's all about the clothes and the music. It's difficult to put into words." He shrugged. "it's just something new."

"How many are there in Margate?"

"Very few, but next week there's a trial Mod dance in Ramsgate."

"Trial?"

"Yeah. Because we are so few in this area the London crowd organise everything for London. So, this is to get more locals aware of it and to see how many are willing to travel. This is just to test the water."

By nine thirty I was getting pretty drunk and contemplating going home when Lenny suddenly stood and waved to someone who had just come in. "It's Ricky," he said. "About bloody time."

I couldn't just clear off home at that point, not now Ricky had turned up. Besides, I was looking forward to a natter. It's hard to remember the last hour of the evening. I remember most of the chat with Ricky but not leaving the pub. I vaguely recall throwing up on the way home and falling backwards on the grass verge and gazing up at the stars in a black sky. One thing I remembered clearly was being in a phone box vainly trying to ring Ollie and dropping most of my change over the floor.

I also recall quite clearly, Alf calling me a drunken little shit and yelling at me to get to bed.

Then it was back to the land of hazy recall. Waking up drunk in the middle of the night in the dark and groping round the wall trying to find the door, while bursting for a pee, was no fun. Then from somewhere in this haze I heard

Ray's voice yelling at me and I snapped awake to find myself in the wardrobe pissing all over his suits.

A couple of days later I went home mid afternoon to find there was no one in and so I made myself a pot of tea and picked up a book that I bought in the second-hand book shop on the way back from Castle's Music. It was a rather dog-eared paperback by Graham Greene, entitled 'The Ministry of Fear'. It seemed Chadwick was still influencing me.

I'd only read a couple of pages before Ray came home. I looked up from my book. "Tea In the pot, bruv."

He ignored me and clumped off up stairs. Five minutes later he was washed and changed and back downstairs. 'Not at work? "

"Early finish." He smiled. "Ready for a spin," he held up the bike keys.

"What, now?" I asked.

"Why not now? What've you got lined up that's so pressing?"

I closed my book. "Where are you going?"

"Does it matter?"

"No, I just wondered, that's all." I fetched my jacket. "If we ain't going far I'll only need this."

He shrugged and left the room. I pulled my jacket on and followed.

He wheeled the bike out to the road and kicked it into life. I got on behind.

"Let's go Cisco," he yelled, and we were off and running.

It had never even crossed my mind that he might not be able to ride the bloody thing, but within minutes I was feeling nervous. First, he set off with a nasty wobble and then he had a bit of difficulty changing gears.

"Do you think this is a good idea?" I shouted over his shoulder. Have you got a licence?"

He ignored me and opened the throttle.

After a few minutes he seemed to be getting the hang of it and I relaxed a bit. He motored round toward the park and headed round the back of the Margate football ground.

He gunned the engine a bit more and we were going a bit faster than I was happy with. I tapped him on the shoulder and Shouted. "Steady on Ray."

"Piss off ya big girl. She's just warming up.

The road swung round to the left, a long sweeping curve and we were hitting it much too fast. I just knew we weren't going to make it,

Luckily there was almost no traffic on the road because he took the bend so wide we were on the wrong side of the road,

Then it happened. I felt the bike twitch and with that I was rolling head-over-heels towards the kerb. I remember the sound of my head cracking against the kerbstone and I must have been knocked out briefly because when l came to we were on a grass verge and Ray was pushing a wet handkerchief down the back of my neck. I saw the bike laid on its side with the handlebars bent and the clutch lever hanging off.

"Come on you little twat!" he said swapping the handkerchief to my forehead. "There's nothing wrong with you."

I detected a shaking in his voice. My vision was slightly blurred, and I blinked several times trying to clear it.

"One word to mum or Alf and your fuckin' dead." He threw the handkerchief away. "Got it?"

I managed a nod before throwing up.

The lump on my forehead was the size of a tennis ball and Ray insisted I combed my hair forward to hide it.

I managed to get through tea without a hitch although my mum did comment on my hair.

I felt Ray's eyes boring into me as if to remind me of the threat made earlier.

"It's all the rage," I told her and that was accepted and no more was said.

The problem came when, after tea, I went for a bath.

I soaked in the hot water for ages and felt a lot better, though very tired and light headed but when I went to get out of the bath the room suddenly spun round, and I was aware of the floor coming to meet me.

The sound of me hitting the floor was enough to send my mum scuttling up the stairs. Somewhere in a strange haze I could hear her shouting at me, asking if I was okay, and then she was sat on the bathroom floor with my head in her lap and she was yelling for Alf to come. Alf crashed into the room. "What's all the bloody ….?" He stopped mid sentence. "Oh, hell! You all right son?"

I nodded.

"What's that lump on your head? How did you get that?"

I tried to think what to say but my senses were still all over the place. I saw Ray standing in the doorway.

"I ran into a lamppost," I managed at last.

"Well," boomed Alf. "Would you believe it? You ran into a lamppost on the very same day your brother came off his bike. What a bloody coincidence!"

"Yeah, I know it looks that way, but it's true."

Ray winked.

"And the bruise on your arm," Alf said. "And the graze on your leg?" He looked over at Ray. "Big bloody lamppost." Alf didn't believe in hospitals or doctors unless you had a limb hanging off or a lorry parked on your head, so I was put to bed. "Let's see how you feel in the morning," my mum said, guiding me out of the bathroom.
A good sleep worked wonders and when I woke I felt okay. My lump was the same size and a slight bruising had formed but I walked down stairs with no dizziness which meant I felt confident there was no need to see the doctor.

With a week left and the weather holding, I decided to ring Ollie to arrange our day out, but his mum answered saying he was in bed with a touch of flu. "Oh, bloody charming," I said to myself; Lenny was working all week and spending his weekend in London, Ollie was in bed with flu, Denise was in Maidstone and my guitar was in camp. It seemed that my leave was going down hill rapidly.

Chapter Seven

Leave came to an end leaving me with mixed feelings. Ray had shown he was a bigger nutter than even I'd thought possible. Firstly, trying to kill me on a bike he couldn't ride and then making me cover up the injured head and risking drowning in the bath when I passed out. All I could think was if I hadn't fallen out of the bath, what then? I'd practised my drum patterns as often as I could, remembering Red's advice to start very slowly. Smacking hell out of a cushion isn't the same as rattling round a nice drum kit but it was all I had.

Sunday afternoon I was finishing off my packing and Ray poked his head round the door. "That it then? Off back to playing soldiers, are we?"
I ignored him. When I looked up he was gone.
Next morning, I braced myself ready for whatever stupid game he had up his sleeve. To my surprise he simply said, "See ya then," and picked up my kit bag and carried it downstairs for me.

I had a hearty breakfast, kissed mum goodbye and set off to catch the train. I was early, but I preferred having to wait at the station rather than get hot and bothered in a last-minute rush.
I was sat on the bench with my kit bag on the bench next to me when I glanced down and noticed the side pocket was half open. My thoughts went back to Ray carrying my bag down stairs. I had been surprised when he just picked it up and took it downstairs without saying a word and, just briefly, I thought he was up to something. I reached down and slowly opened the pocket all the way. I was right to think he'd been up to something. What had he set up now? I looked inside. An envelope was snuggled in the corner and I took it out cautiously and tore it open.
A note read: *thanks, bruv. Have a beer on me.* And there was a pound note inside.

I was knocked sideways. I could only think it was appreciation for my lying to mum and Alf about the crash but surely, he wasn't so stupid as to think they fell for that rubbish? And besides, I kept quiet about it because he threatened me. I smiled, maybe it was my payment for washing his suits.

I boarded the train at Margate and found an empty compartment. I didn't really expect to get all the way to London with it to myself, but I allowed myself the hope anyway. I just needed to think, to get my head straight, because it seemed the more I weighed things up the more nagging doubts moved in.

My hopes of the compartment to myself lasted no further than two stops down the line. At Birchington Station a young lad slid the door open, nodded, and threw his hold-all up onto the luggage rack. I couldn't help noticing it was an RAF bag the same as mine.

The train rattled along, and he sat smoking and I was enjoying my book. After a while I couldn't resist it any longer. "Where you stationed then mate?"
He smiled. "You a Brat then?"
I frowned. "A Brat?"
"Yeah, Boy Entrant."
"Oh, right, never heard that before."
"Really? You surprise me."
"Anyway," I said, "how did you know?"
"Well you don't have to be Sherlock Holmes. How old are you? Sixteen or seventeen?"
I nodded. "Coming up seventeen."

"So, there you go. Seventeen with a short back and sides you wouldn't have out of choice and an RAF hold-all up on the rack."

I laughed. "Fair enough."

"And to answer your question, Waddington."

"What's it like?"

"What Waddington?"

"Yeah, well no, I mean the RAF? What's the life like?"

He sat back and drew on his cigarette and then in the next two or three minutes he turned my mood around.

The RAF, he explained, was just like any other job. As long as you turned up for work on time and did your bit, your life was pretty much your own. The pay was pretty good, the work was interesting, and you had some really good mates. The longer he talked the better I felt. "And of course," he said, coming to the end. "No parents to ask what time you got in or where are you going?" He stubbed his cigarette out and smiled. "It's not a bad life. Not bad at all."

I could have kissed him. He couldn't have any idea of what he'd just done. After that we both settled down to read our books. We said goodbye at Victoria Station and I felt fortunate to have met him.

When I entered the hut, it was obvious from things thrown on beds that I wasn't the first, although the only person in the hut was Monkey. I went over to my bed and dropped my bag. "Where is everybody?" I asked looking round the room.

"I've just got here myself," Monkey called back.

I began unpacking.

Monkey got up and walked over to my bed. "No point doing that, we're moving to the Wings tomorrow. Good leave?"

"So, so." I replied and left it at that. I arranged my washing kit ready for the evening and put my bag straight in the locker ready to take with me to the new huts tomorrow.

I checked my watch. It was gone three. "D'ya know what Monkey? I'm gonna take a walk into Llantwit. Stretch the old pins after all that traveling."

Monkey nodded. "I'm in."

I looked out of the window. "Oh, bollocks! It's starting to rain."

Monkey leaned close to the window and peered outside. "Sod me, Mark. It's hardly pissing down. We can risk it."

The rain had all but stopped by the time we left the camp and the clouds were thinning out. By the time we arrived at the war memorial in Llantwit it had turned into a pleasant afternoon. We sat on the bench and shared Monkey's cheese and pickle sandwich.

I got up and looked around for a bin to chuck the rubbish. "Oh, that's interesting," I said, tapping Monkey on the shoulder. "Tasty little ladies nearby."

He turned to look. "Ah, right. Yes, I see." He wiped his fingers on a grubby looking handkerchief. "Very nice."

Then, to my horror he called out, "Good afternoon ladies."

He stuffed his handkerchief back into his pocket and went over to them. I followed feeling a bit foolish.

The blonde-haired girl whispered something to her friend who giggled and nodded.

Monkey bowed gracefully. "May I introduce my friend and I?"

"Why?"

80

Monkey smiled. "We can't buy you a coffee if you don't know us."

They both giggled. "You can't buy us a coffee any way,"

"And why would that be, pray tell?" he said, in a stupid posh voice.

"I could tell you one bloody good reason why not," I hissed in Monkey's ear. "I can't afford it, that's why."

"The café is shut," the blond girl's friend said. "And it's rude to whisper."

I grunted. "I didn't notice it bothering you a minute ago."

The blonde girl looked at me with a hint of a smile. "Ooh, touchy aren't we." She tossed her hair back. "Go on then," she said.

"Go on what?" I asked.

"Like your friend said, introduce yourself."

The blonde-haired girl was Tina and her friend was Cheryl and they were from Barry. They'd come to Llantwit thinking there was a traveling fair only to find out it was next month.

We walked around the village chatting. Before long we somehow split into couples. Monkey and Tina had stopped to look at something in a shop window and Cheryl and I kept walking.

She was a couple of inches shorter than me with shiny auburn hair tied in a pony-tail.

Time flew by until the girls announced they had a bus to catch. I was quite relieved; me and Monkey had a canteen to get to and I hadn't eaten anything since breakfast except half a cheese and pickle sandwich.

We waited with the girls for the bus. I leant over to Cheryl and asked if I could see her again, but she shook her head.

"I don't think so, Mark. I enjoyed this afternoon, but I'm not bothered about going out with anyone at the minute." I was taken aback, and she could tell. "It's nothing personal, you seem like a nice lad. It's just that…." She cocked her head to one side and smiled. "I'll tell you what, if you come to the fair next month we can say hello I suppose."

I smiled. "Okay. Great."

The bus came into view. "I'm not promising," she quickly added, "we'll see."

Monkey and me set off at a brisk pace back to camp. "How did it go?" I inquired.

He shrugged. "Nah, no good. You?"

"No, me neither."

But I hadn't thrown the towel in yet. Oh no, I rather fancied that Cheryl.

At last we were on the move. We were moving huts and leaving ITS behind us. No longer would we be the new kids. It was a great feeling.

The first two days were relaxed.

The first was mainly an introduction to our new environment with a long chat from one of the civilian teachers about what was expected of us: where we'd start, how we would progress, what instructors we would be assigned to us and what exams, or, as the instructor called them, Progress Evaluation Tests, we could expect.

The second day we were issued with a pair of khaki overalls and a notebook and pencil for use in the workshop.

That and afternoon Corporal Evans explained about that we would soon be practising rifle drill in readiness for a very important parade to welcome a new station commander.

After lunch we were assembled in the camp cinema and shown a film on hygiene and safety in the work place. Then, rather surprisingly, we were given a strange warning.

Sergeant Sharpe walked up to the stage. "Up to now you have been billeted in your own little world of I T S. Now you are in the wings. Up to now you won't have had much to do with the entry pecking order. What do I mean by the entry pecking order? Well I'll tell you. First, let me say, it is frowned upon and if detected dealt with. But there is no use saying it doesn't exist because we are all too aware it does. What it means is the Senior Boys are inclined to see the more junior entries as fair game for a bit of fun. You are the most junior and therefore the most vulnerable. It's recommended you steer clear from any unnecessary contact.

However, if any of you feel at any time these antics are excessive or amount to bullying of any kind, it must be reported. It will not be tolerated."

And, as if to prove his point, that very evening we had a visit. Five lads from the new Senior Entry strolled into the hut. The leader looked around the room. "Now then, you shiny new people," he said in a Scottish accent. "This is a nice tidy hut you have here. Yous guys are obviously top-notch lads at cleaning which is handy as that's why we're here. You can call me Tosh and me and my pals are here because yous are to be given the highest honour we can bestow on a Sprog.

He waved one of his comrades forward and he handed him a pair of drill boots. I noticed that they all carried boots. "These boots need of a bit of spit-and-polish. And I mean spit-and-polish till you can see your ugly little faces in them and you are the men to do the job"

He nodded to his friends. "Choose your man lads."

They walked along the room, and each stopped at a chosen bed and deposited their boots.

When one of them stopped at tall, red haired Andy Braithwaite's bed and said, "Here ya go Ginger, just for you," I think we all expected a bit of a tantrum; Andy hated being called ginger and would fly off the handle, but he just stared.

Another delivery bounced on to Bonner" s bed. We all held our breath. All eyes were focused in the same direction.

"I'll collect then tomorrow evening," he said.

Bonner looked at him and shook his head. He picked up the boots and dropped them on the floor. "Before I clean your fuckin' boots I'll see you lick my fockin' arse."

The lad looked flustered. He turned to the leader.

The boy called Tosh went over to Bonner. "Now your being silly. It's not worth getting into a situation here, it's simply a tradition. If you feel that way, then just remember we've been through it and when you get to Senior Entry you'll be able to do it." He pointed to the others in the room with boots on their bed. "Your mates are playing ball."

"Not my mates. Not my problem. Now tell yer man there to pick up his boots and fock off."

Tosh nodded. "Fair enough. But don't think that's the end of it. It's not acceptable and you're out of order."

"And?"

"As I said, it won't end here."

Bonner pushed his face right up close and hissed, "bring it on Jock. Whatever you have in mind, just bring it on"

The Scots boy backed away and waved the other four out. As they left, the boots intended for Bonner landed on my bed. The door shut and there was silence in the hut. Then Geordie burst out laughing. "Fuck me rigid Bonner, you really are a twat at times."

Bonner smiled. "I know."

Colin Masters poked his head out of his room to see what was going on. "Everything okay lads?"

We all mumbled yes.

He smiled. "Good, because I was just coming to show you something."

"Whatever it is it's making you smile like a cat that's got the cream," quipped Monkey.

"Ta-daaa." He held up his tunic. He had shiny, new Corporal stripes sewn neatly in place. "Meet Corporal Boy Masters."

We gave him a cold bath as a way of congratulations.

When, the following evening, the Senior Entry returned they came in numbers. The one called Tosh hadn't lied when he warned Bonner that it wasn't finished.

The door flew open and in they came. One lad was carrying a large sack. They hurried over to Bonner and in seconds he was pinned to his bed and the sack boy moved in to pull it over his head. Ollie looked over at me and then to Geordie.

Ollie and Geordie moved as one. I was right behind, I called for Monkey as I grabbed one of the boys round the waist and pulled him off Bonner. To my surprise the other lads pitched in. There wasn't a fight, no fists or feet flying in, just one big tag team wrestling match. The room rang with shouts and cursing and grunts.

It was a swarming mass of bodies all piled on Bonner's bed.

Then a whistle blew.

The writhing and wrestling stopped, and all eyes were on the would-be referee. It was Corporal Boy Colin Masters. "That's enough," he yelled. Stunned faces stared at him as if not sure what to do.

Tosh straightened his clothing. "You might be a Corporal Boy in here mate but you havenae jurisdiction over us."

"I don't give a toss. You're out of bounds here."

"We're not interested in whether or not we're out of bounds. This guy here needs sorting sooner rather than later. He can't be allowed to kick against tradition."

Colin shrugged. "It's just a silly game?"

"You lads are new. You haven't had enough time to get into the spirit of things. It's not a silly game it's far from it, it's tradition."

He turned to Bonner. "I'm telling you now, you may be a hard man and willing to risk the consequences of all this but how are you going to feel when the all of the other Wings black this Entry. Because I can assure you they will. Imagine that. Your life here will become a living hell; picked on wherever you go. Do you not think the others are soon gonna get pissed off when they find out why?"

He turned to the room in general. "Think about it. Because of one bolshy sod in this hut your whole entry will be marked men, scared to go to the camp cinema scared to go to the NAAFI. Well, I think you get the picture. He turned once again to Bonner. "Right, your game, our rules."

Bonner flopped heavily on to his bed. "Okay, okay. Give me some fockin' boots, f'chrissake."

Monday morning, after breakfast, we were marched to pastures new; a five-minute march to the workshop
 The workshop was massive. There were bits sectioned off as classrooms and, on the main floor, benches with bits of aircraft and racks of tools. Boys in khaki overalls were busily drilling, filing and hammering everywhere you looked.
I found our first day rather strange. I'd set off all those weeks ago to join the RF with very little idea of what things meant. I loved aircraft, that much I knew. My friends and I spent many hours laid in the grass verge outside the fences of USAF Manston, a short bike ride from Margate, watching the American jets coming and going.
But now, standing, in the workshop, I realised I had a trade to learn and I hadn't much of a clue as to what it entailed.
Our first lesson was with a short, rotund civilian instructor who peered at us through wire framed specs. According to my paperwork he was going to teach us all about tools. His name was Mister Stokes.
We sat round at our desks as he opened a book on his desk and cleaned his glasses on his handkerchief. After a while he looked up. "Good morning lads." He put his glasses on. First off, any questions?"
I put my hand up.
He nodded to me. "Name?"
"Draper sir."
"Okay Draper what's your question."
"Please sir, what's an Airframe Mechanic?"

He stared at me in disbelief. "Are you telling me you applied to be a Boy Entrant and train as an Airframe Mechanic without knowing what it involved?"

"No sir, I applied to be a motor mechanic but when I took the entrants exam, at RAF Cardington, they said I had higher grades than necessary and if I changed to Airframe Mechanic I'd get a more interesting and useful career."

Mister Stokes shook his head. "Is that true?"

"Yes sir. Straight up."

"That's not right, they shouldn't do that. Anybody else?"

"Me too," said Tommo.

"And you are?"

"Thompson, sir. I wanted catering."

"Catering?" he said. You applied for catering and got Airframes?" He slapped his forehead in a dramatic way. "My god what is it coming to? Mind you," he added. "It could be useful. We could always get Draper to drive into town in the morning for bacon and eggs and get Thompson to do us a fry up before class."

We all laughed.

I leant over to Ollie. "I think I'm gonna like him.

Ollie nodded. "Yeah, I know what you mean. He seems a right comical Charlie

I told Ollie about seeing Cheryl in Llantwit. We were spending the evening playing darts in the NAAFI. "She wasn't a cracking looker or anything, but she had a lovely smile and, well you know, we just sorta clicked"

Ollie chalked up his score. "No, Draper, you *didn't* click." He looked at me and grinned. "Or you'd be going out with her." He nodded at the scoreboard. "Double sixteen."

"You what?"

"You, ya dozy pillock. It's your chuck and you need double sixteen."

I grabbed my darts from the table. "Okay, okay, keep your wig on."

"Listen, my faithful friend," he drawled, lighting a cigarette. "She just said you *might* see her at the fair *and* you might say hello. Is that right?"

I nodded. "Yeah, that's about it."

"She's not really interested is she Draper?"

"You don't reckon she'll be there, do you?"

He shook his head. "Be honest. Do you?"

"I really don't know. I'm just saying I really fancied her."

"But she don't fancy you. Bit of a problem, eh what?" He put his arm round me. "Of course, this time I'll be there," he said, squeezing my shoulder. "She probably won't be there, but, if she does turn up I'm gonna be there with you."

"Oh yeah? And what good will that do?"

"Well, you introduce me, and she'll take one look at me and she won't want you anyway; hey presto, problem solved."

I laughed. "Fuck you, ex friend." I walked to the board. "Anyway, Ollie, what if we can't get off camp that weekend?"

He shook his head. "You really are a twerp at times Draper. We're not in ITS anymore. We can get a pass whenever." He looked at the dartboard. "Now throw them bleedin' arrows before we both die of old age."

The following night I went to bed with a bit of a sore throat. Sometime in the night I had a very vivid dream. I was laying on my back in a wood staring at tree branches about a foot from my face. Woven across these branches was a large web with a great big spider right in the middle. I was petrified. I loathe spiders. Then there was a low-pitched humming noise in my ears. The humming became a pulsing noise and with each pulse the spider got nearer and nearer. Sweat began to trickle down the side of my face. His whole web was like a rubber trampoline and the spider pulsed in and out in time with the humming. The nearer the slider got the more sweat broke out. Then, just before this great monster reached my face I woke up.

My pyjamas and bedding were soaking wet and I felt lousy.

When the six-thirty mayhem started I was soaking wet and shivering. Bodies bounced out of warm beds with the usual groans and grunts, but I just pulled the bedding up snuggly under my chin.

Colin Masters kicked my bed. "Come on Draper, up you get.

I groaned and shook my head.

Masters kicked the bed again. "You'll be in the shit if the Corporal gets here and finds you..." his voice tailed off, and he came to my bedside and pulled the bed clothes down fun under my chin. "Oh, bloody hell. You look terrible."

The next hour or so was like sleepwalking. I found myself dressing, closely watched by a face I didn't recognise, and then loaded into a Land Rover. I hardly remember getting put to bed.

I was half aware of things going on around me, being woken to take tablets, rubbed all over with a wet cloth and then towelled dry. I briefly recall waking up shivering, another time sweating.

When I eventually returned to some kind of normality I was told I'd had bad bout of flu and my temperature had been sky high.

"Welcome to the land of the living." The tall, spotty faced medic who had been nursing me was taking my temperature. "You've had a rare old time. I've never known a fever take so long to break."

I asked how long I'd be confined.

"As I said, you've had a nasty bout of flu, so you'll be feeling washed out for a while. Normally a case like yours is a couple of weeks at least."

"At *least*?"

When I got the all clear to receive visitors Ollie and Geordie arrived bearing a bottle of coke, a couple of bags of Liquorice Allsorts, a get well soon card and a book.

"It's from all the lads," said Geordie."

"That's right," Ollie chipped in. "Even Bonner coughed up."

"Only, thing is, Mark, Tommo wants his book back when you've finished."

"Oh, yeah, before I forget," Ollie said, pinching one of my Liquorice Allsorts. "It's confirmed. We've got a sodding Church Parade Sunday, but the afternoon of the fair is free.

I nodded. "I'll settle for a church parade if it means I'm out of here."

"Why aye, you'll be out in time for the fair," Geordie said. "Nay sweat."

A day short of two weeks I was discharged. The spotty faced medic was right, I felt totally sapped.

I was excused square bashing for the following couple of days and given light duties.

The following weekend, when we set off walking to
Llantwit Major, I still felt weak.

The fair was just outside Llantwit on a nice green field.
The weather was being kind for once;
No rain and barely a breeze. We found a spot slightly away
from the fair on a bit of a hill. There was Ollie, Monkey,
Geordie and me. By the time we were settled it was a little
after one. I don't know what we expected but looking
down at the fair was disappointing to say the least. Mostly
it was stalls like fishing the ducks or throw a dart at the
playing cards. There was even a coconut shy.
The only rides were a couple of roundabouts and the
Octopus.
"Bloody hell," Ollie groaned. "Not much is it. There's
only the Octopus worth looking at."
"Good job too," Monkey said. "We couldn't afford to go
on if we wanted to."
We all agreed on that one.
Ollie nudged me. "Can you see her?"
"Bloody hell Ollie, give us a chance we've only just got
here."

After an hour or so it seemed pretty certain she wasn't
there. We decided to take a walk down and get a bag of
chips but one look at the price and we settled for two bags
between the four of us.
We wandered round the fair and Geordie decided he could
afford a throw of the darts. Weighing the darts gingerly in
his hand he shrugged. "Bit lightweight."
"Never mind that ya big lump," Ollie said. "You'd better
make it good."

Geordie frowned. "Why? Are you in need of a goldfish in a bag or something?"

"No"

"Well then. What's the big deal?"

Ollie grinned. "This may just turn out to be the highlight of our day."

Back at the hill again we sat glumly watching the goings on. Around three the skies began to darken, and we decided to head back to camp for a game of snooker. And that's when Monkey saw them.

It was Cheryl and Tina with two other girls.

"Right," said Ollie getting to his feet. Let's get down there."

But I suddenly had my doubts. What if I said hello and she walked off, talking with her friends. She'd every right to, she only said we might say hello. How stupid was I going to look in front of Ollie and Geordie?

But Monkey was already on his way.

She looked different. It was her hair. Last time she had a pony tail but now it was free, and I was surprised to see it was long and curly. It framed her face and she looked rather more attractive than I remembered.

I'd hung back a bit with Ollie and Geordie and Monkey was already chatting to Tina when we joined them. At least he hadn't been given the elbow.

Cheryl turned and smiled. She took me to one side. A good start; or so I thought.

"This is a bit embarrassing," she said, biting her lip.

Oh, shite, I thought. Here it comes. The big heave-Ho.

"I'm so sorry, but I've forgotten your name."

I was so relieved I laughed.

93

"Not angry?"

"No, not a bit. It just goes to prove what people always say about me."

"Which is?"

"I'm so forgettable."

She smiled again. "Don't do yourself down." She cocked her head. "Ah, now maybe ...." She closed her eyes for a moment and then smiled. "It's Mark, isn't it?"

That made me feel more relaxed but then, just as I was going to answer her with some quick-fire witty reply, I became distracted. Out of the corner of my eye I noticed the other three girls were walking away and Monkey was standing, hands in pockets, watching them go.

Tina called back over her shoulder, "coming Cher?"

Cheryl glanced back at the departing girls. "One minute." She turned back and shrugged. "Gotta go l'm afraid."

"So, I gather. But I'm gonna try my luck one more time anyway 'cause I'd like to see you again"

She shook her head. "Nothing's changed, Mark. Sorry."

"Bugger" I said quietly.

As she walked away she called back, "I'll tell you what; if you're going to be at the dance I promise I'll have a dance with you."

"Dance? What dance?"

But she just waved. "Got to go. Bye."

And that was that

  "What friggin' dance is she on about," I said to myself as I watched her catch up with her friends.

Back on our place on the hill Ollie turned to Monkey. "Did that Cheryl bird say something about a dance?"

It was the question I was about to ask.

"Don't you lot ever read the notice board?"

94

"Only when the duty rosters are due," Ollie replied.

"It's the Senior Entry's Graduation Ball," Monkey said. "The famous Camp dances."

"First I've heard of it," I said.

"Well," began Monkey, clearly enjoying being the font of all knowledge. "When there's a camp dance they bring in a bus full of girls from the local laundry and what-have-you. This's what she'll be talking about. She's obviously got an invite."

Ollie lit a cigarette and inhaled deeply. "Anyway, what do we do now? This is not turning out to be a great success, eh what?"

Geordie ignored him and got to his feet. He was looking out into the crowd and frowning. He looked concerned about something.

"What've you seen Geordie? More crumpet?"

He shook his head thoughtfully. "I might be wrong but the three guys standing by the Octopus are talking about us."

"I always said your lugholes resemble radar scanners," joked Monkey.

Geordie ignored him. "Lads, I think it's time we left."

I looked into the people milling around the octopus. I was just about to say I couldn't see anything when I saw them. They were looking our way. And they didn't look particularly friendly.

Without even discussing it we turned away from the fair heading the long way around rather than straight through the crowd. As we made our way along the edge of the field it looked like it a false alarm. They weren't following.

At the far end of the field we turned down toward the gravel path and headed for the main road.

Then we saw the them coming up the path towards us.

"Oh, shit," I groaned. "There's four of them now."

"Five," added Geordie. "There's one behind us now."

I glanced back. "Bollocks, he's right."

Ollie nodded. "Just keep walking. We're gonna have to face them by the look of it. Let's just see what happens".

The guy behind us appeared to be hanging back. I was all for turning; one to deal with instead of three, but Ollie walked towards them.

A squat, red faced guy appeared to be the leader. Behind him stood a stocky, greasy haired lad wearing a black bandana. Alongside him were two tall, gangly older boys, almost certainly brothers.

Red face spoke first. "You boys are new here?" He looked at us and grinned. "Yes, I believe you must be. You see the rules are quite clear. You can come and go here as you please, but you stay away from the girls."

Ollie smiled. "In that case lads, there's no problem. We got the big elbow anyway."

We all nodded in agreement.

I realised I hadn't been breathing and let out a long sigh of relief. But my relief was short lived.

"You're fuckin' lying." Greasy hair snarled. "That's the trouble with you bastards, you come here to our little backwater in Wales and assume us locals are all a bit simple."

"We ain't lying" Ollie said sounding quite calm.

"Fuck off!"

"What's up? We told you the truth. We got nowhere with the girls."

"And I said fuck off!" He took a step nearer Ollie and produced a flick knife. I felt a flow of ice run through me. Monkey tucked himself in behind big Geordie.

The knife was taking this confrontation to another level. The squat lad joined him. "We heard the girls arranging to meet at a dance and don't fuckin' well deny it." But then something distracted them.

The one who was following behind had strolled up. It was Bonner.

"What the fuck do you want?" Greasy hair snapped.

Bonner held his hands up in mock surrender. "Leave me out of this I'm just passing."

"We ain't stupid," the squat round-faced lad said. "You're one of them. It sticks out a mile." He waved Bonner past. "Keep walking."

"Me? One of them? Fock off." He gave a grunt. "Listen, if yous is gonna kick seven bells out of these twats then I want to watch."

Greasy hair looked hard at Bonner. "We know your one of them so what's your game?"

"These fockers is no mates of mine thank you very much. I wouldn't piss on 'em if they were on fire."

Geordie stared at Bonner. "You bastard."

Bonner laughed. "I can't wait to see how hard man Wilson does here."

Greasy hair smiled and pushed his face up close to Ollie. "Oh dear. Not your lucky day, is it?"

That was his big mistake. Ollie slammed his forehead into the boy's face. Then all hell broke loose. Before I could make any kind of move I found myself facing one of the gangly brothers and he was wearing a nasty looking knuckleduster. A fist came out of nowhere and the lad dropped to the floor. I looked to see who had saved me and found myself looking at Bonner. He grinned and leapt on to the other brother.

Then there were fists and boots flying everywhere. Knowing Bonner was with us gave me a surge of confidence and, as the guy that Bonner had hit scrambled to his feet, I lashed out and caught him high on the cheek. He fell back to the ground. I readied to hit him again if he got up again, but then I quickly pulled away. The pain that suddenly shot through my hand was excruciating.

It was all over in no time at all.

Ollie held his hand out to Bonner. "Cheers Jim."

Bonner shook hands and half smiled. "It's just perked up a dull weekend, that's all. It don't make us amigos."

Ollie shook his head. "F'chrissake Jim, what is it with you?"

But Bonner never answered he simply turned away and set off back towards the main road.

Ollie watched him go with a puzzled look. "He came especially," he said to no one in particular. "If not then why come this way at all?"

Geordie nodded, "strange bloke."

"We all okay?" Ollie called. "Good. Let's go get a game of snooker."

We set off walking.

I looked at my hand, it was swelling up visibly and throbbing like mad.

Part Two: Just Finding Our Way

Chapter Eight

"Bugger me backwards, Mark," said Chas, looking at my hand. "How long before it's back in action?"

"A good while. It's a broken bone f'chrissake. What do you expect?"

"You're not going to be playing the guitar with that wrapped up like that."

"Err, no. I think that we can safely say that much." I said, wondering if I should tell him about my drumming. I had already asked Red not to say anything.

"The problem is Paul has bought his new guitar back with him."

"Okay, no need to say it." I sighed. "I'm out of the band."
Chas nodded. "Yeah, sort of."

"It's okay. I wasn't anywhere near good enough anyway." I could see the relief on his face.

I was kind of relieved myself. It meant I could stop thinking about guitar chords and concentrate on drums. Besides, I liked Paul, he was an easy-going kind of bloke. He spoke with a hint of a Geordie accent although he was from Yorkshire, Middlesbrough I think he said. He was lightly built with wavy, dark brown hair and a mischievous grin. If I had to get the boot from the band then Paul was the bloke I was happy to see taking my place.

I was looking forward to the dance and seeing Cheryl but when the big day arrived I started having doubts: she'd turned me down already; would another rejection make me look like a bit of an arse?

All the same, I started getting ready early.

As I stood combing my hair in the mirror on the inside of my locker door Monkey's face appeared over my shoulder. "Getting all dolled up, are we?"

I turned. "Look at you ya cheeky sod. Hardly the village tramp."

"You gonna try and get off with that Cheryl?"

"Funny you should ask. I was just thinking about that."

"And?"

"I'm having second thoughts. I'm really unsure." I slipped into my jacket. "In truth I've probably been kidding myself thinking she's likely to go out with me. She ain't interested."

"What about having the dance she promised you?"

"I may have the dance. As you said, she promised, but I'm just gonna play it by ear. What about Tina?"

"Fuck that. That was never gonna happen. I knew from the start." He ruffled my carefully combed hair and grinned. 'But there's bound to be some lonely lass just waiting for a hunk like me. Yeah?"

I nodded. "Without a doubt."

We got there a bit early, but the doors were open, so we went in. We pulled two tables together against the side wall. There was Ollie, Geordie, Monkey, Tommo Thompson and Colin Masters.

The hall filled steadily and by seven-thirty it was over half full. Just before eight the doors opened and in came the girls. The room was suddenly alive with chatter.

The band was on stage tuning up and the whole room took on a new atmosphere. It felt like a dancehall should feel.

"Oh, bugger," I moaned to Ollie. "I've just realised. I can't see the stage from here."

"So?"

"So, I can't see the band."

"You mean you can't see Cheryl."

"No, clever dick. I mean I can't see the band. I don't give a toss about Cheryl."

He raised an eyebrow. "Good lord, Draper. I do believe you mean it."

"Yes, I bloody well do. Now is it okay if I go and watch the band for a few minutes?"

They were brilliant. I only intended to have a quick look at them but found myself rooted to the spot.

After the first three songs I thought it time to get back to the others but, just as I went to leave the floor, I felt a tap on my shoulder. I turned expecting to see Ollie or one of the others but found myself looking at a smiling Cheryl.

"Oh, hi," I shouted. "How's it going?"

She pointed to her ears and waved me to follow her. We made our way to the back of the room. "That's better," she said. Then she pointed to my hand. "I heard a rumour that you and your friends met some of the locals at the fair. Is that right?"

I shrugged, trying to look nonchalant. "Yeah, well, something like that."

She giggled.

"What's funny about that?"

"Sorry, just never saw you as a hard man."

"No?"

"No, you seemed so timid when we first met. Rather shy."

I simply shrugged.

She pointed to my hand again, "What's the damage?"

I held it up. "Broken bone. It's well on the mend now."

She gave me a mischievous grin. "And the other guy?"

I laughed. Was she changing her mind about me? Did she like the hard man image?

I decided to test the water. "I expect he's wondering if it was really worth it," I said, trying to sound cool.

"Anyway," she said, changing the subject. "I owe you a dance. Let me know when you want it."

But my head was still locked in the new me. The hard man. "No, I'm always chasing you, you come and find me when you're ready."

"What?" She snapped. You want me to come to you?"

I sensed I'd misread the situation. "Yeah, when your ready. I'll wait for you."

"Let me say, You're in for a long wait there."

I went back to my seat and flopped down heavily. Ollie leant over. "What's up?"

I waved him away. "Don't ask."

The band announced their break. I went and stood near the stage. One of the guys from the band, set up the microphones for Chas's acoustic guitar and Paul and Jumbo plugged in to the amps. But that wasn't where my real interest lay. My eyes were glued to Red and the drums.

Then a voice boomed round the room. "Ladies and gents, boys and girls, we have a special treat for you now, a

102

group of your very own. Let's have a big hand for Sky-High."

Then the amplified guitar of Chas, with his immaculate picking, rang out loud and clear and they played the country instrumental he'd shown me. Then a couple of Shadows hits and lastly another country picking tune I didn't recognise.

Red made it look so easy. I noticed the way he held the sticks and the crisp, sharp sound he got by using his wrists and not his arms.

As they left the stage people were patting them on the back and clapping loudly.

Chas came up to me grinning from ear to ear. "How'd it sound?"

I gave him the thumbs up and he reached for my ear, but I caught his wrist. "Stop doing that."

He just grinned even more.

As he left I saw Cheryl looking my way. I mouthed, "Sorry."

She smiled and signalled for me to join her for a dance.

As we walked back to the hut Ollie put his arm round my shoulder. "I see you and Cheryl were hitting it off. I'm chuffed for ya mate."

I nodded. "Yeah, she's a bit of alright."

"When ya seeing her again?"

I shrugged. "We haven't arranged anything yet, but she's given me a phone number."

"Really?"

"Yeah, it's her work place"

"Well, there ya go." He squeezed my shoulder and chuckled. "A telephone number. Wow, that's love, that is."

Whenever I had a free moment I'd try playing the patterns Red had shown me. It all looked easy enough when he did it but when I tried it seemed impossible. He'd promised me it would suddenly fall into place. "One day you'll think you're never going to get it," he'd said. "And then the next day, voila, there it is, you've got it! I hadn't got it yet, not by a long way," but, with his words in mind I refused to give in; not even with a painful hand.

 But, as sure as I was I'd get it eventually, it was the fact that I hadn't got it yet made me keep it a secret from Chas.

 One evening, having chatted for ages about our first few mornings in the new surroundings, me and Ollie settled down to a game of cards in the hut. Ollie lit up a cigarette and took a long draw.

"D'ya know what Draper?" he said from behind a curtain of grey smoke. "I think life has just got a whole lot better."

"In what way?"

"Well, learning a trade is a damn site more enjoyable than all that boring crap we were fed in ITS." He smiled. "The History of the RAF my arse."

 "And the theory of fight." I added and we both laughed."

"And what's really great is next weekend it's me and you off to good old Barry Island."

"Bloody too right."

Then, completely out of the blue, Ollie put his cards down and stretched. "Draper, old son, what's happening with this drums lark?"

I stared at him. "What's that mean?"

"Well, you're a bit faddy. One minute your busting a gut to learn some guitar chords, and its practise, practise, practise and now you're doing it all again only now it's with a pair of drumsticks?"

"I still don't see what you're getting at?"

He sighed. "It's like this; I don't know how long it takes to learn to play the bloody things but what's the point of you trying? For one thing, we heard how good the lads were with the ginger haired lad on the drums."

"Yeah, and?"

"Do you really believe they're gonna wait for Lord only knows how long for you to be good enough. You don't think that somewhere on this camp there isn't a decent drummer just ready for Chas to find?"

His message hit me right between the eyes.

Ollie scooped up the cards and started shuffling. "Just something I think you ought to maybe consider?"

I groaned. "Okay, point taken."

"Another thing," he said. "Why do you keep putting your small change in a jar, like a little old lady?"

"That's easy. Every time I buy anything I put the small change in the jar ready for the Fairground. Got almost nearly a pound so far," I said. "That should help."

Ollie groaned. "I ain't very flush I'm afraid"

"Do you want to scrub it this week and go another time?"

"Fuck no. We never got to Dreamland last leave, so we will just have to make up for it. The funfair is supposed to be shit-hot."

I nodded. "Role on Saturday."

I never mentioned my pound from Ray. It was in an envelope in my locker. I'd decided to start a savings fund to go towards a drum kit somewhere in the future.

Wednesday morning at breakfast I noticed Chas, a couple of tables away, trying to attract my attention.

I looked over. "What?" I mouthed silently.

He got up and came over. He looked a bit edgy.

"Got time for a quick chat before workshops?"

"Leave it till break time."

He nodded and scurried back to his table.

"Here it comes," Ollie joked. "You're getting the big elbow."

I smiled. "He did that already. So, your wrong there."

By the time break came around I was intrigued. I was just taking a swig of my coke when Chas arrived by my side.

"I've had a word with Paul," he said, plunging his hand into a bag of crisps. "He's really chuffed about the band." He licked the last of the crisps from his fingers. "He's pleased you're okay with it, I think he was feeling a bit guilty."

I shrugged. "It's okay."

"Well, what I wanted to tell you was we had a chat, and all agreed that if you want to practise with us to help improve your guitar work then you're more than welcome." He beamed. "What d'ya reckon?"

I laughed. "That's funny, I was going to talk to you about joining the band."

Chas frowned. "No, no, no Mark," he said quickly. "No. I'm sorry, I didn't mean you could..."

I stopped him mid-sentence. "Relax. I know what you meant."

He frowned. "Eh? What's that mean?"

"I'm offering to be in the band again only this time, as the drummer."

He looked at me as if waiting for a punch line. "What? Are you saying you can play the drums?"

I nodded. "I am."

Suddenly he was twiddling my earlobe again. "Now then Mark," he said, with that funny growl of his. "You're pulling my leg."

I knocked his hand away. "Pack it in!"

"Actually," he said. "I've been asking around and there doesn't appear to be any takers, so I thought we'd go without one."

"There is now," I said smiling.

"What are you saying, here? You can actually play drums?"

I shrugged. "Okay, maybe not *actually* play them, no, but I'm learning."

"How?"

I explained about Red's lesson and how I was practicing the basic patterns. "I'm getting there," I told him."

I don't think he was too impressed, in fact he suddenly looked very disappointed, but break was over, and I left him to ponder it and made my way back to the classroom. I took my seat and scanned through my notes so far.

After a few minutes I became aware of someone standing behind me. Then a hand rested on my shoulder and I felt my earlobe being squeezed.

I brushed it away. "Fuck off Chas."

"But I thought you liked it?"

I looked round quickly and there, grinning like the proverbial Cheshire Cat, stood Ollie. "Is that not right?"

I punched his shoulder. "It's bad enough him twiddling my ear without you joining in."

"Oh, shut up Draper, you love it."

On Saturday afternoon we picked up our permits from the gatehouse and caught the bus to Barry. We'd decided to walk from the bus stop in Barry to Barry Island not realising how far it was. We could see the funfair as we walked but it seemed to never get any nearer.

Finally, when got there, we weren't disappointed. As we stood in the entrance looking around Ollie clapped me on the back. "This looks pretty good eh? Yes, I think we could manage to enjoy this place."

I nodded.

"Come on then young Draper, let's have some fun."

Chapter Nine

We did a tour of the park, working out what we liked most and what we could best afford. At first, we were both very aware of the fairground cowboys after the fiasco in Llantwit Major but that was soon eclipsed by the goodies all around.

When we stood watching the Scenic Railway I had a flashback of being in Dreamland, with a rickety, old wooden roller coaster that had seen better days.

That was first choice. After that I had my eye on the Dive Bomber but much to my surprise Ollie wasn't keen. "I don't want anything that has me upside down, thank you Draper"

"This doesn't really get you upside down. Just before you start to turn upside down ..." I couldn't think of a way to explain it clearly. "Come on it's easier to watch it than explain."

Ollie watched as the two pods dipped and turned on the end of two long arms, each pod rotating on its axis, twisting and turning and giving the sensation of riding in a dive bomber. It was clear he still wasn't keen. "Hey, Ollie if you don't fancy it then it don't go on. It don't matter mate. It's pointless wasting your money like that. I can go on my own."

He fished in his pocket for a cigarette. "Don't talk daft. If you're getting on it then so am I." He lit his cigarette. "I have to look after you." He smiled and drew on his cigarette. Just at that moment two young girls screamed loudly as the bomb rotated in the top position.

"I think maybe we should get it out of the way first." Ollie said still looking unsure.

The ride came to a stop and we took our seats, closely watched by a gang of youngsters. The operator told Ollie to get rid of his cigarette and then lowered the wire mesh cage. Ollie grabbed the safety bar and his knuckles began to turn white straight away. And then we were off.

First the pendulum stroke, arcing gently, then a little higher, then higher and higher with each swing, nearer and nearer to the top. At the top of the stroke we swivelled to the upright position, then, as we set off on the down sweep the capsule swivelled again.

Something hit my cheek. Then a noise like something metallic bouncing off the wire mesh. "Shit, Draper the bolts are shearing!"

Another metallic ping, then another. A sixpence piece landed in my clothing. "Ah, bollocks!" I yelled. "Bollocks, bollocks!"

"What's up?" Ollie shouted, gripping the bar even tighter. "My fucking change. It's my fucking money!"

The ride swept through its arc again and I saw more coins bouncing about the cage.

Then I heard him, Ollie was laughing his bloody head off. We searched the ground around the area but there weren't any coins to be found.

"Ollie stop looking," I said. "There's no way we're gonna find anything."

"I figured that," he said. "And I know what you're gonna say."

I nodded. "Yeah, me and Lenny used to be proud of the fact we knew the best place to stand to catch the skirts getting blown up in Dreamland."

"Exactly. And you saw them little sods watching us get on board same as I did." He smiled. "The buggers knew exactly where to stand."

I nodded. "And now I'm skint."

My mishap was soon general knowledge. Ollie was happy to share a good laugh with anyone willing to listen. Everywhere I went for the next day or two I was the butt of the joke:

"Hey Draper, if I pull your arm will you pay out?"

"Hi Mark, it makes a nice change seeing you."

"Draper its time for a change."

"Hey Mark, do you know the words to Three Coins in a Fountain?"

And one that, I must admit, made me smile, "Hi-Ho Silver, away"

One evening me and Ollie were playing darts in the NAAFI with Bonner and Geordie when the guy called Tosh came in with another lad. They bought their drinks, found a table and began playing cards.

Our game came to a finish and we went to our table to join Monkey, Tommo and Colin Masters. We chatted away about this and that until, out of the blue Tosh walked over to our table.

"Oh shit," Geordie said quietly to Bonner. "Here comes trouble."

Bonner stared straight down the table.

Tosh arrived at our totally silent table. He looked at Bonner. "Can I have a word?"

"About?" Bonner said, eyes straight ahead."

"You wanna go somewhere quiet."

"Here's fine."

Tosh looked a little flustered. It would be hard to describe Tosh. He had no distinguishing features at all. He was medium height, medium build and when he spoke it was with strong Scottish accent. If I could pick on one thing it would be his eyes; pale greyish blue but with a hint of menace. He cast an eye over our little assembly and shrugged. "Okay. If you prefer."

Bonner just nodded.

"I suppose it wouldn't be a bad thing for your pals to hear this. The thing is …..." He seemed to be looking for the right words. "This is not easy. I know what I want to say but I'm not sure how to say it."

Bonner said nothing.

"What's your name?"

"Jim. Jim Bonner."

"Okay," he pulled up a chair and sat down. "Listen Jim, I was raised in the Gorbals, in the heart of Glasgow's ganglands. I've seen a good few hard men in my time and they're all the same; they'd die rather be seen to back down. The sort of man you'd rather have on your side than have to face. And, when I see you, I see a hard man.

"It was painfully obvious you were happy to take on the whole world and its brother the other night and I'm not so daft as to think you backed down in fear of the reprisals or anything like that. I think, just from what I've seen of you,

111

it was a massive climb down and, correct me if I'm wrong, it hurt like hell."

Bonner looked up at him for the first time. I held my breath while waiting for the response. Just where was this going

"You're right, I'm not in the habit of backing down, no, so what's your gripe?"

"I'm not here to gripe, Jim. I'm here because I wanted to say thanks. Everyone's aware of how it could easily have got out of hand. And I do think you climbed down for the sake of the other guys in your huts getting caught in it." Tosh held out his hand and stood up. "I just wanted to say it was appreciated, that's all"

Bonner looked at the hand being offered. He stood up, pushing his chair back with a clatter. Oh, shite I thought, here it comes. But I was wrong, Bonner nodded and even managed a hint of a smile "Is that you finished?"

"It is."

Bonner took the offered hand. "Tosh isn't it?"

"James Macintosh."

"Right James. I think we're sorted."

Tosh nodded. "Yes, we're sorted." They shook hands. Tosh turned to leave then hesitated. "I'm in hut 06. Why don't you come on round sometime for a chat?"

If the handshake hadn't stunned us Bonner's response certainly did.

"Yeah, okay, I might jost do that."

Geordie was one of the few lads Bonner talked with at length, most of us settled for the odd grunt, so it was no real surprise that come lights out it was Geordie who raised the subject of the conversation with Tosh. "What did you think of Tosh's little chat, bonnie lad?"

112

There was a silence. I assumed Bonner was ignoring him but then he spoke. "That guy Tosh said that the Gorbals was a hard place to grow up, well the area I was raised in was harder than that. Men were known to end up face down in the gutter for nothing more than a wrong word in the pub."

You could almost touch the tension in the dark. Bonner had just delivered the longest speech we'd ever heard from him. But there was more to come.

"It was a place where the wrong religion could get your house torched, where the wrong political belief could cost you your kneecaps.

I was the youngest of seven boys and the son of a Belfast hard man: hard as granite, hard working and hard drinking. The only way to have a peaceful life was to keep my head down. I was happiest left alone. It made me a loner and that got me bullied at school. One day when I came home from school I was met by father who'd heard about me getting bullied and the going over I got from him was far worse than I'd ever gotten from any school bully. When I recovered I knew that I'd never get bullied again.

My da told me to stand up for myself. His advice was drummed into me, never to be forgotten: if I got threatened by a bully I should take him on, and if I came of worse one day, then the next day I had to take him on again and again, every day until I got the better of him. That's been my way of life ever since."

He paused. "I joined up because I wanted to get away from home and away from all the hate and nastiness and try to live a normal life. But I didn't realise how playing the hard man for so long had made it ingrained in me. I rather liked being hated and feared, it was only when I realised I was risking becoming just about the most hated boy on the camp, and that I was putting everyone else on our Wing in danger of having to suffer the consequences, that I knew I had to back down. I think Tosh is the first person to understand how hard that was."

"And how do you feel about it now," Geordie asked.

"Ask me in the morning."

And that was that.

I lay in the dark thinking that when I wake this will all have been a dream. Surely? This can't be Bonner. But then it occurred to me that, for all the things he was, he was still just another seventeen-year-old lad finding his way in a strange environment. We were all just finding our way.

I'd been drumming after tea one evening and returned to find Ollie waiting with a message from Chas. He wanted to see me as soon as I got in. I'd promised Ollie that I'd be back in time for a couple of frames of snooker and now Chas wanted to see me.

"It sounded pretty urgent," Ollie said.

"Err, well, it's gonna have to wait. We're booked in for the snooker."

"Don't talk like a twat. This is about the next dance."

"Dance? What about the …"

He waved me away. "Just fuck off and see him."

"Bloody hell, Ollie. You've changed your tune."

Ollie winked. "Perhaps I'm looking forward to seeing my mate up on that stage. Eh?"

I laughed. "Hey, watcha know; my first groupie.

I set off to find Chas, puzzled by Ollie's reaction. No sarcastic comments, no complaining about spending time with the band, no moaning about deserting my mates. What the hell had gotten into him?

I found Chas laid on his bed, toying with his guitar. When he saw me enter he swung himself into a sitting position.

"Ah, great. Just the man I want to see."

I plonked myself down next to him.

"I've had a chat with the other two and they're all for it."

"For what?"

"Playing at the dance again."

"Just the three of you?"

"Ah, that's the thing I want to see you about."

I sensed his hand heading for my earlobe. "NO! Don't even think about it!"

"You say you aren't a drummer but you're always in the Band Hut. Can you play, or can't you?"

"Good question."

"Flight Lieutenant Copperfield was asking."

"Who?"

"Copperfield. He's the entertainments Officer. He's also in charge of the Band Hut."

"What the fuck are you talking about?"

"Flight Lieutenant Copperfield is the man who says whether or not we can use the place to practice. You really should have a permit to use the drums."

"Oh, thanks!" I grumbled. "Now you tell me."

"Okay, I'll sort it. We need to keep him sweet. He's also the man who says whether we can play at the dance or not."

"Oh, I see. Are you playing the next dance then?"

"Ah, well, now there lies the snag. He doesn't want us playing as a trio."

"What are you gonna do.?"

He grinned, made his growling noise, and reached for my ear.

I stared in disbelief. "And you've told him I can play?"

115

"You get a fair bit of practice."

"You bloody well have!" I snapped. "You told him I could play."

He shrugged. "Well can you?"

I sighed and gave him the truth about my progress. To my surprise he seemed quite pleased. "If you think you're getting the hang of it then maybe we can make it work."

"Or not!" I said.

"I'll set up a practise session."

Through nobody's fault but my own, I was being pressured into working as hard as I could on the drumming. Somehow, I had to get up to speed in time for our four numbers at the dance. The very thought of it sent me into a cold sweat.

The days came and went with very little to separate them. We went to workshops and classes, we cleaned and polished, we marched, and we ate and we slept and all the time my drumming progress was slow but positive. I was now in need of more than a pillow; I needed more time on an actual drum kit, but then we heard Chas's request for a practice session was turned down because the Station Band were rehearsing for a concert in the officer's mess.

Thursday morning, as we arrived at the workshops and were making our way to our classroom I heard my name called out. I looked to see an officer waving me over. "Oh shit," I said. "What have I done?"

He was standing in the doorway of the Education Officer's tiny office. Pointing to a chair he waved me to sit and introduced himself as Flight Lieutenant Copperfield. "Boy Entrant Draper?"

"Yes sir," I replied, recognising the name.

He pushed a sheet of paper my way. "You requested permission to use Band Hut equipment?"

I was about to say no when it dawned on me. Chas. "That's right sir."

"Right, just read this permit request and sign it"

It occurred to me this was all rather strange. Why had he come to me rather than send for me to go to his office? As if he was reading my mind he explained he was away all week as of this lunchtime. "Boy Entrant Charles seemed to think it urgent for you to have the permit, so you can progress with your rehearsing. I'm looking forward to hearing you play when I get back."

As I walked back to the classroom his words sunk in. I groaned. I had a little over two weeks to get it right.

On Sunday me and Ollie decided to go to Barry Island Pleasure Park again and it was heaving.

"Bloody hell" I laughed. "Where they all come from?"

"It's Sunday," Ollie offered. "It's probably the only place open."

We queued for ages to get on the roller coaster and by the time we finally got our turn we were ready for a hot dog. When I lost all my change on the Dive Bomber Ollie had shared his last pennies helping me out and so I offered to buy the hot dogs.

"Thanks, my friend but don't go skinting yourself just to pay me back. That's daft."

I pulled Lee's pound note from my pocket. "No worries."

Ollie frowned. "I thought you were saving your change because you were as skint as me? Where the hell did that come from."

I told him the story. "So?" I said when I'd finished. "The Drums will just have to wait. Hot dog?"

"Yeah," he laughed. "Why not?"

When we'd finished I took the rubbish to a nearby bin. When I returned I found Ollie watching something near the kiddie's roundabout.

"What you lookin' at?" I asked, hoping it wasn't trouble.

He nodded in the direction of the ride." keep looking over there," he said. "You'll see in a minute."

And he was right, I saw her. Cheryl. "Bloody hell, fancy that."

"You gonna say hello?"

I shrugged. "I suppose so. Yeah, why not?"

She smiled when she saw us approaching. "Good lord, it's the heavy mob."

She lifted my hand and examined it. "All better I see."

"I should blinking well hope so."

She cocked her head to one side. "You haven't come to ask me for a dance again?"

I ignored her. "On your own?"

"No, Tina's just popped to the loo."

"I was going to ring you. Are you going to the dance Friday week?"

She giggled. "So, you *have* come to ask for a dance." Then she saw Tina coming. Tina said hello and the girls linked arms.

 "We gotta go," Cheryl said. "Hope to see you at the dance."

They set off but but only got a few paces when Tina turned to look at Ollie as if she'd just seen him for the first time.

"Are you going to ask me for a dance "she said cheekily?

"'Cause for you, I might just say yes."

118

Ollie smiled nonchalantly. "We'll see."

Cheryl slapped her friend playfully. "What are you like?"

"Okay. It's agreed. We'll meet at the dance," I said. Then I quickly added. "After I've finished playing"

Cheryl frowned. "Playing what?"

"Oh yeah, my band's playing." I turned away. "See ya then."

After a few yards Ollie started laughing. "My band? I don't believe you, I really don't." He shook his head. "My fucking band. Did you really say that?"

"Will you shut up?" I said, but I had to smile.

Chapter ten

It was Wednesday afternoon, sports afternoon, before we got a full band practise in the Band Hut. I was pretty poor. I wondered what the other three were thinking. I didn't imagine it would be very flattering.

But, it wasn't a disaster and that was something.

I thought I had the drum pattern for The Savage worked out, but I was wrong. I could see the look of horror on Chas's face as he heard this awful noise banging out behind him.

"You call that the Savage?" he said turning to face me. It's nowhere near.

He was right; it was all wrong and my timing was still dragging. It was Jumbo who came to my rescue again.

"Chas, why persist in trying to play things Mark isn't ready for? There are plenty of numbers we can do with a basic drum pattern?"

Paul agreed.

I could see Chas was disappointed but as the afternoon wore on and more songs were added to our list, he seemed happier.

After we'd finished and tidied I walked back to the hut with Jumbo and I thanked him for helping.
He nodded. "You're going to be okay, Mark. You just need to find the right way for you, and not for Chas?"
I smiled. I think I know what he meant. "Listen Jumbo, I realise you're learning the same as me, but you always seem so calm, so confident. Chas has one of his rants and it just washes over you. If you get a bit wrong, the next time it's perfect. How do you do it?"
He gave a little chuckle, "I just do. No reason."
We arrived at the huts and the stopped and smacked his forehead. "Bugger, "he snapped. "Paul was going to lend me something to read."
I shrugged. "I've got some books in our storeroom if you wanna look?"
"Oh, yeah. Please."

I emptied my bag of books and he picked about for a while. "Aha!" he said. "I see you like Dennis Wheatley."
"I used to like that stuff, but I've sort of moved on from that rubbish." I replied.
He shook his head. "It's not all rubbish, you know."
"No?"
"No." He held up Dennis Wheatley's 'Strange Conflict'. "You read this?"
I nodded.
"Astral plane stuff, not like in this book , I grant you, is real."

I studied his face, waiting to see if he was pulling my leg. There was no sign of him being anything but deadly serious.

"I'm not going to tell you about it, Mark because I know you won't believe me. What I will say is you just asked me how I remain so calm. Why I don't have butterflies, Remember?"

I nodded.

"Well" He hesitated, "I meditate."

I looked at his face. He was definitely serious.

"You're looking at me as if you can't make up your mind," he said, smiling.

"No, no, Don't think that for a minute." I said. "It's just that I don't get the connection with astral plane stuff."

He pursed his lips, thinking. After a short while he sighed. "No, you'd never believe me."

"Oh, come on Jumbo, I'm intrigued now. You can't leave me hanging here."

"I shouldn't have said anything. Forget it."

"But you *did* say it and now I want to know. Come on."

He laughed gently. "Oh, what the hell. You can believe I or not. All I will say is if you laugh at it or tell anyone else, that's it with us, Okay?"

I nodded.

"Well, it's like this; I am learning to meditate into a state where I can actually leave my body. Only for a few seconds, I grant you, but it's coming, it's taken over three years go get this far." He studied my expression

"Shit! The astral plane?"

"That's it. Now don't ask me any more."

I held up my hands. "Not a word."

"Right," he said. "What do I want to read?"

After he'd gone I sat thinking over what I'd just heard. I realised had anybody else had told me that I would have laughed. But somehow, coming from the big guy, I found myself believing it.

The following week I decided to use the whole of Saturday and Sunday afternoons getting it right. There was no point asking the others; Chas had a date with a girl he'd recently met and Jumbo and Paul didn't think rehearsing without Chas was worth it.
Monkey, Geordie, Tommo and Andy Braithwaite were all going in to Barry. Tommo had discovered a weird bohemian coffee bar where the local Beatniks hung out that he wanted to try. "I only had a quick look," he explained. "But it's all little booths and candles. Looks really good." The others were all up for it.
When I asked Ollie what he had planned he just shrugged. "I'll probably tag along with the others."
"You're okay with me deserting you like this?"
"I bloody well am," he grinned. "You need to get this drumming lark sorted out or come the dance I shall have to deny knowing you."

The weekend spent practising was worth it. With time getting short I needed to be good enough to play during the band's break. At last there was a glimmer of light at the end of the tunnel. I was glad Ollie had gone in to Barry with the others. I know I'd have felt guilty spending the weekend in the Band Hut while he was left kicking his heels. I just hoped they had a good time.
Drumming on my own was working a treat when it came to the patterns Red had shown me; the problem was now my timing. But then, by sheer luck, I found the answer.

I was setting up Sunday lunchtime when I noticed the Equipment Room door was slightly ajar and, being the nosey little sod I was, I went to look around. It was full to the brim with things like music stands, marching drums, chairs and shelves full of assorted instruments. Then I noticed, right at the end of one of shelves, a metronome. It meant I had to play quietly in order to hear it, but it was strict timing and that's what I wanted.

Sunday evening, I was laying on my bed reading when Monkey came over and sat on my bed. "Any idea What Ollie's up to?"

"What?" I slipped a bookmark in and closed my book.

"Has he said anything about this weekend?"

"Sod me Monkey I've hardly seen him over the weekend. Why? What's up?"

Monkey slid up nearer me as if he had some great secret to share. I was suddenly intrigued but it was a bit of a let-down. They'd been to the bohemian café in Barry but felt so out of place they cut the visit short. Then, later, when they were contemplating getting back to camp Ollie said he wasn't ready to go back and went off on his own. "He only just made it back to camp on time."

'So what? Where's the big mystery?"

Monkey waved his watch in front of me. "He went in to Barry again this afternoon on his own and he's not back yet."

"He went in on his own?"

"Yeah, really weird."

I shrugged. "I wouldn't say it's weird. Not really. Unusual, yeah, but that's all."

As if on cue the door opened and Ollie came strolling in.

Monkey nudged me. "Here he is," he whispered. "Find out."

As he got up from my bed I said, "fuck off. Ask him yourself."

Ollie looked up. "Ask who what?"

"Monkey wants to know what you've been up to in Barry."

Monkey groaned. "Thanks Draper. Thanks a fuckin' bundle."

Ollie just smiled. "I can honestly say no monkey business." He laughed at his own joke. "Get it? Monkey business?" He shook his head. "Oh, sod it. Please yourself."

I frowned. It would seem something had put him in a very good mood.

Naturally, Monday morning on the way to breakfast, I just had asked him what the big mystery might be. He came to a halt. "No mystery Draper. The others were all going on about how out of place we were in that coffee lounge, but it didn't bother me, I was okay in there. I felt pretty well at home, and that's it."

"But they said you went back into Barry on your own?"

"So what? I went back on my own. No big deal, okay?

"Fine"

"Good, now that's cleared up let's go eat."

As we reached the Mess Hall I stopped Ollie at the door. "Ollie?"

"Now what?" he said impatiently.

"What is it you're not telling me?"

With less than a week to go we I was much improved but not quite ready. Chas had grudgingly agreed to drop the songs I struggled with and replaced them with less

124

complicated ones. We were told we had enough time for four or five songs. But then our application to use the Band Hut to get another two rehearsals in was rejected, with the exception one hour after tea on the Wednesday before the dance on Friday.

"What do we do now?" Jumbo asked. "We need a bit more practice somehow?"

Chas had the bright idea of doing a sort of show in the NAAFI one evening but that was quickly torpedoed when it was pointed out that the Station Band would be using the drums for their own rehearsals and Paul pointed out we didn't have adequate amps to play anywhere.

And so, it was back to the Drying Room. My heart sank. "How can that help?" I asked. "It's a bloody poor substitute for a drum kit and it's more time on a drum kit I need."

"True," Chas said. "But we can work on your timing, and that's the important thing at the moment." He smiled. "We'll get you sorted." I didn't mention the metronome, I didn't want to raise their hopes just in case it hadn't worked.

I was quickly finding out what being an Airframe Mechanic meant. To my utter amazement I found myself really enjoying it. There were hydraulic systems to learn, pneumatic systems, liquid oxygen systems plus all types of riveting. There were wheels and tyres including brakes. Then we had flaps and ailerons and elevators and more besides. There wasn't much of the aircraft we didn't work on.

My exam had scored seventy-three and I was happy with that, but I knew I couldn't sit back relax, we were learning so much and at such a pace it was keeping us on our toes.

The instructors were a mixture of civilians and NCOs. Corporal Billington was a National Service leftover who taught Aircraft Control Systems. He hated it. Rumour was he was a university lecturer before being called up.

He had a reputation for being a bit eccentric and our very first lesson with him proved it to be true.

He was a good six foot with a mess of dark, wiry, hair. He wore his glasses on the end if his nose and when he looked at you he peered over the top. He looked every inch the textbook university professor.

He strolled into the room, picked up a piece of chalk and banged it against the blackboard. He then chalked round and round in a tight circle until there was this blob of white in the centre of the blackboard. After that he took a book off his desk and held it up. He said nothing, he just peered over his specs at the room full of bemused pupils. After what seemed an age he spoke. "This class is Aircraft Control Systems which is basically Advanced Theory of Flight. This in my hand is a very good book that I am halfway through and very much enjoying." He went to the blackboard. "And this is a chalked spot."

He spun on his heels and stared, wide eyed, at a classroom full of frowning pupils.

"Any Boy here who has the slightest interest in Advanced Theory of Flight please raise your hand. If more than half the room shows in favour we start the lesson; less than half, then I get to read my book. So, to start with please focus on the the white chalk spot."

He sat down in his chair, put his feet up on the desk and opened his book. Again, we were kept waiting. My arm was tiring by the time he waved us to put them down.

"Right, it seems you all want a lesson. If you'll simply gaze on the chalk spot while I finish this chapter and then we'll commence."

Once he got going he was terrific. He made it interesting and funny.

"You can tell he was interesting." I said to Ollie as we left the classroom. "That hour just flew by."

'Oh, very witty Draper."

'You what?"

'Flew by? Get it?" He laughed." The Advanced Theory of Flight? Flew by?"

He really was in a good mood.

Ollie had completely ignored my question about him being less than forthcoming about Barry. I decided he'd tell me in his own time. That was, of course, if there was anything to tell. And, as it turned out, there was.

It was Friday, the evening of the dance that he decided to fill me in. In all honesty I was so nervous about the evening ahead it would be the weekend before I would get the full significance of what he had to say.

He had met a woman in the coffee lounge. She was serving behind the counter. I heard him call her a woman rather than a girl although it didn't register. When he said she was not just a woman she was a married woman I remember thinking wow, I must have misheard him. I even said. "What?"

"You heard," he replied, but I went straight back into my own little world again thinking about the gig.

"See Draper," he said. "Now you know why I don't want the others to know. I'm trusting you to say nothing." He looked at me. "Okay?"

127

I nodded although I'd hardly heard a word.
"How does Apache start?" I asked. "I've gone blank."

My nerves were all over the place. I had hardly touched
my food since breakfast.
Chas poked his head round the door after tea to ask if I had
a white shirt. I said I had, and he told me to wear it on
stage. The words 'on stage' set my nerves jangling. I tried
not to show him how terrified I was. I lifted my shirt off
the hanger and held it up for his approval. He gave me a
thumbs up. "Black tie?"
I nodded.
"Excellent. See you over there. I'm going to check out the
gear. You should do the same. Check out the drums before
they start playing." He gave the thumbs up again. "This is
it. We're gonna knock 'em senseless."

I pulled on my white shirt, but my fingers were trembling
so badly I couldn't fasten the buttons. As I wrestled with
them Jumbo came in to the hut. He watched me for a few
seconds. "Struggling?"
I nodded, not daring to try to speak.
He fastened the last few buttons. Standing this close
together I was reminded of what a big guy he was. His
hands were perfectly calm, no sign of nerves at all. "I just
thought I'd pop in to see how you're doing."
"How do you do it?"
"Do what?"
"Meditate like you were on about? It obviously works, you
stay so calm. Aren't you ever scared?"
He turned up my shirt collar ready for my tie. "Yeah, I had
a few butterflies first time, I admit, but no, I'm not scared.
Excited, yes."

I took a deep breath and exhaled slowly.

He handed me my tie. "You'll be fine. Come on, get the tie on and I'll walk over with you."

It was a warm evening and at half past seven as we walked over to the dance I felt a line of cool sweat run down my back followed a second later by a trickle from my armpit. "Bloody hell, Jumbo, is it me or is it muggy."

He laughed and patted me on the back. "It's you. It's your ..." He pulled his hand away "Stone the crows, Mark, your shirt is soaking wet."

"F'fucksake sake I can't do this. I'm not ready."

The band were called The Renegades and they really looked the part all dressed in red jackets with black velvet collars. Chas was on the stage talking with the guitarist and I went to look at the drums. It was a much bigger kit than the one in the Band Hut. It had a beautiful silver glitter finish and on the front of the bass drum was the name of the band. They were immaculate.

A voice from behind me said. "Don't touch anything."

I turned to find myself facing a pale faced youth sporting long sideburns and Buddy Holly style glasses. "I've got it set exactly as I want it."

He walked round the kit and sat on the stool. Pulling a pair of drumsticks from a holder he did a roll round the kit. It was so smooth and so powerful I almost took my breath away. I noticed his arms moved very little, it was all in the wrists. He did a couple of other patterns and said. "You can move the stool and that's all. Got it?"

He sounded as if he resented me touching them at all and that gave me an idea. Maybe I'd found a get out of jail card. "Okay, I understand what you're saying," I said. "I think maybe it's best if I leave it all together. The guys have played without drums before. They won't mind."

 He looked a bit shocked at my reaction. "Don't be daft. No. Get on the stool and have a feel."

But all I could see was my way out with no blame on me. "No, no. Listen mate, I can see you're not too keen on me using the kit and I can appreciate that. it's a lovely kit. If you're not happy then I'm not bothered, so I'll just tell the lads I'm sitting this one out." I left the stage.

In one bound he was by my side, holding my elbow. "You've got it all wrong. I didn't mean don't touch full stop." He was looking a bit sheepish. "I simply meant that I'd rather alter them for you."

My idea hadn't worked. I swore under my breath.

With our need to get the gear sorted out with The Renegades we were way too early. We settled down at one of the side tables out of the way, and, as we sat chatting, Ollie appeared.

"How did you get in?" I asked. "The doors aren't open yet?"

"I told the Corporal Boy on the door that I was on vital band business." He swung his arm round from his back. "There ya go."

He handed me my drumsticks. "You might need these." He pulled up a chair and looked at the other three. "The fact is I'm worried about my young mate here. He's a nervous wreck."

"He'll be fine." Chas said. "Once he gets up there behind that kit he'll be great."

My insides froze as he mentioned the drums and my stomach began griping. "Excuse me gents," I groaned, "but I need the loo.".

"Bloody hell, Mark," Jumbo said. "You look terrible. You okay? You've gone as white as..." but he was still talking as I dashed past him and headed for the toilet.
I sat waiting for my stomach to erupt but nothing happened. After a few minutes Ollie came in to see if I was okay. I assured him I'd be out in a minute although I just wanted to sit there for ever. I heard The Renegades start playing. I hadn't realised I'd been sat there for so long. When I eventually emerged from the toilet I decided that as much as I wanted to watch the band, fresh air was what I needed.

Outside, in the cool evening breeze, I stood searching my brain for something that I'd done so many times it should be automatic, but no matter how hard I tried I couldn't remember the intro to the very first song, Apache. I was close to tears. I wanted to be anywhere but this bloody dance.
A voice behind me made me jump. "Hi, there. I thought I saw you sneaking out here." It was Cheryl. "Where were you earlier?"
I didn't want her to see me like this. I clenched my fists, took a deep breath and turned.
"Sorry, been tied up."
"I wasn't going to come tonight, I've got such an awful cold." She covered her face in her hanky. "Don't look at my nose."
"So, what made you come?"
She wiped her nose. She had her hair the way liked it; loose and curly framing her face. Her nose was red. "I wanted to see what you meant about your band?"
"Sorry, silly thing to have said. It's not my band."

"But you *are* in a band tonight?" she asked in a voice that said she'd be disappointed if I said no.

"I am. Yes."

"What do you play?"

I was tempted to tell her that I didn't play at all, that I was just a learner, but I quickly dismissed the idea. "The drums."

"Drums," she said clapping her hands. "I love the drums."

"Listen, I'm on soon," I said checking my watch. "Chat later?"

"Of course." She kissed my cheek. "I'm so excited." She turned to leave and then giggled. "I bet I've just given you my germs."

I smiled. "It was worth it."

As soon as she left I was amazed at just how much that short chat had calmed my nerves. It was time to go back in, but I felt a fair bit calmer. I went to join the others and listen to the band on stage.

As I walked across the dance floor I even managed a bit of a smile. All I could think was Cheryl had said she was excited.

Then, all too soon the band announced a short break and left the stage. Flight Lieutenant Copperfield took to the stage and tapped his microphone a few times and then, if that wasn't proof it was working he said, "one two, one two, testing."

He pointed at the stage. "We enjoyed them so much the last time that they're back again to play for us again. Put your hands together for your very own Sky-High."

And we were on.

There was a crowd rapidly forming in front of the stage. I was aware of Cheryl standing at the very front.

Jumbo turned to face the drums. I watched his foot for a few seconds to get the timing. I had the intro clearly in my head but then, with no warning, my nerves were back again. My arms were frozen to my sides.

Chapter Eleven

We left the stage to the sound of clapping and cheering. Chas slapped me on the back, "I knew you'd be alright," he said. I even let him twiddle my earlobe.
All I could think was thank fuck for Jumbo. It was all down to him.

What had begun as nerves had soon became sheer panic. Once the panic had set in I was lost. I couldn't get my arms to move and if I had managed to move them I couldn't think what I was supposed to play.

I could see Jumbo's foot giving me the timing, but I couldn't respond. He looked at me and clearly saw the abject terror etched on my face. Then he nodded. It was just a slight tilt of the head, but it seemed to say, 'don't worry we'll get you out of this'. And with that he began playing the intro on the bass guitar. 'Bomp, bomp, bomp, bomp. Bomp, bomp, bomp, bomp.' And then I could hear the war drums as clear as could be.

It was a brilliant idea. Within seconds I'd joined him. He nodded again as if to remind me of our conversation earlier. I would have nodded back to say thanks, but I was concentrating like crazy, watching his foot again. It might not be great, but I didn't care: I was on the stage and I was drumming.

Later, after I'd nipped back to change my shirt, I went looking for Cheryl. As I made my way across the dance floor people were patting me in the back and congratulating me. I felt ten feet tall.

I saw Cheryl sat with three-other girls. She hadn't seen me, so I watched her for a while waiting for a slow song before asking for a dance. When the band started playing a nice smooch number I made my move.

We shuffled slowly round the floor. I put my hands round her waist and pulled her close. She put her hands around my neck. After a while I asked her what she thought of the band?"

She put her mouth close to my ear. "I thought the guitarist was really good."

"Who, Chas? Oh yeah, he really is good. So, you liked it then?"

She leant back slightly. "Yes, it was really good, but what happened to you at the beginning? I thought you weren't going to start,' she said frowning. "You looked scared to death. Like you didn't know what to do."

I stopped dead in my tracks. It was like a punch in the stomach.

She saw the expression on my face and quickly kissed me on the cheek. "Oh, Mark, I'm so sorry, that wasn't nice." She stepped back. "Sorry."

She sneezed into her hankie.

Her nose was red and looked rather sore and her eyes were starting to run. We stood facing each other in silence. She really did look poorly. Then I realised the band was now playing a faster song and people were dancing round us.

I took her hand and guided her off the floor. She tucked her hankie up her sleeve and squeezed my hand. "I could kick myself sometimes. Sorry. Are you angry?"

I shook my head. "No. It's okay? You're entitled to your opinion. You obviously didn't think I was very good, eh? Well, that's amazing 'because I thought I was bloody awful!"

She started to laugh but it turned another sneeze.

She was still holding my hand and I squeezed hers' "Can I kiss you?"

She looked a bit taken aback. "No. Of course not! Don't be silly."

I felt a bit like a scolded child the way she snapped it out but then she said. "I'm all snotty and nasty. You'll have to ask me when I'm better."

My evening was made. That was an invite for a date if ever I heard one.

I was amazing what a pick-me-up it was knowing that I was now making real progress with Cheryl and at last the drumming was coming together. I was feeling on top of the world and now there was summer leave to look forward to. But before that we had exams, including our first practical exam. Classroom stuff was straightforward when it came to studying, but practical tests were do or die. We had spent a fair bit of time learning how to file a piece of metal into a perfect square and how to use hand drills as opposed to power tools but not a lot besides so what the exam would involve was a mystery.

The Saturday before the exam I was laying on my bed doing a bit of last-minute studying when Ollie came over and stood at the foot of my bed combing his hair. "Bloody Nora, Mark, you're keen, aren't you?"

"I haven't studied anything like enough, what with the drums and all that. l don't want to be the only one to fail the exams."

"Ah, right, I suppose so."

"Ollie," I ventured cagily. "changing the subject somewhat, did I hear you right the other day? Did you really say you were going out with a married woman?"

"I wouldn't say we were going out f'chrissake. I've only just met her."

"Yeah, but you did say a married woman?"

He nodded and gave me a mysterious grin. "I did,"

"So how old are we talking here?"

He frowned. "At a guess I'd say around thirty."

"Bloody hell!" I gushed.

"Shush! Keep it down. And don't go telling anyone. Now subject closed."

"Fair enough."

"Anyway," he said, lighting a cigarette. "I was just wondering what you fancy doing this afternoon? I find I'm at a loose end cos my lady friend is working, and I don't fancy staying here all afternoon."

"Bog all," I said. "I'm taking Cheryl to the flicks tomorrow and that's about me broke."

Ollie frowned. "You've spent the rest of your brother's quid already?"

"No, of course not"

"So, you're nowhere near fuckin' skint then."

"Well no, but I thought I'd put that away as a kind of a top-up fund for the times I take Cheryl out."

He groaned. "Bloody hell."

"What's that meant to mean?"

"Let's face it, Draper, you're ..." he stared up at the ceiling. "Oh, never mind. Forget it."

I should have left it there and done what he said: forget it, but I wanted to know just what he was going to say.

"No," I said. "I can't forget it just like that. Out with it!"

"Alright, you asked for it." He sat down heavily on my bed. "You've known this bird five minutes, had a couple of dances and a kiss in the cheek and suddenly you're acting like a lovestruck schoolboy. This is some bird who you've never actually taken out on a date yet, and has told you, if you remember, she doesn't want a boyfriend at the moment. Am I right?"

I threw my text book into my bedside locker and grabbed my wash bag. "Fuck you Ollie!" And I stormed off to the washroom.

That afternoon the majority of the lads were either off camp somewhere or over the NAAFI. I lay on my bed and watched Ollie get ready to go out. His bed was opposite mine and so it was hard not to watch him, but we were both avoiding eye contact.

He was definitely not headed for the NAAFI. Not with his best shirt and a smart tie. I wondered where he'd suddenly decided to go.

I just wished he hadn't had to make me feel so bloody small earlier? That was crappy? But now, now I'd calmed down, it was crystal clear that he was right. And now we weren't talking and that was my fault. He slipped his wallet in his back pocket and took a last look in the mirror.

"Just before you go," I called as he made for the door.

He turned.

I was about to say I was sorry, but he got in first. "No, leave it Draper, I know you're pissed off my mate, and you're entitled to be but I just wanna say I was out of order and I'm sorry."

"Yeah, well, so am I."

He came back and held out his hand and we shook. I flipped his tie with my finger. "You're still going out I see."

"No flies on you my son, eh what?"

"Where you off?"

"Guess."

"I thought she was working today?"

He winked. "I might just go for a coffee, anyway."

Sunday was a bit of a luxury; no church parade. The whole day to ourselves. I persuaded Andy Braithwaite to bring me a couple of slices of toast back from breakfast and settled down ready for breakfast in bed and a read of my book. When Andy came back he was clutching two slices of buttered toast and a mug of hot tea. "Here you are, your lordship," he quipped in a posh voice. "Breakfast as ordered." He grinned and added, "Tha' really is a lazy begger."

I thanked him and smiled to myself as he walked away; what a lovely way to start the day. Despite acknowledging that Ollie was right about me acting silly over Cheryl I was still getting quite excited about seeing her. I had no idea what film we were going to see, and I didn't really care.

Eventually I got up and made my way to the washroom. I brushed my teeth, showered, had my weekly shave, dried my hair and twenty minutes later I was dressed and ready to go.

Ollie looked at me with a smirk on his face.

"What's wrong with you?"

"Where are you going?"

"I told you yesterday, I'm taking Cheryl to the pictures."

He looked at his watch. "Well, you can set off now if you really can't wait, but I'm just wondering whatcha gonna do for the hour and a half before you're due to meet her?"

I looked at Ollie rather sheepishly. I was at it again. I grinned. "Lovesick schoolboy?"

Cheryl was waiting at the bus stop and I was pleased to see she was over her cold. She saw me and waved. She came and kissed my cheek which was a good start and we held hands as we walked but, when we arrived at the cinema, she stopped dead in her tracks and let go of my hand. It was a horror film starring Oliver Reed as a Werewolf and Cheryl didn't like horror films. She stood staring at the advertising board shaking her head and then suggested we do something else instead. I was devastated, I had waited a fair while to get a chance to get nice and cosy on the back row with the lights all dimmed. What's more a good horror film was an unexpected bonus; she'd definitely need a manly arm round her.

"We can't go anyway even if I wanted to." she said, pointing to the poster. "It's an X certificate and I'm not sixteen."

This was going down the pan rather quickly. I couldn't just walk away and give in, not when I had such high hopes. I persuaded her to let me give it a try and, providing we got in okay, if she found it too frightening, we'd leave. Getting in was a joke. The young lass in the ticket booth never even looked at me, I could have been a school kid in short trousers for all, she cared; she just pushed the tickets out and carried on noisily chewing her gum.

When we came out I was walking on air. It had worked to perfection. We'd cuddled tight whenever Oliver Reed grew his gruesome fangs and I buried my face in her hair breathing in the fragrance of her shampoo. When, toward the end of the show, I tried for a kiss she came to me eagerly and it was heavenly. The last fifteen minutes or so we hardly saw the film. I made a tentative move to touch her breast, but she moved my hand gently away. I left it at that.

By the time we'd had a kiss and cuddle at the bus station I had an ache in my trousers fit to bust and I spent the entire twenty minutes bus journey back to camp wearing a stupid grin on my face.

Just like a lovesick schoolboy.

Leave was looming fast. As much as I was looking forward to it I was sad not to be seeing Cheryl for so long. The Progress Evaluation Test turned out to be simply a bit of filing and drilling and that was job done.

We wouldn't get the results until after the summer leave, but everyone seemed confident that they'd done okay.

Me and Ollie were walking back from the Mess Hall after lunch on the day before leave when I suggested to Ollie that we liaised with each other to get the same train coming back.

"Yeah, normally I'd say yes, but I can't this time."

"No? What's up?"

He looked around to make sure there was no one in ear shot. "I'm trusting you here, Draper, f'fucksake keep it to yourself."

"Come on Ollie, what do you think…"

"Yeah, Fair enough." He draped his arm round my shoulder as we walked. "The fact is I'm coming back on the Friday."

"You can't. The huts are all locked up till Sunday."

"And who mentioned the huts?"

'What?"

"Listen, I'm coming back to spend the weekend with my lady friend. Her sister lives just outside Cardiff and I'm staying there."

"But what about hubby?"

"Him and the sister hate each other. Long story there. Another day perhaps. Anyway, he won't go near her sister and the sister doesn't care about us being together 'cause she quite likes the fact he's being cheated on."

"Fuckin' hell, you're sleeping with her?"

He smiled and nodded. "Naturally, my son."

"Bloody Ollie, if you fell in shit you'd come up smelling of roses."

He just laughed."

I shrugged. "Seriously though mate, I hope you know what you're doing Ollie. I really do."

"If my memory serves me well, Draper," he laughed, "I know a damn sight better than you."

,

Chapter Twelve

The very first day home I woke early. I heard Ray getting up although I pretended to be asleep. As soon as I heard the back door shut I got out of bed and quickly dressed. The house was quiet with just my mum tidying up after the men had gone to work.

"Early bird again," she said as I entered the kitchen. "Getting to be a habit."

Mum was a tiny woman with pink cheeks, a peach like complexion and thinning hair. She had a wicked sense of humour and the warmest smile I've ever seen.

She was wearing a faded green apron and had a tea towel draped over her shoulder. "Breakfast?" she asked as I sat at the table.

"Toast and tea would be nice, ta."

"Have you spoken to your brother?" she asked, putting a couple of slices of bread under the grill.

"Not yet. Why?"

"Then you won't have heard."

"Heard what?"

"About your brother. He's getting married."

"Married? Ray?" I said louder than I meant to. "Since when?"

"He told us last Friday. October or November apparently."

'Who's the desperate woman?"

"Now Mark, stop that." She set about making a pot of tea. "Her name's Bernice and she works in the office on the farm."

"Bit of a surprise was it?"

I caught a hint of a smile quickly come and go. She knew what I meant.

"Well?"

She turned the toast over. "I don't know. If she is he hasn't said as much."

"Ray getting hitched," I said shaking my head. "Who'd have thought it?"

"Who indeed. We never even knew he was courting."

"Mind you, mum, it'll be great for you and Alf. Place to yourselves."

She handed me the toast and started pouring us both a cup of tea. She looked me straight in the eye. "I suppose so."

Three little words, yes, but delivered in a way I could only call, frosty. I stared at her, looking for something more but the moment had gone. Sometimes getting anything from my mum was hard going.

I decided to test the water. "You don't seem too thrilled mum."

She passed me the tea and smiled. "We'll see."

I sensed that she wasn't going to say any more on the subject. I ate my toast in silence. "Any plans today?" mum asked.

I nodded. "Thought I'd have a coke in the Pelosis for a coke and maybe read a few pages of my book."

"You still love your books then?"

"Oh, yeah. Although I've changed quite a bit just lately. A bloke at camp got me into different stuff." I wondered what she'd say if I told her about Adrian trying in on with me?

144

The Margate beach was fairly full, the early ones picking their favourite spot, but I knew that in an half an hour or so it would be packed. I walked along the front, stopping now and again to play on the arcade machines. Following the road round past the clock tower, toward the harbour, I made my way to the Pelosis coffee bar and bought a Coke. In amongst my change was a sixpenny bit so I slid it into the juke box and selected Roy Orbison's Dream Baby and Sandy Nelson's Let There Be Drums.

I sat idly toying with my straw and gazing out if the window when a voice behind me said, "going by the haircut I'd guess you joined the Army?"
I turned. "I always said you was a bright girl Mary, but it's the RAF."
Mary Foster was my first taste of young love and, without doubt, the first girl I kissed. We went out for walks together and the occasional afternoon in the cinema back when we were only fourteen. It was ended when her family moved away somewhere. Oxford, I believe.
She pulled up a chair and sat beside me. "The RAF must suit you, Mark, you're looking really good."
I smiled. "Apart from the hair cut."
She laughed. Mary was a pretty girl in a strange sort of way. Her face was round and chubby looking, whereas she was actually quite trim. Her hair was very similar to Cheryl's, all loose curls, but Mary's was darker and longer. She had totally kissable lips, soft and full, and I'd always found her attractive and now, in a smart white

summer blouse and short skirt she had clearly filled out very nicely and was even more attractive than ever.

"When did you move back here?" I asked.

"We haven't. We're just here for a few days visiting. We're staying in Aunty May's boarding house."

"I don't suppose you fancy, maybe the cinema or something."

"When?"

"I'm free full stop so it's up to you."

She pursed her lips. "Mmm, tonight is out." Another pause for thought. "Tomorrow seems to be favourite."

"Fine with me."

She smiled. "Just like old times, Mark."

I laughed. "Apart from the fact that I'm paying."

"Ah, well, that's even better."

At tea that evening I grilled Ray about his girlfriend. Was he bringing her home to meet everybody? How long had they been courting? Where would the wedding be?

All the time what I wanted to say was: how far gone is she? What do you want a boy or a girl? I steered clear of that idea.

Ray was happy answering my questions until I asked about where they planned to live and then he looked a little uncomfortable. First, he glanced over at mum and then Alf and I knew what was going on. "We're not exactly sure yet. Got a couple of ideas."

And I understood mum's frosty look at breakfast,

Mary wanted to go into Westgate to see 'A Taste of Honey'. I wasn't fussed what film we saw, I was just looking forward to a replay of my back-row fun with Cheryl. However, it wasn't too long before it came clear

146

that wasn't about to happen. Mary wanted to watch the film. I managed to put my arm round her but twice I moved in for a kiss and twice I was brushed gently away. Luckily it was an excellent film and I wasn't too disappointed.

But the 'B' film was totally different. An awfully boring crime story. I thought to myself she can't be watching this rubbish, so I decided that it was worth one more attempt at a kiss. Surely, she wouldn't turn me away now this crap was on. She sensed me moving towards her and put her finger to my lips. I sighed heavily trying hard not to sulk.

"You don't want to watch this rubbish, do you," she whispered?

"You must be joking."

She smiled. "I got that impression."

She kissed me. It was a fleeting effort, her lips brushing mine like the flickering of an eyelash. "Come on, let's go for a walk."

Along the cliff top we found a seating shelter and Mary suggested we sat for a while. I put my arm round her shoulders and she held my hand. When I eventually kissed her, she allowed her tongue to probe my lips. The next time we kissed I opened my mouth slightly and our tongues touched. Then it took over completely and I couldn't believe how exciting it was.

After a while I slowly moved my hand round to her breast as we kissed. She seemed okay with that and so I slid my hand inside her top and felt her breast outside her bra. Mary was quite happy with it and seemed to be enjoying our kissing.

I tried sliding my hand up inside her bra, but it was too tight. I tried sliding in from the top with the same result. The only thing left to try was undoing the bra.

I found the clasp or whatever it was, but could I work out how to unfasten it? No, not even close.

She laughed gently in my ear. "Here, let me."

And then I was holding a bare breast and it was wonderful.

I walked her home to her Aunt's place and we kissed for a while at the garden gate and asked if I could see her again.

"I've enjoyed this evening," she said smiling. "I really have, but we're only here on a flying visit. So, I can't see you again."

"Oh, right," I said. "That came out of the blue."

"Yes, sorry.

I kissed her for the last time. "Just my luck."

She watched me walk to the end of the road and waved. As I waved back she blew me a kiss.

I'm a Margate man through and through and Ramsgate was always the poor relation. I hardly ever bothered going there and it was a fair bet I wouldn't have gone this leave but for a strange fluke.

I was making my way along Margate sea front when I saw a rather amateur looking flyer stuck on the railings above the stairs to the Gents toilet. It caught my eye because it was simply an RAF roundel with the date and venue. I thought it must be advertising some kind of RAF function, but then I remembered Lenny talking about Mod symbols and the roundel was one. Also, the venue was in Ramsgate and that was another thing he'd said.

The more I heard Lenny enthuse about this Mod thing the more intrigued I was becoming. I checked the date. It was the next day. I had no other plans and thought it might be amusing to surprise old Lenny boy.

But then, when it came to what to wear, I was stuck. I had nothing in my wardrobe remotely like the gear Lenny wore. In the end I settled for my olive-green trousers and a white shirt with my favourite V-neck jumper which I carried in case the evening cooled later, and, with one last check in the mirror, I was ready.

I set off straight after tea which meant I arrived in Ramsgate way too early. I decided to take a stroll along the front to kill time before the do. I assumed it was a dance but really hadn't a clue what to expect.

I made my way to a familiar spot along the cliff tops looking down on the Western Undercliff. This place held vivid memories of being ten or eleven and standing up against the railings with mum and Alf and looking down onto the prom and the motorcycles competing in the Sprint Trials. It was an event Alf loved.

I stood on the prom looking up at the cliff I recalled the horrendous racket of screaming engines as the riders gunned their machines to the limit and, no matter how hard I jammed my fingers in my ears, I could never keep out the noise. And then there was the smell. A mixture of petrol, hot Red-X and burning rubber, all combining to form a blue haze that crept up the cliff side and assailed the nostrils. I smiled to myself. Just for a brief second there I could have sworn I caught a whiff.

I turned away from the memories and made for the Marina. I loved walking round the Marina and at the ice cream parlour on the corner I bought something called a Super Whip ice cream cornet. It was the latest taste sensation apparently, but I think it was just a fancy name for an ice cream that melted faster than the others.

Just after eight I made my way to the venue. According to the tatty flyer I'd taken from the railings along Margate front, it kicked off at seven thirty.
Another home-made poster, outside the venue read:
'The Mods are coming.'
The First Meeting Outside London.
Don't miss it.
I smiled to myself. Once again folks, Mark Draper is in at the birth. Although looking at the sparse gathering in the hall I wasn't sure what was being born.

The first thing was to find Lenny. I was looking forward to seeing his girlfriend.
I was also looking forward to seeing his face when he saw me there.
But a couple of laps of the room made it clear he wasn't here yet, otherwise I would easily have found him.
I got served at the bar no problem and stood in the corner off the hall drinking and watching.
It really was a different world. I've never seen boys so immaculately dressed. Some in suits, some in cardigans and all with similar hair styles fairly short and centre parting. The girls seemed to favour short, shapeless dresses and fairly short hair not that dissimilar to the boys.
The music was new to me also. Record after record I'd never heard before. I knew 'Will You Still Love Me Tomorrow?' and 'You Always Hurt the One You Love,' and one or two others but that was it.

After a couple of pints, I was getting bored. No sign of Lenny and this was not really my cup of tea. Then I saw three girls sat at the other side of the room. I'd spent enough time already this evening watching the strange, almost dreamy type dancing so I thought I'd give it a try. To my surprise the first girl I asked said yes; she even stayed on the floor for a couple more dances. Then, well pleased with myself, I went and bought another beer. Around nine it started to fill up a bit. I was drinking too much and decided I was bored with it all. There was no sign of Lenny. It was time for a pee and get the next bus home.

I had a long overdue pee and was leaving the toilet when someone barged into me. I assumed he was pissed. "Steady on mate," I laughed. "You'll have us both on the deck." He glared at me and stabbed his finger in my chest. I was a bit drunk but not so drunk as to not smell trouble when it was near.

"Stay away from that girl," he sneered. "Okay?"

"What girl?"

"We seen ya dancing," he said.

"Okay, fair enough pal," I said. "Message received and understood. I didn't realise she was your bird."

"She's not my bird but she's one of us and you ain't."

I stared at him. "What?"

"This is a Mod dance," he pointed at my clothes, "And you ain't anybody's idea of a Mod."

"Oh, I see." I said. He was a weedy looking thing. A good sneeze would blow him over.

I stared at his freckled face. "I hear what you're saying pal but unless you want a smack in the mouth I'd fuck of out of my face."

He stepped back. "If that's how you want it then away you go." He smiled and opened the door for me.

I was fuming. That puny little twat wasn't telling me what to do. I went back inside and bought another beer. I drank it quickly and then walked over to the girl and asked for another dance. She shook her head and turned her back on me.

As I walked away I became aware I was being watched, like the mysterious stranger in a cliched cowboy film, who, when he enters the saloon, causes all conversation to stop and all eyes to focus on him. I was tempted to whistle the theme tune from 'The Good, The Bad and The Ugly' but I resisted.

It was time to leave.

The last pint had really been one too many. I was nowhere near as drunk as the night I peed in the wardrobe, but I was a fair way from being sober.

I lurched out of the hall and leant against the wall outside taking in a lung full of fresh air. Once I felt sure I wasn't going to throw up I chanced walking. Thankfully I was reasonably steady.

I walked carefully in the direction of the bus stop.

I had no idea how long I was going to have to wait for the bus but the longer it was the better. I could do with a little time I to get myself together. I didn't think the bus conductor would be too happy if I threw up all over his bus.

Just down from the bus stop was a lamp post and I propped myself up against that and settled down to wait for the bus.

I never saw them coming and by the time my brain registered what was going on it was too late.

I sensed, rather heard, running feet. Before I could even think about what was going on a fist hit me square in the mouth. Another hit my cheek and my face was rammed into the lamppost. Four sets of fists rained into me.

As I fell to the floor I heard a voice shout:" Woah, stop, stop, for crying out loud, It's my mate." Lenny's face appeared in front of me and I was being lifted to my feet. "Oh, fucking hell, Mark. "I'm so sorry. I didn't realise it was you or …. Oh hell."

He wiped my face with his handkerchief. "Sod me. What a mess." Two of the Mods walked away but the third seemed to be a mate of Lenny's. "What the hell are we gonna do with him?"

Lenny looked a bit confused and vague. "Eh?"

"Face it Lenny, they won't let him on the bus like that." That's when I threw up.

They took me back to the dance hall and into the toilet and washed me down. The general opinion was I needed to go to hospital, but I refused.

Somehow, after what seemed hours, Lenny managed to find a lad with a car and persuaded him to drive us back into Margate. The only condition being that we took a roll of toilet paper in the car with us, so I wouldn't bleed all over his car

Chapter Thirteen

When I got home mum and Alf were in bed and Ray was
not yet home. I went straight to bed. I thought I'd find the
first aid kit in the morning and get a couple of plasters.
I must have gone straight to sleep because the next thing I
knew it was morning and Ray was leaning over me. "What
the fuck have you done?" he yelled, before charging out
the bedroom calling for mum.
I tried to sit up, but my face was glued to the pillow
somehow. I eased my face free of the pillow and looked
down at the dark red goo. Blood. The pillow and the sheets
were soaked in it. Then Ray and my mum were running in
and Ray was ranting on about what a mess I was. My left
eye wouldn't open. When I touched it it was caked with
dried blood.
"Oh, my good lord, Mark. What happened?" Mum cried.
"What have you done?" She pushed Ray to the door.
"Water and towel."

"Hurry Ray," I shouted. "I'm having a baby." I laughed at my own joke, but my mum was not amused. "This is nothing to joke over."

Her voice was slightly shaky, and she was close to tears. "What have you done?" she asked again.

I gave her the nearest thing to a smile I could manage. "I was picking my nose and I slipped."

Ray arrived carrying a bowl of water and a towel. "What's he done?" he asked handing mum the bowl.

"I have no idea. He just keeps making silly jokes."

She began gently washing my face. The crust of blood over my eye was too thick to wash off and she prised it gently away. "Oh, Mark, this needs stitching."

As more of the blood washed away the more upset she got. I was now aware my lower lip was badly swollen and hanging out and, now the crust had been removed, blood was running freely from my eyebrow. My mum was crying. She dabbed my lip and asked me again what had happened. I gave her a quick outline of the evening's events and tried to sound upbeat. I hated to see her upset.

Ray borrowed the farm's delivery van and drove me to the hospital. I had a stitch in my lip and two in my eyebrow and my nose was broken leaving me with me with a shadow of two black eyes. Ray had to get the van back and I told him I'd be okay walking home.

When I left the hospital, the sun was shining in a clear blue sky and I was happy walking but then, after only a hundred yards or so I suddenly started shivering from head to toe. It came totally out of the blue. As if that wasn't embarrassing enough, I started crying. People walking by were staring at me and I thought what a sight I must look with an enormous bottom lip, two black eyes, stitches in my eyebrow, shaking like a shitting dog and blubbering like a baby. I made my way home the long way using the back streets. The less people seeing me in this state the better. The shaking and the tears had cleared by the time I reached home.

Lenny called on me that evening after work and he was quite shocked to see how much damage they'd inflicted in such a short time. "If only I'd seen you sooner," he groaned.

"Where did you appear from anyway?' I asked. "I looked several times and never saw you."

Lenny explained how he'd waited for his girlfriend to arrive by train, but she didn't turn up so then he tried phoning but couldn't get an answer. He'd eventually arrived at the dance when his mate Steve and a couple of the other guys were setting off to find me. "I just tagged on behind Kenny," he said. "Shit luck really."

I nodded. Shit luck yes, that about says it all. Every time I feel life is plodding along quite nicely, I always manage to run into shit luck.

First, I find myself in bed with a very willing young lady and I'm short of a bloody Johnny, then I try to get closer to brother Ray by admiring his crappy motorbike and end up in the roadside unconscious and concussed and now, when I decide to give Lenny a surprise by turning up at his Mod dance, I end up getting the living daylights kicked out of me.

When we were granted two weeks leave it seemed like a long break, but it had flown by and as the the end drew near I thought of Ollie shacking up with his married woman on the last weekend while I hadn't even gotten close to getting a bit. Jammy sod.

The break had given me plenty of time to think about things and plenty of things to think about. Thinking about Ollie with his mystery woman got me thinking about my sex life, or lack of it.

It was early days with Cheryl, I hardly knew her, but I had the distinctive impression she wasn't thinking how she'd really like to jump my bones anytime soon.

No, as much as I was looking forward to seeing Cheryl again I felt pretty sure I needed to accept that she wasn't Denise, she wasn't going to invite me into her bedroom; she wasn't Mary, she wasn't going to undo her bra for me; she wasn't a married woman with a bed to share, she was Cheryl and she was lovely, and that's all she needed to be. Also, I had decided that I was a drummer. I still had plenty to learn, but it was what I now wanted. I understood if it hadn't been for Paul being so much better on guitar I would never have dreamed of playing the drums and it was just my way of getting back into the band, but now I was certain it was what I wanted. The money I was saving in my Post Office Savings Book would be the start of saving for the drum kit.

I decided I was going to travel back on the Sunday rather than Monday and as I had to get up early Sunday morning, I had a quiet evening in the pub with Ricky. Even though I was not late back, Mum and Alf had already gone to bed. The first thing I noticed in the morning was that Ray's bed hadn't been slept in.

I packed my stuff roughly into my bag and went down stairs. Mum had promised me a full breakfast to keep me going and a sandwich to go in my bag for when I got back to camp.

Alf was drinking a mug of tea and mum had poured me one ready. I pulled up a chair and took a sip of tea. "Ta, mum," I said. "Best drink of the day."

Then I felt it. The atmosphere. You could have cut it into pieces and served it up for breakfast.

I looked at Alf, but he was just staring into his mug. I glanced over at mum, she was putting sausages in the frying pan.

"Was it something I said?" I joked.

Alf just grunted, and my mum said nothing.

"I see Ray's bed's not been slept in." I looked over at Alf. "I suppose he slept at his girlfriend's place, did he?"

"Ask your mother."

'Mum?"

The sausages began sizzling and she fetched a pack of bacon from the pantry. She glared at Alf. "I told you I don't want to talk about this in front of Mark. Just leave it alone for now."

"You would say that!" he sneered. "Anything to avoid facing it."

Mum ignored him and turned the sausages

But he was straight back in there again. "Your son asked you a question, are you going to ignore him?" This was the Alf I was happy to get away from; nasty and spiteful. He was determined to get her back up and he succeeded.

She banged a plate down angrily on the work surface. "All week I've been trying to get an answer from him," she said icily "And do I get a decision? No, of course I don't. And then last night when Ray brings it up he sides against me!"

"I just made a decision. That's more than you can say."

"*You* decided? No, I don't think so. Bernice you mean; she had you weighed up completely, you old fool."

Alf stormed out if his chair sending it scuttling across the room. His temper was nothing new to me; it had come my way too many times. "This is so fucking well like you woman! Always someone else's fault."

Mum spun round, almost dragging the frying pan from the cooker. "Don't use that language in this house!"

But Alf was at the door. "Balls to you!" he yelled as he snatched his boots from the cupboard. "Balls, balls, balls."

"That's it. Here we go. The same as always. Can't handle it so clear off out. Where is it this time? Can't be the pub it's too early so I'd guess the allotment "

The door slammed, and he was gone carrying his boots in his hand.

I stared at my mum. She was holding back the tears.

"Bloody hell mum, what was that all about?"

She added a few rashers of bacon to the pan. "After breakfast."

And, sure enough, it was not mentioned until we'd eaten breakfast and washed the dishes. Only then did she tell me: All week she had been trying to get Alf to discuss Ray and Bernice's situation. Mum felt sure Ray was going to ask if they could live with them. There were problems that needed sorting out, but Alf just said that she had no reason to assume that Ray was going to ask and, even if he did it could be sorted.

Then, last evening Ray had brought Bernice home to meet mum and Alf and to say that they were struggling to find a place, and could they move in with them.

"Bernice was all over Alf. She kissed him on the cheek as she arrived and then said all the right things." She grunted. "It was well rehearsed."

She turned to me. "I couldn't believe it. I simply could not believe it. Suddenly, he's saying yes, of course they can move in. No problem."

I frowned. "What is the problem?"

She sighed heavily. "You."

"Me?"

"Yes, of course. It's a two-bedroom house. What happens when you come home on leave? Where are you going to sleep?"

I nodded. "Good point."

After breakfast I finished my packing, checked I had my travel warrant in my bag, and I was ready to leave.

I was about to kiss my mum goodbye when Alf came in with Ray and Bernice. The door was hardly shut behind him when he started, "Ray and Bernice have agreed to B and B it when Mark is on leave. So, as I said before, there is no problem." He nodded and looked around as if expecting a round of applause.

I got my first look at Bernice. She certainly wasn't what you would call attractive. Her nose was the first thing of note; too large and bony. Her hair was a dull brown and needed a good brushing. She wore no make-up.

"We're not asking for a permanent fix, Mum," Ray said. "We *are* looking for somewhere else. Honest."

Mum just stood looking at the trio.

"We won't be any bother." Bernice chipped in. "Really."

Mum half smiled. "Oh, I know that dear. You won't bother me because I won't be here."

"Now what are you on about?" Alf said gruffly. "Won't be here?"

"That's right my love." She took off her apron and threw it on the chair. "I'm leaving!"

"Leaving?" Alf repeated sounding perplexed.

"Yes, Alf, leaving."

"One little tiff and you're off? Don't talk daft woman."
She turned away and combed her hair in the mirror. "If
you think I'm walking out over just this issue, Alf, then all
I can say is you must have been sleepwalking through this
marriage for the last few years."

She left the room and I heard her clumping up the stairs.
"Where will you go ya daft bat?" Alf yelled after her,
"You can't just walk out like that. For a start you've no
money and then where you going to stay?" He shook his
head. "Silly bugger." He smiled lamely at Bernice. "Give
her a minute and she'll be fine."

But she wasn't fine.

I went upstairs to see if she was okay and found her
carefully packing a small suitcase "Where are you going?"
I asked

She told me she was going to my Aunty Annie's in
Maidstone and so I said I'd get the train with her. I was
going to miss mine anyway.?

We walked to the station in comparative silence. We had a
bit of good luck and found a compartment to ourselves.
Once we were on our way I asked her what Aunty Annie
thought of all this.

Aunty Annie lost her husband just over a year ago and
mum told me that when she had phoned her sister some
weeks previous she was told to come anytime, she'd love
the company. I asked mum what she meant by 'some
weeks previous' and that's when she opened up to me and
it all came flooding out.

"It's not about Ray wanting to move Bernice in. That's just
a grain of sand on Margate beach. No, it's much more than

that." She sighed heavily. "I'm forty-two Mark, I'm still alive, and I want to stay alive, but that man is killing me. I want to go dancing, I want to go out to the cinema occasionally. I want to go out to a nice restaurant. All I ever do is listen to that miserable sod snoring in front of the television all evening. I want a holiday, anywhere, I don't care. I haven't just decided to go it's been coming for over a year.

"How long are you gonna keep him sweating."

She looked at me her jaw set hard. "I'm not keeping him sweating. It's not a game, Mark, I've left him."

And that was that. I gazed out the window at the Kent countryside flashing by, mulling over all that had been said, and we passed the rest of the journey in near silence. As the train slowed into Maidstone station she took her bag from the rack and smiled at me. "Don't think about it too hard, Mark. I know what I'm doing. I'm only surprised I left it this long." She kissed me on the cheek. "I'll write."

I nodded. "Yeah, that'd be good."

She watched until the train set off again and stood on the platform waving.

I waved back. All I could think was how small she looked.

I was so wrapped up in what had gone on with mum and Alf I forgot I was still bearing the scars of battle. As soon as I got in the hut I was reminded. Geordie came in about twenty minutes after me. "Ha'way man. Whose fists have you been battering?" He laughed and came over for a better look. "What the hell happened to you?"

"You should see the other guy."

His eyes widened. "Really? Who, how, when, where?"

"Nah, I'm bullshitting you."

I related my tale.

Ollie got back Sunday evening. He took one look at me and grinned. "Fuck me Draper, I leave you alone for two weeks and look what happens. He threw his bag on to his bed. "So? What *did* happen?"

"I'll show you mine if you show me yours."

"What?"

I laughed. "I'll tell you what happened to me if you tell me about your weekend."

Ollie's story was far more interesting than mine. "Listen Draper, he said, "I keep saying it I know but I'll say it again. This is just between...."

I cut him short. "Piss off, Ollie. You know I'm safe." I looked around making there was no one in hearing range and said, "but just tell me again about that bit in the bath."

When things had settled down and the stories all been told I pulled my book from the locker and flopped on my bed. I'd hardly read a couple of pages when Paul charged into the room with a grin right across his face. "Hey, Mark, you've got to see this," he blurted, skidding to a halt at the foot of my bed.

I grunted. "Can't you just tell me."

"No. Definitely not."

I put my book down. "Okay, but this better be good."

His grin widened. "It's better than that."

Now I was hooked. "In that case, lead on plum duff."

Paul took us to Chas's room where Chas and Jumbo were looking at something on Chas's bed. I couldn't see what because the two were in the way. When I got to the bed I couldn't believe my eyes. There, laid on the bed, was a bright, gleaming new Fender Stratocaster Guitar just like the one Hank Marvin used in The Shadows. It was beautiful. For a while we looked in silence and then Jumbo laughed. "It's amazing. I can't believe it's real."

"Oh, it's real okay," Chas nodded. "You too could own such a machine. All you need is a year's salary."

I stared at him. "What? Are you serious?"

"I'm exaggerating, of course, but it's still a bloody expensive piece of gear."

"If it's not a rude question," Jumbo said. "How did you manage to afford it then?"

"My dad left me a fair bit of money for my eighteenth birthday."

"Ah, sugar. Sorry Chas," Jumbo said quickly. "I didn't know you'd lost your dad."

Chas coloured. "I haven't."

"Eh?"

"My dad left home when I was a little kid. I didn't even know he'd set up a fund for my eighteenth. Anyway," he mumbled shutting the case. "we're in danger of wearing it out staring like this."

As we left the room I put my hand on Paul's shoulder. "Don't ever drag me away from my book for something as trivial as that again."

He laughed. "I promise."

As if to remind us that leave was over, Monday morning we had a kit inspection and then, Tuesday morning, we were down for an hour of rifle drill with Corporal Evans. It was as if we'd never actually been away.

"It has to be done on purpose," moaned Tommo as we got ready for rifle drill. "Why couldn't we get nicely eased back in with classroom Monday morning and workshop on Tuesday.

Colin marched us to the parade square and then, a couple of minutes later Corporal Evans came marching on to the square with a rifle and snapped smartly to a halt. He was a tall barrel of a man built more like a rugby prop forward than a drill instructor. Straight away he proceeded to shout orders to himself while demonstrating the moves.

"Corporal. Corporal order arms!" he shouted. Then "Corporal. Corporal shoulder arms."

He went through the whole sequence of the drill yelling orders and reacting to them. Monkey began sniggering. Than someone behind me joined in and that got me going. I tried in vain to keep a straight face.

Corporal Evans suddenly stopped and stared into the ranks. I quickly realised he was staring at me. "Boy Entrant Draper, "he called. "Out here on the double."

I ran smartly out to the front and came to a halt in front of him. "This here," he shouted to the others. "Is Boy Entrant Draper. Now Boy Entrant Draper likes a good laugh. And why not? We all do when it comes down to it."

He stood beside me and I felt the full enormity of the man; he really was big. "Your pals here agree Draper, we all like a good laugh. So, when you're ready lad, joke please."

I stared at him. "Corporal?"

"A joke if you please. We all want to laugh. Nice and loud so we can all hear."

was stunned, was he serious?

"Come on Draper we're waiting."

Yes, he was serious.

I took a deep breath. "An elderly couple meet on a holiday cruise and get on very well.

On the last day of the cruise they discuss the possibility of marrying and the man says they need to know more about each other. He asks if she likes dancing and she replies that she likes to go dancing often. He suggests the cinema and she says yes, now and again. He asks about fine dining and she says yes, very often.

Finally, he takes a deep breath and asks about sex.

She pauses and then says, 'I like it infrequently.'

He ponders this for a few moments and then asks, 'was that one word or two?'

Silence. Then a few laughs, and then more and more got the joke. Even Corporal Evans laughed.

"Excellent Draper." He waved his hand. "Okay lads quiet now." He smiled at me. "You see Draper, we all laughed. It was funny, and we laughed. When we hear a funny joke, we laugh. Agreed?"

I nodded wondering where this was leading.

"Now you Draper, you were laughing at me." He leant over me. "So? Am I a joke lad?" he bellowed in my ear. "Well? Am I?"

"No Corporal."

"Louder!"

"NO CORPORAL."

"Then save your laughter 'till one comes along. And remember this: if you laugh, or even crack a smile, on my drill sessions again I'll have you doubling round this square every morning for a week. Now fall in.

The following Saturday afternoon I stayed on camp. I'd rung Cheryl at work to arrange a date but she was going visiting relatives with her mother and so I got a permit to use the Band Hut for some drum practice. In the evening I had the hut to myself and enjoyed a good read in peace and quiet.

Between half eight and half nine the lads drifted back in after their day out. Geordie came back in a good mood. He sat on his bed smiling to himself and looking round the room as if checking to see who was in. He saw me looking at him and nodded. "And the winner is," he said, getting up and walking my way, "the one and only, Mark Draper." He raised my hand and made a noise of a crowd cheering.

"What the friggin' hell are you on about?"

He'd been to Barry to see some film or another. Geordie often flew solo so that was no surprise. What was a surprise was him going to a pub on his own.

"I just missed the bus and fancied a bit of a stroll round town," he explained. "I saw a pub and thought a swift half and a packet of crisps wouldn't break the bank."

He sat on the end of my bed. "Well, I saw an empty stool at the bar and parked my arse down, it was only as I ordered my drink that I noticed a glass in front of me and it was almost full. I figured I'd sat in someone's seat. No sooner had I twigged than I got a tap on the shoulder. I turned, expecting to see a fellah and there's this lass." He smiled. "And I wouldn't climb over her to get to you, bonny lad, if you get my drift?"

"Yeah, I get the picture. Get on with it. What have I won?"

"Patience. I'm getting to it," he said. "Anyway, I got in first I told her I'd just realised it's someone's place and am about to move." He smiled to himself and shook his head. "She just gave me a lovely smile and gestured me to sit. Before I could say anything, she went and returned with another stool."

At that moment Ollie arrived back. He took one look at us both sat on my bed and said, "what deadly plot are you two planning?"

"Shush," I hissed. "Geordie's telling me something."

"Well you'll just have to wait 'till he's filled me in."

167

I waited patiently as Geordie ran through his tale. "So, there I am, sat next to this lass, supping my half and wondering what to say when she she says she likes my accent and where was I from? And then we sort of started chatting. Her name was Avril.

"What was she like?" Ollie asked.

"She was about the same height as me, although she was wearing high heels, really short cropped blond hair. I say blond, more bottle blond than the real thing. I quite fancied her, but I was a bit unsure."

"Unsure in what way?" I asked.

"Well, in some of the pubs around Newcastle, the only birds seen in a boozer on their own, looking like her, are carrying a price list in their handbags."

"Okay," said Ollie, sounding a little impatient. "You're sat on a barstool chatting up a possible floozy, What next"

"And why have I won something?" I added.

Ollie raised an eyebrow. "What?"

I shrugged. "Don't ask."

"Well, first she buys me a drink, then we chatted for a while and she told me she was a hairdresser in Barry. I told her about life in the huts and she laughed when I told her about having to be back by nine. When it was time to go she walked with me to the bus stop. I asked her if I could see her again and she seemed keen. I asked her when and bugger me she suggested tomorrow afternoon. So, I thought, why not? But then, just as the bus came into view she remembered she was meeting her friend. I thought shit, that's that down the drain, but as I was getting on the bus she shouts bring a friend."

I suddenly realised what he was on about. "Hang on here Geordie," I said. "You ain't wanting me as a blind date? You're not saying that's what I've won?"

He grinned. "Yeah, why not? It could be a laugh."

"Ask Monkey or someone."

"Ha'way man, don't want anyone else. I want you. What harm could it do? Come on Mark, say yes."

I sighed. "Where are you planning to go?"

"No idea."

"I suppose it'll get me off camp for a few hours."

"Is that a yes?"

I nodded. "Oh, balls to it okay."

He slapped me in the back. "Excellent,"

"Hold on a minute Draper," said Ollie. "Are you forgetting the lovely Cheryl? What would she say?"

"Oh, piss off Ollie she'll never know."

He shook his head. "For your sake you'd better hope not."

Chapter Fourteen

Sunday morning brought with it a bit of a change of heart. As we filed out to get ready for church parade I slipped in beside Geordie. "Geordie," I said quietly. "I've been thinking."

"No."

"Listen, I think you'd be better…"

"No."

"Just shut up for a minute."

"Still no."

"What about Tommo?"

He looked at me and shook his head. "No, I don't want Tommo, I don't want Monkey, I don't want Bonner, I want you, and you've already agreed bonny lad."

I groaned. "Yeah, okay."

All through church parade I had a bad feeling about my blind date. I'd never been on one before, but I'd heard stories from other lads who'd had huge disappointments. And what if she was okay and it was me who was the disappointment? I tried to dismiss the doubts and simply wait and see.

Geordie was looking forward to it, but then why wouldn't he, he knew his date? On the way to the bus I asked him to describe his Avril again, but he just shrugged. "You'll see for yourself in a wee while bonny lad." He squeezed my shoulder. "I bet this lass of yours is drop dead gorgeous. She's bound to be."

We were met by the girls at the bus stop. I figured straight away which was Geordie's from his description and so my eyes locked on to her friend. My date.

She was far from ugly, in fact she was strangely attractive. I say strangely because she was rather a large girl and her face was too full to be naturally pretty, but you could see how attractive she could be. Her hair was tied up in pigtails and that did her no favours at all. With her heels on she was a little taller than me. Her name was Nerys.

To my relief when she came to shake my hand and say hello she gave me a lovely smile so maybe I wasn't the disappointment I'd feared. Then she said, "Goodness have you got black eyes?"

I smiled, "I did have. Almost gone now."

"What happened?"

"Long story."

She shrugged, "Fair enough, you can tell me later."

The walk from the bus stop in Barry to Barry Island was a good twenty minutes walk, but it was the girls' suggestion and it would save me a few pennies, so it suited me. Although, at the same time, Barry Island meant the Pleasure Park and the Pleasure Park meant spending money. As we set off I noticed Nerys was carrying a backpack. To my surprise and delight as we neared the park Geordie looked at Avril and said, "I must warn you Pet, that I'm rather short of money, I looked at Nerys and shrugged. "Same here."

The girls assured us we'd be okay. "We'll just have a wander around here," April said and then we'll have a bit of a picnic and a beer and later maybe a dance."

I was a bit perplexed. How was that okay? A picnic and beer then a dance? That didn't sound cheap. Then I realised it was Sunday. "You won't get a beer on Sunday. The pubs are shut."

Avril winked at me. "My wonky donkey over there isn't just carrying a backpack for the fun of it,"

I looked at Geordie as if to ask what the heck is going on and he shook his head.

171

We spent well over an hour just walking round the Park watching the rides. Nerys was quite chatty and her Welsh accent was one of the strongest I'd yet heard. What Geordie hadn't told us was how much older the girls were than us.

As we strolled around, Nerys linked her arm in mine. "So, why are you both so broke?" she asked.

I explained about the joys of being a Boy Entrant and she laughed gently. "So, how old are you?"

I told her seventeen and she smiled. "Avril didn't tell me I'd be cradle snatching."

"Why? How old are you?"

"Twenty"

"Are you're not a bit disappointed?"

She stopped and turned to face me. "No, I'm not disappointed at all. Your age doesn't bother me one bit. I've got a steady boyfriend and I don't need another one, so this is just a nice way to spend a boring Sunday when he's out on the road. Avril often does this sort of thing and I am quite happy going along. Anyway, you seem like a nice enough person to while away a Sunday afternoon with."

I was chuffed to ribbons. Me, a nice enough person. I smiled to myself.

When we finally chose a ride we all agreed The Scenic Railway and joined the queue. As we waited I asked Nerys to explain the picnic and dance.

She tapped her nose. "Secret."

We walked all the way back into Barry, Geordie and Avril in front and Nerys and me behind. Nerys asked me why I joined the RAF, did I have a girlfriend, what hobbies I had, did I like Wales? She seemed genuinely impressed when I told her I was a drummer in a pop group. She called to Avril: "would you believe it, I'm only going out with a drummer in a band?"

"Oh, wow! A drummer."

Geordie looked over his shoulder and grinned and said nothing.

Avril led us to a hairdresser's salon and fished in her handbag for a bunch of keys. She unlocked the place.

"I assume this is where you work?" Geordie said as we filed in. Avril nodded and pulled down a window blind. It was a fairly big salon and the air was full of the odours of shampoo and hair sprays.

Nerys swung her backpack off and knelt on the floor and opened it. She produced a can of beer for each of us and a pack of rather squashed sandwiches. Finally, she took two more cans and put them in a small fridge in the corner.

"We'll have to share these," she said. "Couldn't carry any more."

Avril called from a back room, "you did pack the tin opener I hope?"

"Yes, I did, and the napkins."

Avril reappeared carrying a Dansette autochange record player. "How do you like your music boys? Hot or smooth and sexy?"

She selected a few records and slid them onto the autochanger. "Music to eat to first I think."

The first record dropped noisily onto the turntable and Nerys handed out sandwiches and paper napkins accompanied by Buddy Holly singing 'Not Fade Away'.

Having eaten the food and supped the beers, Avril put a fresh stack of records onto the spindle. With all the window blinds down the lights had been on but as the first record started playing Avril turned them off.

The room was now dark, but the half light was enough to see clearly, and I saw Geordie smile at me in a knowing way. I only hoped he couldn't see the fear in my eyes. I felt way out of my depth. Watching the girls setting things up so smoothly made it clear that this was not a one off.

Nerys kicked off her shoes and motioned me to dance. I took a deep breath and joined her. I wasn't sure if I was scared or just excited.

After a few smooches I looked over at Avril and Geordie. They were almost stationary and kissing with a real passion. Then I saw Geordie's hand fondling her backside. Was Nerys expecting me to make a move? I remembered Mary and how much I enjoyed the French kissing and made a move to kiss Nerys. She responded straight away. We smooched gently through another couple of songs and then Cliff came on singing 'The Young ones. Nerys sighed in my ear, "I can't stand this record." She held my hand and led me into another room.

It was a large storeroom and somewhat darker than the salon.

Without a word she pulled a pile of pillows from a shelf and laid down. I lay next to her and we were kissing again. There was no doubt in my mind as to where this was heading, and I was getting more nervous the further we went.

She sensed it. "Relax," she whispered, "you're doing fine." She sat up and slipped out of her blouse and bra and pulled my hand to her breasts.

Then it got a bit frantic. It seemed that one minute I was feeling my way round her ample breasts and then we were tearing off our clothes and kissing like crazy.

I slid my hand slowly down, down over the satin smooth skin of her slightly chubby belly, down towards the triangle of curly hair then down into the wetness down below. I rested my hand between her legs and she was breathing heavily. She opened her eyes and looked into mine. She smiled, just for a second or two, and then she closed her eyes again.

I took this as as a sign of approval and I found myself getting more confident. She reached down and squeezed me gently, and I heard my heart my heart pulsing in my ears.

 I slid my leg over and she released me. "Have you got anything?" she panted. My heart sank. Did I learn nothing from Denise?

"Oh, shit. Sorry."

I went to slide my leg back, but she pulled me on top of her. "You'll just have to pull out." With that she gently guided me in.

It felt so wonderful I could have cried. She kissed my neck and moaned.

I was concentrating like never before. I'd heard people talking about making yourself think of something boring. I chose my times tables and found it working.

For a good while I was in control, doing well and feeling confident. Then she reached down and clutched my buttocks in both hands and somehow took over. It was fatal. My seven times table shattered into fragments and was gone. I knew I wasn't going to be able to last long with her doing that.

Sure enough, very soon I was struggling. I bit my lip hard, determined not to let it happen but I was in trouble. I had a feeling she could sense it. "I'm sorry," I whispered miserably.

But she clutched me tighter, thrusting up to meet me. "Not yet," she panted. "Not yet."

But it was too late. The sensation came from my toenails and up through my body.

I tried to pull out, but she held me too tightly and there was nothing I could do. I felt myself shudder. She must have felt it but still she kept thrusting up at me and groaning. I tried to keep going even though I was spent.

Just as I felt myself losing my hardness she dug her nails in my bum cheeks. "yes," she hissed through a clenched jaw. "Oh, please. Just a little more."

She thrust herself up at me in sharp, jerky movements, and then her body arched, and she let go of me and flopped back on the pillows.

I was walking on air all the way to the bus stop. What a blind date that had been. Not only had I lost my cherry, as Ollie would say, but I was confident I'd kept Nerys happy in the process. As we waited for the bus Geordie and Avril were discussing meeting up again.

I was just thinking of asking Nerys when she said. "I've enjoyed today." She kissed me. "Thanks."

It was a brief kiss, but it said so much; our date was over and there was to be no more.

Ollie couldn't wait to find out how I'd got on and I'd hardly got through the door when he was on me. The problem was so were Tommo, Andy, Monkey and several others.

"Come on," urged Monkey. "All the juicy details please."

I laughed. "Fuck off, ask Geordie."

"I will in a minute but right now I'm asking you."

Geordie flopped heavily on to his bed. "Ha'way, ya randy little sod tell them all about your mucky afternoon." He laughed to himself,

"That's not fair on the girls."

"So? You're never going to see Nerys again."

"No, but you're seeing Avril again."

He beamed. "Oh yes, without a doubt."

"Well then?"

He hitched himself up on one elbow. "Aye bonny lad, but it's not hearts and flowers, it's pure unadulterated sex."

"Ah-ha," said Monkey nodding madly. "So, you did get your leg over. Come on, let's hear it."

After I'd finished, the nosey buggers all gravitated down to Geordie's bed for his version of events.

Ollie stayed and sat on the end of my bed. He smiled. "So, my good friend Draper has lost his cherry." He fished in his pocket for his cigarettes. "Where does this leave the lovely Cheryl?"

"Nowhere. I mean nothing's changed." I was a bit disgruntled. "Why do you have to put a damper on things?"

"You what?"

"You bring Cheryl into it like we're getting married or something. She's just a bird I've seen a couple of times. That's all. Nothing special."

"Bullshit Draper. That's what I told you. From the first moment you met her you've talked about her like she's the love if your life." He jabbed his finger at me. "If you're telling me she's nothing special then I'm telling you that's bullshit and if you're telling me that *and* believing it then you're lying to yourself."

I said nothing.

"Okay, now I've pissed you off." He lit his cigarette.

"Sorry."

I waved the apology away.

"Right then," he said, blowing a plume of smoke my way. "do you want to hear about my weekend?"

I nodded and smiled. "Go on then. If you must."

Ollie grinned. "I don't know if I should. I think you're possibly underage for this."

"Sod off granddad," I laughed. "And get on with it."

It didn't take long before I realised what Ollie meant. When he'd finished I said, "It sounds as if she's been storing it up just waiting for you."

"I think you could say that my friend, yes."

"Yeah, But the question is how do you feel about her?"

He shrugged. "She's all right. I like her."

"She's *just* all right?"

"No, in fact she's really nice. Is that better?

"Careful Ollie. Just be careful."

He ruffled my hair and laughed. "I've got it by the balls."

I gave him a concerned look and shrugged.

There was a rather nasty accident during workshops on Wednesday afternoon and I'm ashamed to say I found it quite hilarious.

We were working in pairs using pop rivets. The idea was a fuselage repair was needed and it was carried out by one pair at a time. Monkey was paired off with Andy Braithwaite. Monkey, being the smallest, went inside the metal fuselage and it was Andy's job to use a power drill and make four holes in a metal repair, one in each corner. Monkey would hold the plate in place and clamp the holes with a holding pin once the drill was through.

Andy called out, "ready?"

Monkey shouted "ready."

Andy called, "top left?"

Monkey shouted, "top left."

The drill whizzed through the metal plate with ease, but the high-pitched noise of the power drill was suddenly joined by a high-pitched scream from Monkey. He tumbled out from the fuselage holding his hand and staring at his thumb with a hole right through the flesh and up through the nail. "Bastard!" he yelled. He took another look at his thumb and turned a nasty shade of pale. "you bloody idiot Braithwaite," he said, sinking to his knees and watching the blood drip on to the cold floor. "Top left you said."

Braithwaite was staring open mouthed at the hapless Monkey. He pointed to the fuselage. "That is top left." Monkey groaned. "*My* top left you…." And then he fainted.

That evening Chas called for a practice and said he had some news. He sounded excited and come the evening I was so intrigued that I set off early. Whatever it was Chas had to tell us wasn't the real issue with me. I was just chuffed to be part of it at last. Up until a short while ago I'd felt like there was a band consisting of Chas, Jumbo and Paul and then there was me. I had no sense of belonging. Now I'd thought it all through and decided I was a drummer it was different. I wasn't just a drummer, I was the drummer in Sky-High.

It occurred to me as I made my way to the practise, that we were okay together without being friends. We got on well enough and I thought Jumbo was a great bloke, really helpful, but we never knocked about together outside the band. He was was a bit of a mystery, keeping himself to himself, and yet he seemed a very popular bloke with the boys in his hut. I enjoyed his company but never went looking for it. Yes, I liked him. In fact, now that he'd told me about his meditating, not only did I like him, I found him really fascinating.

Paul was simply a nice bloke, easy to get along with and pleasant to chat with, but that was as far as it went, I'd never seen him on the bus to Barry at the weekends. When I did see him in the NAAFI or the mess hall, it was a quick hello or sometimes just a nod.

Then of course, there was Chas: fussy, demanding and a bit of a perfectionist.

On the one hand he was amusing and slightly strange, I was thinking mainly of his thing about tweaking my earlobe, and, on the other hand, he was quick to flare up when things weren't going the way he wanted. In the early days I'd found him a bit of a clever sod, I remember our first encounter in the Drying Room and how rude I thought he was. But now, having seen how good he was, more so with the new guitar in his hands, I could understand It. He was a class above the rest of us and having a far from competent drummer holding him back must have been frustrating.

I got to the Band Hut to find Paul was already setting up. "I thought *I* was early? Look at you."

He sorted through his plectrums. "I'm dying to hear what Chas has got up his sleeve."

I went over and watched him. When he plugged his guitar in and started tuning up I asked how he was getting on with the it.

He strummed a chord. "I love it."

"It certainly looks nice," I said. "How much?"

"Twelve quid."

"Wow. That's good."

He nodded. "It's second hand but you wouldn't think so. Anyhow thanks for letting me use yours. I'll bring it to your hut after we wrap up here?"

At that point Chas and Jumbo came in to the hut. "Come on Mark. Are you setting up?" Chas called. "We've got a busy evening ahead."

I waved. "Okay, don't panic."

When we were all set up and tuned, Chas put his guitar down. "I've got some great news." He lit a cigarette and took a long draw in his cigarette. "Two bits of great news to be precise." He pulled a piece of loose tobacco from his tongue.

"Come on then," urged Paul. "Get on with it."

"Okay, listen. I had a meeting with Copperfield. His request I hasten to add. Well, it seems he's really fired up by the idea of having, as he put it, the camp's own pop group. It's never happened before. Anyway, he said as it is now we only get to play four or five numbers every three months at the dance. What would we think about putting on a show once in while in the camp cinema?"

"Bloody hell Chas," I said. "What did you say?"

"What do you think? I told him we'd love to."

I stared at him. "You're mad."

"Why?"

"Why? Because we've nowhere near enough material ready." Chas smiled. "Then we better get practising."

"You said two things?" Jumbo reminded him.

"I did indeed. I told him we couldn't manage playing the cinema with your knackered bass amp and he's gonna order one for The Band Hut."

"That thing you and I play through isn't exactly brilliant," Paul said.

"Ah, right, I might be able to do something about that soon."

Paul raised an eyebrow. "Eh?"

Chas tapped his nose with his finger. "we'll see."

Chas wanted to try 'Walk Don't Run' despite it having a couple of tricky drum breaks. I would rather not try it but having already got 'The Savage" scrapped I felt guilty at the thought of getting a second of his numbers thrown out but, by keeping to straightforward songs we stood much more chance of quickly building a program for the cinema. stubbed his cigarette out and picked up his guitar. "Let's get started."

Toward the end of August, the weather was terrible. It was almost as if summer was over and done with but then, right at the end, summer suddenly returned full on and I spent the last weekend of August taking Cheryl out to the cinema or a café or Barry Island but often just walking. I loved being with her.

With Ollie visiting his lady all the time and me meeting Cheryl we spent less and less time together. He didn't seem to mind, and I know I didn't.

Everything was going well; workshops were interesting, drill with Corporal Evans was bearable and inspections seemed to come around less often. The hut had been cleaned so many times that all it needed now was a sort of maintenance program and it was ready for any kind of inspection you care to mention.

Every time we came in to the hut we removed footwear and used thick wads of cleaning cloth as skates. The lino was still a shitty brown colour but now it was a shiny shitty brown.

Sunday morning coming back from church parade Ollie, Geordie and me were walking back to the hut after being dismissed by Corporal Evans when Ollie pulled his sleeve up. "Hey, lads," he said holding up his arm. "What d'ya reckon to this?"

He was wearing a rather nice new watch.

"Yeah," I said, grabbing his arm to get a closer look. "Very smart. Where d'ya get that?"

"A present."

"A present?"

'That's what I said."

"Stone me," I cried. "Not from your mystery lady?"

"Got it in one."

"She must be in to you in a big way," Geordie said.

Ollie flung his arms wide open. "What woman wouldn't be?" He laughed. "I'm a lean, mean sex machine."

I frowned. "To quote something back at you: I hope you know what you're doing?"

He dropped his arms. "I know exactly what I'm doing, Draper. Worry not."

I shrugged. "I'm just saying it sounds dangerous, that's all."

"Dangerous?"

"Ollie are you forgetting she's a married woman?"

Geordie stared at Ollie. "Married?"

I groaned. "Oh bugger. Sorry Ollie."

Geordie mimed zipping up his lips. "Safe with me," he said. "But I will say this, If that's true, then I'm with Mark. Fucking around with a married woman, especially one who buys you presents. Dangerous."

"Ah, fuck the both of you!" he huffed. Then he walked off. As he walked away I looked at Geordie. "I've got a bad feeling about this."

Chapter Fifteen

The mail arrived one evening and there were two letters for me. I was intrigued; it was rare I received any mail at all let alone two.

The first letter was from Lenny just to say hello how are you and catch up with any news. Lenny didn't usually write but, I think he was still feeling guilty about me getting thumped.

The second appeared to be a card. I tore open the envelope and sure enough I pulled out a card. It was an invite to Ray's wedding on the 6th November at the Margate Registry of Births, Deaths and Marriages.

I shouted down the room. "Anybody know when our autumn break is?"

A voice shouted back. "October."

"Yeah," I called back. "I know that. But when?"

Tommo was walking past on his way to the washroom. He flicked my feet with his towel.

"Thirtieth."

"Sure?"

"Certain."

"Ta."

Then I noticed a letter in the envelope. A single page. I nearly missed it tucked away like that. It was from my mum to say that Ray and Bernice had found a flat in Garlinge, just outside Margate, and would be moving in there right after the wedding.

I couldn't believe the timing. It was perfect.

She also said Alf had sought her out and they'd had a good chat. I smiled when I read that they were actually going to the cinema next week.

It seems, reading between the lines, that Alf had paid me mum a visit, cap in hand and apologies at the ready, asking her would she come home? She said she would. I was pleased, I didn't care much for Alf, but I loved my mum totally and if she had stung him the way it seemed then maybe a nice restaurant and bit of dancing would follow the cinema?

When Tommo returned from the washroom I was busy whacking my pillow with my drumsticks and he stopped at the foot of my bed watching for a while. "Is it dead yet?"

"Eh?"

He pointed at my pillow. "You're thwacking that poor pillow hard enough aren't you? What are you trying to do?"

I put the drumsticks down and told him how Chas had the idea that we each chose a number to learn for the camp cinema. The problem was that Chas was still wanting 'Walk Don't Run'. "Now, in all honesty," I said, "I love that number, but it has a tricky drum intro and to make it worse the intro is repeated halfway through the song."

"So why are you trying then?" he asked.

I took a deep breath. "Because, Chas reckons if I learn to play it really slowly, a few beats at a time, and then gradually build up the speed, I could probably manage it."
"Right, I'll let you get on with it," he said. "I've got trousers to iron."
"And I've got a letter to write," I said. As he wandered off I picked up the drumsticks to give it one more go. Right, here we go, I thought, one more time, nice and slow.
My doubts were slowly fading. Things that not many days ago were difficult we're starting to come easily. I was getting there.

No sooner had we stopped taking the piss out of Monkey and Andy Braithwaite over their drilling fiasco than another funny thing happened.
There was a lad in one of the other huts called Terry Henderson. The only time I recall being aware of the guy was the time St Athan hosted a boxing evening against RAF Cosford and we all went along to cheer our lads on. Henderson was our main man. He was a class above everyone else in the ring that evening. What puzzled me was, for a boxer with his skill, how he looked so battle scarred?
His nose was flat and around his eyes he had signs of damage. He was a heavy-set boy with broad shoulders and thick upper arms and, as he moved round the ring, he snorted loudly. He certainly wasn't the kind of guy you'd want to bump into on a dark night and yet people in his hut said he was a quietly spoken lad who wouldn't hurt a fly. Outside the ring, of course.

We were in the classroom having a lecture on hydraulic systems.

187

The instructor was Mister Shaw, he was one of the oldest instructors there. It was the last lesson of the day and poor old Terry was struggling to stay awake.

Mister Shaw was pointing out the components by use of a large board, showing the typical layout of an aircraft's system. He was using a long wooden cane as a pointer. Just as Terry lost his battle to stay awake Mister Shaw pointed to the small metal hydraulic reservoir and as he explained the component he tapped it twice with his pointer making it ring like a bell.

In one swift movement Terry was on his feet, fists at the ready, and closing in on the hapless Mister Shaw. As if the sight of him wasn't enough to strike fear into the old gent, it was all accompanied by a barrage of loud snort as he jabbed his fist in the face of some imaginary opponent.

It all happened in a split second and then Terry woke. His cheeks flared, and he stuttered an apology to the pale and shaken instructor.

"Bugger me," a voice from behind me said. "Punch drunk at seventeen. Would you believe it?"

Terry returned to his desk looking somewhat abashed and Mister Shaw left the room mumbling to himself. I felt so sorry for both. Terry looked devastated as he sat staring down at his desk and I imagined poor old Mister Shaw was frantically looking for a nip of brandy.

"Hey, Terry," Geordie called. "Which part of the hydraulic system was it that you found most offensive?"

From this point on life suddenly became rather hectic.

I suppose it began with Colin Masters putting up the latest duty roster. For the first time since ITS we had drill almost every day. Most of it rifle drill.

As we all stood round the notice board grumbling Colin explained that Saint Athan was getting a new commanding officer after we get back off leave and we would be doing a demonstration of rifle drill and that meant a load of practise.

Monkey grunted. "Why us?"

"It's not just us," Colin explained. "Each entry has something to do."

There was a camp dance coming up as well, and Chas had us practising as often as possible because, on top of the dance, shortly after we returned from leave we had to get ready for our gig in the camp cinema.

Also, of course, there was a Progress Assessment Test to look forward to.

These were busy days but also better days. After the autumn break we would be allowed broaden our horizons. For one thing, not only would we be allowed to travel to Cardiff, we'd get a pay rise.

But before that there was a fair bit of square bashing. The first half-hour of rifle drill for the open day routine was taken by Sergeant Sharpe. We'd seen almost nothing of him since being introduced; he normally spent drill practice working with the senior entry, getting them in shape for their passing out parade.

He was a hard taskmaster and quick to flare up. When he did flare up he sent out a spray of spittle. He had almost no lips and his eyes were set back giving him a pinched look. He soon gained the nickname 'Weasel'.

At the end of the half-hour he stood shaking his head. "That's not good enough! Not nearly good enough! On the big day you have to believe you're the most important part of that parade and, if you believe it with all your might you *will* be. From the moment you stand ready to perform your drill before the Air Commodore, to the moment you march off behind the band, you are the centre of attention. You are numero uno." He allowed a hint of a smile to cross his lips. "Only don't let Band Master hear you say that, he might not agree."

That produced a ripple of laughter."

"All right lads," he called. "Settle down. "So, what I'm saying is you have got to work hard and then a bit harder, that's all there is to it." Then, as an afterthought, he added. "You have it in you, I'm certain of that; we just need to draw it out."

At that point Corporal Evans came marching on the square. The NCOs said a few words and Sergeant Sharpe marched off.

"Oh dear, not good enough I hear?" He walked up and down for a few moments, thinking, and then stopped. "There are things that people tell you and you think no, not for me, no way. Well I'm going to tell you something now that you are going to scoff at. Not might do; will do. And then I'm going to make you change your mind. As it is now you're all here to learn a trade and drill is just something you tolerate." He nodded. "Am I right?"

We all shouted, "Yes, Corporal."

"Well I'm here to prove you wrong. I'm here to prove to you that drill can make you feel alive, excited and even moved. But most of all proud"

We spent the whole thirty minutes going over and over the drill. He ran around adjusting a slightly wrong rifle position, yelling at someone else to stand straight and at someone else for lagging behind the timing. All in all, it was a very intense thirty minutes.

The next morning began with Corporal Evans again, and again Corporal Boy Masters marched us to the parade ground where Corporal Evans was ready and waiting. Then, without saying a word he had us drilling.

We'd been going through the moves of the rife drill sequence for around ten minutes when he halted, stamped his foot angrily and yelled for us to stand easy.

He screwed his hands up into two fists. "Timing, timing, timing. That's what we're working on here. One movement, one sound."

He stood looking at the squad in front of him and I soon found myself on the other end of his stare. I thought about the last time he singled me out and my heart sank. Not me again? What had I done this time?

"Boy Entrant Draper. Yes, just what I need."

He beckoned me to join him. I marched out to the front.

"Am I correct in saying you're something of a drummer?"

I frowned and nodded. "I'm learning Corporal."

"That's good enough. What's your favourite song to play?"

I blurted out the first thing that came into my head.

"'Apache' Corporal."

He looked pleased. "Ah, good. That'll work. Now, I want you to sing it to me."

I stared in disbelief. "It's an instrumental, Corporal. I can't sing it; there aren't any words."

"I know what an instrumental is Draper!" He snapped. "Just sing the tune."

I wasn't sure if he was serious or not. "I don't understand Corporal."

"Ye gods," he said banging his head with his hand in a comical way. "Sing me 'Apache' Draper, it's not too complicated is it? On the big day you'll have the band playing but, as we don't have the band today, you can do the job. Right? So sing."

I took a deep breath and began singing the tune, much to the amusement of the others.

He wanted it louder and so I started again. He raised his rifle and began slapping the strap against the rifle with the palm of his hand in time with my singing. After less than half way through the song he waved me to stop.

"Excellent Draper. Excellent." He went into the squad and took my place. "Alright, lads, do as I've been doing and follow Draper's timing. Right Draper off you go, loud as you can.

I nearly burst out laughing but just managed to keep it in.

I began to sing. "Da, dee, da da, da, da de, da."

It was really weird. Corporal Evans joined in Singing along with me, all the time smacking the strap on his rifle, making sure the boys around him were keeping time.

Then he started to call out the drill moves. "Order arms, present arms, shoulder arms."

As the squad ran through the moves he continued to hammer the strap of his rifle sharply against the wooden stock with his hand, keeping it in time with my singing. To my amazement the sound emanating from the drill was much crisper and sharper than before.

Eventually he came out to the front and I went back to my place. He was beaming.

"One movement, one sound. Did you hear it? The song became our conductor. From now on you'll always keep that song in your head when doing rifle drill. Well done lads. Hence forth this squad is to be known as The Shadow squad."

As we marched off the square, rifles on shoulders, Corporal Boy Masters

called: "Rig-a-dig," and we all joined in the chant: "Oy, oy, oy."

We left the parade ground and made our way to the huts. Ollie put his arm round my shoulder. "Dy'a know what, Draper?"

"No, what?"

"I do believe Evans might just be winning."

I struck a theatrical pose. "Thanks to me, of course."

"Oh yes," he said smiling. 'Thanks to you."

In fact, everything seemed to be coming good: the rifle drill with Corporal Evans was quite good fun and, as Ollie said, he was winning. Most of us admitted it was a good feeling when we got it right. Sergeant Sharpe seemed to be pleased with the way our marching was coming along, even if he didn't actually say so. He said if we kept at it we'd be ready to impress the new CO.

Sky-High was ready for the dance and well on the way to being ready for the cinema.

Come the weekend I was really looking forward to getting off camp and seeing Cheryl. I had no idea that she had plans, she'd said nothing about it when we spoke on the phone in midweek but, when she met me from the bus and we linked arms, I had a feeling she had something in mind. I looked at her. "Have you any plans for today?"

She squeezed my arm. "Yes, I have actually. I'm hoping you don't mind babysitting?"

It took a few seconds to sink in. And then I said. "Who? Where? What are you saying?"

She giggled. "Don't panic. It's my sister's lad. Megan has to go into Cardiff for a few hours and asked if I'd look after Max for her." She stopped and looked at me. "She's not going out until half past six, so if you don't want to do it we still have plenty of time together before…"

"No, no," I interrupted. "You just took me by surprise, that's all."

We spent the afternoon strolling round town and then stopped for a coffee in a busy little café.

"You're definitely okay with babysitting?" she asked toying with her coffee cup.

I shrugged. "Yeah, we've got no plans otherwise. How old is the kid?"

"His name is Max!" she reminded me sharply.

"Okay, sorry. How old is Max?"

"Just over a year. If it's worrying you then you can relax. He'll be in bed around six."

My mind was soon slipping into overdrive. A house to ourselves for well over an hour. "What time is your sister due home?"

"Between eight and nine so you might have to go to the bus stop on your own."

Her sister was gorgeous: tall, slim, lovely figure and a beautiful smile. There wasn't any sign of a husband or partner. When she'd left I asked Cheryl about it?

"She manages quite well on her own which is just as well as he was long gone before she knew she was carrying. He was some guy in a pop group who were playing a short season in Cardiff. She only did it once poor thing."

We sat in the settee and watched television for a while and I was trying to judge how to play things. "We're off on two weeks leave soon," I said, just for the sake of something to say. "Did I tell you?"

She shook her head. "No. You've never said. It seems to me you're always on leave."

We fell silent. After a short while I decided to test the water, but when I went to kiss her she turned and kissed me. I was a bit surprised but on the other hand curious: had I read it correctly? Was this the good old 'come-on'?

We kissed for a while and then I tried touching her breasts. She seemed okay with things so far and I contemplated trying inside her top. The couple of times I'd tried in the past had ended with the brush off.

I stayed kissing and touching for a bit longer and then I slipped my hand slowly inside the woollen jumper and waited for her reaction. Nothing.

We continued kissing and my hand cupped her breast, enjoying the warmth of her body. Eventually I moved my had up slightly ready to slide inside her bra. She pulled my hand away and put it back outside her bra again. We were kissing all the time.

I left my hand outside the bra for what seemed ages. Then, during one passionate kiss I made a move again to slide into the bra once again.

She pulled my hand away from her breasts and sat up on the settee.

"What's up?" I moaned.

"Nothing," she said, straightening her jumper. "Had enough that's all."

"Bloody hell, Cheryl, what is it with you?" I snapped. "It's not some kind of sexual perversion. People do it all the time."

"What do you want? Why do you have to keep pushing me?"

"I just want to feel your breast."

She folded her arms and stared straight ahead. "You *were* feeling it."

"No Cheryl, I wasn't feeling it; I was feeling your bra."

"All right," she said turning to face me. " I take of my bra and then what?"

"Eh?"

"What next? How long before that's not enough? How long before you want to get my knickers off?"

"Oh, here we go," I moaned, "I can't have a feel of your breast without turning into a raving sex maniac. Well, let's just forget it."

"So now you're going to sulk I suppose?"

I stood up. "No, I'm not going to sulk I'm going to catch my bus."

She glared at me. "All right she hissed. If it's so important to you, here!"

And with that, she reached behind her back, unfastened her bra and lifted her sweater. "Happy now?"

I looked at her alabaster breasts as she sat there with her top pulled up and I was so tempted to sit down again but my stupid pride got in the way. "Thanks, but, no thanks. I'd hate to think I'd bullied you into doing something you didn't like."

All the way home on the bus I had the picture of her sat with her top up and breasts on display and cursed myself for being so bloody stupid.,

I got back to camp early but Ollie was already laid on his bed reading.

He nodded to me as I reached my bed. "Early?"

"That's rich coming from you," I countered. 'How long you been in.?"

He shrugged, "half hour, there's about."

I knew something was wrong. "What's up old mate?"

He looked drained. "I dunno, I really don't."

"What's that mean? If you don't know nobody does."

He tried a smile, but it died almost before it started. "I thought I was such a bloody star. You know, bedding an older woman. Young stud on the loose." He rubbed his eyes and sighed. "Just look at me now."

"F'fucksake Ollie, what's wrong?"

"She says she wants to leave her old man and shack up with me as soon as we graduate."

"But you can sort that. Surely you only have to tell her to piss off? She can't do bog-all."

He lit a half-smoked cigarette. "Couple of problems here Draper old son. One, she thinks she might be up the duff, and two, if she is and she tells her old man, he's gonna come looking for me."

"Oh, fuck me! Preggers? What a bugger." I didn't know what to say. Then something occurred to me. "Ollie, her old man can't come onto camp."

"Oh yes he can."

"How's that?"

He grinned lamely. "He lives on camp. Over in East Camp."

"Oh shit. What's he do?"

"What the Fuck's that got to do with it?"

I frowned. "I thought you said they lived in Barry."

"Yeah, I did, that was just a way of keeping it all secret. Just a smoke screen. I used to meet her in Barry."

"So, whatcha gonna do?"

197

"Hang meself from the nearest oak tree." He shook his head and stubbed out his cigarette. "I'm fucked if I know." I never told him about me and Cheryl. Later perhaps.

Chapter Sixteen

The Friday after the baby-sitting incident was dance night. I'd phoned Cheryl in the week as usual but whoever answered it said she couldn't come to the phone. I never bothered trying again, I'd half expected it. She was clearly pissed off.
Chas, Jumbo, Paul and me set off early to arrange the equipment with the band; 'The Diamonds' according to the posters. It was a wet, miserable evening with fine drizzle drifting around on a chilly breeze as if to remind us that summer was well gone.

Once we'd sorted things with The Diamonds we sat down to wait for the evening to start. I don't know why I was so edgy but every time the doors opened I looked up to see if the girls had arrived. I thought it best to get in an apology straight away, may be even try and talk her round. Either way I owed her an apology.

Ollie came striding in with Tommo and Monkey about a quarter past seven. They stood looking round to find where we were, and I stood up and waved to show them, but as I did the door opened and the girls came in led by Cheryl. The first thing she saw was me waving and she smiled and waved back.

I couldn't believe it. She didn't appear to be angry at all. She kissed me lightly. "You've calmed down now I see."

I felt my face redden. "Yes, sorry about that."

"Forgotten."

"I ought to say sorry before you say that."

"You've said sorry and I've said it's okay. Okay?."

I smiled. "Okay."

The Diamonds were striking up. "I'll catch you later," I shouted.

She nodded and kissed me on the cheek. "Good luck." She mimed drumming and I laughed. As I left I noticed Tina giving me a somewhat less than friendly glare.

Back at the table Ollie had bought me a coke. As I sat down he leant over and shouted. "Believe it or not Draper, I'm jealous. "

"About what?"

"You and the lovely Cheryl." He gave me a wan smile.

"You know how it goes, nice boy meets nice girl, they hold hands beneath the silvery moon and fall in love. Why the fuck didn't I go down that route?"

I laughed. "Piss off you daft wanker. We're not in love."

He suddenly looked sad. "No, neither am I."

The evening was going so well I wanted to bottle it: 'Sky-High' played the interval spot without a hitch and went down a treat, there were even shouts for an encore, and

Cheryl wasn't mad at me. We had a few dances and a kiss and cuddle and agreed to meet the next day. But in the end, the evening finished on a bit of a sour note.

I kissed Cheryl and she got on the bus, but, as I turned away Tina appeared in front of me. "I've been hearing bad things about you," she said with a knowing smirk. "Naughty boy."

At first, I thought Cheryl had told her about the babysitting row and she was just letting me know that she knew about it. Then the realisation hit me like a kick in the gut: she wasn't talking about Cheryl at all; somehow she knew about Nerys!

Saturday, after lunch, saw two total opposites getting ready for the afternoon out. On one side of the room Ollie was getting dressed with a look of someone who would rather be going out anywhere except meeting his lady, and opposite him was me combing my hair and smiling at the idea of my date with Cheryl. I figured if Tina intended telling Cheryl she'd have done so before the dance.

When I was ready to go he was standing in front of his locker door mirror tying his tie. I sat on the end of my bed watching him. "What're you gonna do?"

He turned his shirt collar down over his tie. "I'm fucked if I know. I change my mind every five minutes." He reached under the bed and fetched his shoes. "I need to call it a day if I'm honest."

"But?"

"But I feel like a bit of a shit."

"Do you?"

"Yes, She's lovely. She loves to laugh and has a terrific sense of humour. She says that her marriage had taken all her inner happiness away and I'd…" He thought for a few moments, "What was the word she used? Ah, got it!" He smiled at the recollection. "I'd rekindled it." He slipped his shoes on. 'Yeah, that's about it. She's simply lovely."

I frowned. "So, do you love her?"

"Love? Phew. That's the longest four-letter word in the dictionary that is." He shut his locker and put his cigarettes in his jacket pocket. "Truth is Draper, I don't think so."

I groaned but he just slapped me on the back. "Come on buddy, let's go face the foe."

I sat on the bus with Ollie, Geordie and Bonner. Geordie had a date with Avril and Bonner was just having an afternoon out.

Ollie was sat in the window seat absentmindedly watching the countryside fly by and I left him to it.

The bus pulled into the bus stop and, as we got off, I noticed Tina was with Cheryl. I just hoped she wasn't going to tag along all afternoon.

I said cheerio to Ollie and wished him good luck. As he turned away I smiled at Cheryl and went over to her.

"Stop right there!" She glared at me.

I was a bit slow catching on. Had she got another throat infection or something? "What's up?"

"I don't want you any nearer than that until you answer me something."

That's when the penny dropped. Bloody Tina had dropped me right in it.

"I want to hear you say you didn't go with that Barry bike, Nerys Holding."

I noticed Ollie watching the proceedings. I pushed my hands deep in my pockets and tried to think what to say.

He who hesitates is lost the saying goes, and I hesitated a little too long.

"It's true!" she shouted, causing people to stop and stare. "You lousy bastard, you did!"

She began crying.

I looked over to Tina and gave her a dirty look. "Thanks for that Tina."

She shook her head furiously. "It wasn't me, Mark. Honest." She cast her gaze deliberately to one side and I looked the way she was directing me. Geordie was walking down the street with Avril.

I turned back to Cheryl. "Can we just go somewhere and talk?" I took a few steps nearer. "Please?"

She wiped her eyes. "There's no point?"

"Well I'd like a chance to expl.... "

"Mark!" she snapped sharply. "It's simple. Did you go with her, yes or no, and it looks as if it's yes doesn't it?"

"Five minutes," I pleaded. "That's all. Just give me a chance."

"A chance? To do what?" She wiped her eyes again.

"I told you. A chance to explain."

She shook her head. "Can you?"

"I can but try."

She shrugged and took Tina aside. There was a minute or so of secret chat and then Tina nodded and walked off.

"I don't see what you can have to say that could change anything." she said, putting her hankie away. "But I'll give you a listen. Let's walk."

As we set off I was feeling quite miserable. She was right, what could I have to say that could do any good. "I'm guilty," I began. "But not so much guilty of going with Nerys as guilty of being naïve."

I explained how Geordie had nagged me into the blind date and how, so as not to let him down, I went with them to the hairdresser's.

"I'm not excusing myself for what happened I'm just trying to get you to see the predicament I found myself in. I wasn't expecting any of that when we went to the salon. I was flummoxed. When it started to look as if Avril and Geordie were heading that way it was too late."

"What does that mean? Too late?" She asked icily.

"I suppose it means if I said no and left at that point Geordie would get kicked out as well. I'm pretty sure that's what would have happened."

She stopped and stared at me. "You went and screwed the Barry bike just because you were worried about your friend?" She gave me a look that made me feel like a scalded child. "Are you really that weak?"

At this point I knew I was losing her. I shrugged. "I'm sorry, Cheryl, but it would seem that I am."

But I had to give it one last try. "If I thought it might help I'd tell you how little it meant, and I'd tell you how much I care for you. I've let you down badly and you don't deserve it. I've let myself down and I'm ashamed. But I do care for you; I care a lot."

We walked on in silence. After a minute or so I stopped. "Oh, balls to it," I groaned. "This is pointless. "You're right to be angry, I've no excuse." I turned away. "I'll get the bus."

"Mark," she called after me. I turned back and she walked up to me. "Why have you never said how you feel about me before."

I sighed. "Maybe it's because I thought you'd laugh."

"Laugh?"

"Yes."

"Why would I laugh?"

"Well, because we hardly know each other. The truth is, Cheryl, the thought of you kicking me in to touch today made me realise just how much I really do care. But I do, I really do. I certainly don't want to lose you." I reached for her hand. "What's more, I think you care for me a bit."

She stared at me. "And what gives you that impression?"

"Well, you've called me back."

"And? What does that prove?"

"If you didn't think we had a chance, you'd have let me go."

"Oh, I see. Right," she said sniffling. "But the fact is I don't know what I want to do. Yes, I care for you too, Mark, but is that enough to stop me seeing these images of you and her together? It's torture." The sniffles turned into tears again. I sensed there might still be a chance. After what seemed ages she squeezed her eyes tight shut. "I can't think, I just can't think.' Her eyes opened. "I want you to go now, Mark. Ring me midweek, after I've had a think."

I was about to say something, but she waved me away.

"Shut up now, Mark. Just go, please."

She turned and walked away.

As soon as Geordie came in that evening I was off my bed and over to him. "What's that fucking Avril of yours up to?" I snapped.

He looked a bit taken aback by my sudden assault. "What?"

"Why did she have to go and tell Cheryl about that do?" He took off his jacket and hung it in his locker. "I've no idea what you're raving about bonny lad."

As he spoke a thought came into my head. Why hadn't I thought of it before? "And while we're at it, who told Avril I was going out with Cheryl?"

"Mark, you're beginning to get up my nose. Just tell me what you're going on about?"

I told him about Cheryl finding out about Nerys and Tina pointing to Avril.

Geordie shook his head. "This is the first I've heard about any of this. It's no good asking me."

"But you're the only person who could've told Avril about me going out with Cheryl."

"Oh, give it a rest, Mark."

"No, Geordie. I want you to explain to me how Avril knew about me and Cheryl?"

"Right, Draper," he said slamming his his locker door shut. "Now you're accusing me of something I know fuck all about and I don't like that." He was clearly rattled. "So here it is for the last time."

I was aware of the silence in the hut as Geordie spoke. "I haven't seen Nerys since that blind date and I haven't mentioned you and Cheryl to Avril, why would I? I know fuck all about any of this and I don't like false accusations from you or anyone. Got it?"

"So, who told...."

A finger jabbed into my chest. "Are you deaf or plain sodding stupid Draper?" He looked really menacing. "Leave it!"

I stood looking at him and I heard someone say. "Come away Mark."

I thought that was probably a good idea. I'd never seen Geordie this way before.

Sunday morning with no Church Parade again was nice. A chance to lie in. The mess hall at breakfast was almost empty until the last moment before finish when the mass of boys who had timed their lie in with military precision

205

came ambling in. Ollie had been in no mood for a chat last night and wasn't hungry come breakfast. I knew he'd tell me his news in his own good time and l left him alone.

We did some swatting together after breakfast, asking each other questions in preparation for the tests and then decided to have a game of cards. There were two tables in the hut and the far end table was in use, so Ollie fetched a pack of cards, threw them on the table at our end and went for a pee.

I was putting the study books and folders back in the locker. Just as I finished Ollie came back into the room.

"Oh, fuck off Tommo, we're just about to have a hand of cards."

I looked and saw Tommo sat at our table laying out his cards for a game of Patience. He gestured to the table. "Empty table."

"It wasn't empty. My pack of cards was on it." He pointed out the unopened pack on the corner of the table.

"Oh, them? I never noticed them." He continued dealing his cards.

Ollie swiped Tommo's cards from the table and waved his pack in his face. "Our cards. Our table. Now fuck off."

I have no idea what Tommo was thinking. He surely must have seen that Ollie was getting very pissed off. "No, you fuck off. Having a pack of cards on the table doesn't make it yours."

Ollie grabbed the back of Tommo's chair and flung it backwards. Tommo was just scrambling to his feet when Ollie's fist hit him in the mouth, sending him crashing to the floor again.

In one leap I was at the table and grabbing Ollie from behind, pinning his arms to his side. "No, Ollie," I yelled. "There's no call for that."

Andy Braithwaite jumped up from his bed to help a bewildered Tommo back to his feet. "You great arsehole, Wilson," Braithwaite shouted. "Tha's way out of line."
I released Ollie and he stormed out of the room slamming the door behind him.
We got Tommo to his feet just in time for Ollie to come steaming back in. He strode over to Tommo before anyone could stop him and grabbed Tommo by the shoulders. "Christ, Tommo, I'm so sorry, mate." He looked at the blood coming from Tommo's lip. "Oh shit, shit, shit." He gave Tommo a hug. "I'm so sorry."
Colin Masters came out if his room. "What's going on?" He saw Tommo's blood dripping into his handkerchief as he walked down the hut towards the door. "Tommo?"
Tommo waved him away. "Nothing for you to get concerned about." He picked a towel from his locker and left the room.
"I'll ask again; what's going on?" Masters said. "Anyone gonna tell me what's happened here?"
Ollie stepped forward. "Me I'm afraid. Lost me rag with Tommo."
"If he's hurt Ollie, I have to recommend you for a charge. You know that?"
Ollie just nodded.

As it turned out the lip wasn't as badly damaged as first appeared and Ollie's apology was accepted. They shook hands and Colin Masters seemed satisfied enough to go back to his room with no mention of a charge.
The incident was over, but it had somehow left a strange atmosphere in the room. The hut was nearly always full of chatter but now the silence was so heavy you could almost reach out and touch it. Boys were sat on their beds reading

or polishing buttons, activity everywhere, but no one one looking up and no one speaking.

Then a mischievous chuckle came front Monkey's bed-space. He suddenly sprung up from the bed, put his shoes on and carried his bedside rug to the middle of the room. "Ladies and gentlemen," he called. "We come to the part of the day when the much-awaited star turn is about to perform." He made a low bow and then stopped. He looked down at the bedside rug and shook his head. "Too small. I need two." He nipped smartly Over to Geordie's bed and lifted his rug. "I'll just borrow this if I may?" Back in the centre of the room he began again. "Ladies and gentlemen put your hands together for the amazing all singing, all dancing, all weathers, twice on weekends, Monkey the Marvellous." He bowed again and then, to everyone's amazement, launched into the funniest dance routine I'd ever seen. And, wow, could he dance.
He began with some amazing tap routines, albeit on a soft rug, and then slowly turned it into a full-blown comedy routine. It was brilliant and yet I was not surprised; I'd sensed something deeply comic inside him from the day we met.
When he finished he returned to his bed hot and breathless and the room, minutes ago so deadly silent, erupted. The mood wasn't just broken, it was shattered and banished to the four corners of the universe.

It was late that evening before Ollie came and asked about Cheryl.
"You were there," I reminded him.
"Not right to the bitter end."
I filled him in and then swung the subject round to him.

He gave a gentle laugh. "Me? What can we say? It just doesn't get any easier. I thought it only fair to break it to her gently about calling it a day. The first wasp in the picnic was her relief not turning in for work. I'd gone to a pub for a pint and a drag expecting her to be ready at seven. As it was by the time we got away from the coffee bar it was almost time for my bus." He ran his fingers through his mop of fair hair. "As we walked to the bus stop I said that I thought we should stand back a bit and see how we feel after a break and she grabbed me and hugged me and started crying. It was almost as if she could read my thoughts. She said she didn't want me to even think of it. She said I'm the one thing that keeps her happy and I couldn't be so cruel as to leave her for even a minute. She said that she loved me, that she'd do anything to keep me. Just think of that, Draper, anything. I hadn't got the heart, or the balls, to even hint at ending it."

"So, what next?"

"Ha! If I knew that I'd know twice as much as I know now."

"I know one thing Ollie."

"Go on?"

"You can't go around taking it out on ya mates."

He nodded. "No, I know. I'm so pissed off about that."

Thursday afternoon I was so preoccupied with thoughts of the pending phone call that the lesson on Pre-Flight Inspections was just a blur and when I looked at Ollie I could see he was elsewhere.

When the NAAFI van arrived, I bought a coke to share with Ollie.

"I'm gonna have to be careful," Ollie said, lighting a cigarette. "I can't concentrate on bugger all.

I nodded. 'Me neither."

"Yeah, but at least come this afternoon you'll know how the land lies."

I took a swig off coke. "Oh, thanks a bundle."

"I'm sorry old son, but you have to say it's true, and all I'm saying is one way or another, in an hour or two can clear the old head and move on."

"If only it was that easy."

After classes Masters marched us back to the hut and as soon as we were dismissed I went to my locker and found some change for the phone. Ollie wished me luck and I hurried to the phone box only to find it occupied. I looked at my watch. Cheryl left work at five and it was now a quarter to.

I contemplated telling the guy to hurry it up but noticed he was senior entry and I knew where that could lead.

It was almost five-to-five when he eventually finished. I was in such a panic I dropped a coin and had to get on my hands and knees to find it. I picked up the handset and dialled. It was three minutes to five.

Chapter Seventeen

"Damn, Damn and bloody bollocks!" I banged the phone down on to its cradle. I'd missed her by no more than a minute. One bloody minute.

I stormed back into the hut and collapsed on my bed. Ollie looked over and grimaced. "Oh, dear," he said. "I gather it's bad news."

I stared at my watch. "What time do you make it?"

He checked his watch. "Just coming up to five past. Why?"

"Shit," I said, taking my watch off. "I'm a bit slow."

Ollie nodded. "Ah, I see. You missed her."

"By a bloody minute."

"Oh, shit. Not so clever," he said. "Changing the subject old son, it's our Assessment Test Monday. You wanna do a last-minute swat."

"I groaned. "Yeah, I suppose we ought to."

"Good man take your mind off things."

But it didn't.

After Ollie and me had finished I lay on my bed reading. Geordie came in from the washroom and sat himself on the foot of my bed. "Now Mark do you think we can maybe talk without it becoming a slanging match?"

I grinned. "I did rather attack you I suppose."

"There's no suppose about it."

"Sorry about that my old buddy I was a bit rattled."

He shrugged. "Fair enough." He towelled his hair. "Do you want to explain it to me again. Nice and slow".

I filled him in on the whole episode. When I'd finished he exhaled heavily and shook his head. "None of it makes sense. Firstly, I've never mentioned Cheryl to Avril and, I've not spoken to Nerys since the evening in the hairdressers. Secondly, I don't think Avril knows Cheryl. So, if the girls didn't say anything, and I didn't, who are you you left with?" He raised an eyebrow. ."it has to be Tina."

I shrugged "That's how I see it, but who told Tina?"

He held his hands up in a gesture of surrender. "Not a bloody clue bonnie lad. I just know it wasn't me."

Friday, I rang Cheryl's work only to be told she'd gone home lunchtime with a migraine. It seemed as if it wasn't to be and the gods were trying to warn me off. But then, Saturday lunchtime I received a letter.

When my name was called I assumed it was a letter from home, but the address on it simply said: *Mark Draper, RAF St. Athan*. It could only be Cheryl. I opened it and found a single page letter dated Thursday 25 Oct.

'Mark, I don't know if you tried phoning or not but, whatever the answer, if you want to meet for a chat at the weekend I'll be at the bus station the usual time Saturday. Hope you get this letter okay.

Cheryl.

Tommo was watching me. "You look bemused, Mark.

I nodded. "I am a bit. This letter is not addressed properly and was only posted Thursday evening at the earliest and yet it's arrived already."

"Maybe that's the answer. Get people to minimalise the address."

I laughed. "Minimalise? Stone me Tommo, is that a real word?"

"If it wasn't, then it is now."

I read the letter over again. This afternoon was the last chance to get to see her before leave. I looked at my watch, suddenly realising I needed to get a move on if I was going to catch the bus.

I hurried to the washroom.

Ollie, Geordie and Monkey had left to catch the early bus and by the time I finished getting ready Tommo had left and the only one in the hut was Bonner. I grabbed my jacket and locked up.

"Give me two minutes and I'll be with ya."

I looked up to find Bonner skating down the room. "Quick piss and I'm ready."

I stood watching him leave the room. How weird was this? Me and Bonner going into town together. The lads would never believe it. Come to think of it, I wasn't so sure I did.

It was strange to be sat on the bus with the big Irishman. Although he'd changed so much since his chat with Tosh he still kept himself very much to himself.

We'd been traveling in silence for around five minutes and then he spoke. "I couldn't help hearing about your girl trouble. Is it her you're going to see this afternoon?" he asked, looking out the window.

"Yeah," I replied. "I'm not sure what to think. "I'm trying not to get too optimistic, but I can't help thinking that if she wants to meet me there has to be a chance."

He looked at me and smiled. "It's feckin' obvious she's still keen on yous and that makes you a very lucky man.

"I suppose so."

"Suppose? There's no suppose about it. Just think a moment. If it was the other way around and you was telt that your lass had been screwing some bloke would you forgive her?" He shook his head. "I feckin' think not."

And that was the conversation for the journey.

I thought about what he'd said; he was right. I would never forgive her for that. The question I had to ponder now was she about to forgive me, or was it all down the pan?

I stepped from the bus and Bonner gave me a pat on the back. "Good luck." I smiled as he walked off, thinking that maybe I ought to make an effort to get to know him a bit better.

I turned back and there was Cheryl.

We went to our usual café and found a corner table free. I ordered a coke for me and a coffee for her. She stirred a spoon of sugar into her coffee and I made some stupid remark about her being sweet enough. It was as if we had things to discuss and we knew we had things to discuss but couldn't find a way to start.

Then, just as I decided to dive straight in she also began speaking resulting in a slightly embarrassing moment.

"Go on, Cheryl," I said tentatively. "You first. What were you going to say?"

She sighed. "It's not that simple." She gazed into her coffee for a moment. I think I'd like to carry on seeing you but I ...." She blushed slightly. "I need reassurances."

"Okay, I'm listening."

"Well, firstly I'm just sixteen...."

"I'm only seventeen," I blurted.

"Please, Mark, don't interrupt! It's hard enough as it is."

I mimed zipping my lips.

"I'm just sixteen and a few weeks. Nerys is over twenty. I've never... well, you know, and I haven't, whereas Nerys has a reputation for being a bit easy. My problem now is, are you now going to expect me to do the same?"

"Lord no! Don't even think about it." I reached out and squeezed her hand. "I wouldn't dream of it."

She pulled her hand away. "Well you made a big enough fuss when I stopped you going inside…" She checked that we couldn't be overheard. "Inside my bra."

"I've apologised about that. Besides you said it was forgotten."

"It was, until I heard about Nerys."

"Oh, fair enough." Then I remembered the chat with Geordie earlier. "Anyway, talking of that, who told you? My money's on Tina."

She shook her head. "For what it's worth it was Milly."

I frowned. "Who the hell is Milly?"

"Do you remember when you saw me at the fair with a bunch of girls?"

"I do."

"Then you might remember her; a tall, skinny girl with glasses? Well that was Milly and she obviously remembered you. She told me at work. Anyway, you're changing the subject. I'm talking about us."

"Sorry."

"I've done a lot of thinking and it's occurred to me that almost every time we're alone you have to make a play for my breasts."

"I didn't realise you disliked it so much."

"I don't. Most times I quite enjoy it, but it gets to the point where I wonder if you really care for me or are just out for what you can get. I'd like to go to the cinema and watch the film without having to sit in the back row just because you want a play."

I took a sip of coke. That was a real slap on the wrist and for the life of me I couldn't think what to say next. "Well, there ya go. What can I say?" There was a little devil in my head telling me to tell her to keep her precious tits. I shook the temptation away. "I've told you that I really care for you and you have to believe me because I mean it. The problem here, as I see it, is you say you like it most times, and that's good, but how the hell do I know when you like it and when you don't?"

She sensed I was getting a bit touchy. "Don't start getting upset it's not something we can't sort out."

"So, what's the answer?"

"The first thing is when you try it and I push you away that's telling you I don't want to. Okay? It doesn't mean have a two-minute rest then try again. When I'm in the mood I let you, don't I?"

I nodded. My elation at knowing she still wanted to go out with me was melting like my Super Whip ice cream on a hot summer day in Ramsgate." Yes, I suppose so." I said glumly.

"Oh, come on Mark, this isn't fair. Somehow your making me out to be the villain here."

I sighed heavily. "No, you're right, I'm sorry. "It's just that…"

"Just that what?"

The devil in my head stepped in. I leant towards her. "It's just that I'm a tit man and you have gorgeous tits."

To my surprise she found it amusing. "I think you mean breasts," she said with a smile.

"No," I replied. I definitely mean tits."

At the bus stop we kissed goodbye and I hugged her tightly. "I'm really going to miss you," I said, moving my kisses round to her neck.

She sighed in my ear. "It's only two weeks. It'll fly by."

I pulled away from kissing and looked into her eyes. "Say what you like love, I'm still gonna miss you."

She smiled and nodded. "Yes, I know and I'm going to miss you, but I've got your home address now, so we can write." We kissed again and said our goodbyes as the bus came into view.

Just as the bus arrived so did Bonner. He saw Cheryl and waved. "You're a very pretty young lass," he said. "He doesn't deserve you."

I realised he was drunk.

He wasn't rolling drunk just slurring the occasional word. We sat at the back of the bus and he laughed gently as he sat down. As far as I could remember I'd never heard him laugh before.

"What's amusing you?" I asked.

In drink his accent was really strong, almost comical. "Oí beat the bloody the lot of 'em." he said.

I groaned. "Please tell me you ain't been thumping people?"

"No, no, I'm talking about darts ya daft bugger." He put his arm round my shoulders and gave me a hug. "Do ya know what young Draper, I think you're the kind of guy that I would really like to know better. Why haven't we chatted before?"

"Probably because friendly chat doesn't seem to be one of your strong points Jim."

He took his arm away. "If your gonna have a go oil not feckin' well bother."

I was surprised how quick he was to take offence. "I wasn't having a go Jim. You have to say it's true, you do keep yourself to yourself." I hoped I hadn't said the wrong thing, so I quickly added. "I mean, I'd love to get to know you better."

He leant to one side and farted loudly. Several looks of disgust came our way. "Jim!" I hissed. "Pack it in."

He just chuckled to himself and went to sleep. I looked at him dozing beside me and wondered how he was going to manage to sign back in without them seeing him drunk. He could be in serious trouble.

I woke him as the bus was nearing our stop. The sleep had done him no favours at all. He was now a bit unsteady on his feet. I held his arm and steered him away from camp. "Where the feck are we going?"

"We're gonna have to get you steady enough to pass back into camp."

He pulled his arm away roughly. "Jaysus Draper oim not a feckin' kid."

Then I really pushed my luck; I grabbed his arm even firmer. "Listen to me, ya great lump. If you get pulled up for drinking you're automatically on a fizzer. Seven days and a fine." I pulled him to my side. "You don't want that mate, you really don't, so just for once quit being the big I am and do what I say."

I waited for the worse. Then I heard him laughing again. I let out a sigh of relief and started walking him along the pathway.

He ruffled my hair. "You're a bit of a gem really Mark Draper, so you are. Now lead on mother."

The thought of being on a charge must have sunk in because he let me lead him away from camp and walk around without another gripe.

Although he had a bit of a wobble when signing the book, somehow, we made it.

When we got back to the hut he collapsed onto his bed and I pulled his shoes off. He smiled. "Thank you, kind sir, you've been wonderful. "He let out another resounding fart and began laughing again.

The hut was full of faces looking on in amazement.

I was about to go to my bed when he propped himself up on his elbows. "I need a piss."

"Well, don't look at me mate. You're on your own there." I left him, fully clothed on top of the bedding and laughing gently. Before I got as far as my own bed he was snoring.

"What about him wanting a piss?" Tommo asked. "He might piss the bed if you leave him there."

He had a point. "Oh, bollocks," I groaned. "Who's gonna give me a hand here?"

When he fell asleep on the bus he woke in a worse state than before, now, having gone to sleep on his bed, he was away with the birdies. He was almost a dead weight.

Tommo took Bonner's left arm and I took the right and we headed for the washrooms, but it was impossible to hold him steady.

Geordie came in from the washrooms as Tommo and me struggled. He looked at me and laughed. "Give him to me, Mark, you hold the door.

We eventually got him to the urinals but that's when the real problem kicked in. Who was going to take it out and hold it while he peed?

Come on Mark," Tommo said, grimacing from the effort. "You can do that bit. He's your project."

Right on cue Monkey came in. "Just the man." I said, quickly dragging him over to the urinals. "Do us the honours."

Monkey stared at Bonner's fly then at me. "Why me? What's up with you?"

I gave Monkey my little boy lost face. "Please mate. Help us out here."

Monkey sighed heavily. "If he wakes up and smacks me one, I'll kill you Draper."

I was looking forward to hearing what Ollie had to say but, as so often happened, I fell asleep reading before he got back.

Next morning someone shook me gently. I assumed it was Ollie wanting to know if I was going to breakfast. "You awake?"

I grunted. "I am now."

I looked up to see Jim Bonner. "Coming to breakfast?"

"I didn't expect to see you so bright eyed and bushy tailed this morning, Jim."

I saw Ollie peering over his blankets with a bemused expression on his face.

Bonner stretched. "I feel fine." He looked over at Ollie. "Your pal here was bloody great last night. He saved my bacon, that's for sure."

Ollie sat up. "This I gotta hear?"

Jim related the story to Ollie with most if the room earwigging. He finished his story and then frowned as if he'd suddenly thought of something. He turned back to me. "Did you take me for a piss last night?"

I grinned. 'Me, Tommo, Geordie and Monkey. You're a heavy bugger, you know."

He cringed. "Oh feckin' hell."

I winked. "And such a big boy, Jim."

After breakfast I sat on Ollie's bed. "How'd it go?"

He sat with his hands behind his head and a grin that split his face. "I didn't know anything could feel that good."

"What did?"

He sighed. "Sex." He went into his thoughts. "The things she showed me. Wow. Why her husband treats her so badly I'm buggered if I know."

"Yes, yes, that's all well and good but you were deliberating packing her in last time we discussed it," I reminded him. "I gather you changed your mind."

"And I did try," he said. "I sat her down in the café during her break and told her about how I was beginning to think we should maybe think about where we were going."

"And what did she say?"

She told me to hang on while she made a quick phone call. She came back smiling and said we could use her sister's place after work. We could talk properly then."

"And, let me guess. You ended up in bed and she weaved her sex magic and your cock overruled your brain?"

He laughed. "Yeah, something like that." He fished in his bedside locker for his cigarettes. "Anyway, that's me up to date. What about you?"

I filled him in on how things had gone with Cheryl, although it seemed a bit tame after his adventures.

Monday morning was the exams. There was no doubt that they were getting serious stuff now. I felt fairly confident but, unusually, we wouldn't get the results until after our leave.

As before, Ollie was cutting his leave short and staying with his lady's sister.

Getting away from the crappy hut and the discipline was always a pleasure but going home was losing its charm. For one thing I wouldn't get to see Cheryl for over two weeks and for another the band was coming along and I really loved our practice sessions.

But leave was on us once again and Tuesday morning our transport to Gileston Station rolled up and we threw our bags in and hauled ourselves in after them.

As the convoy pulled clear of camp Masters called out. "Rig-a-dig-dig," and the answering chant came. "Oy-oy-oy," as we trundled on down the hill to the train station the chant rang out from all the lorries.

It had been raining earlier and as I jumped down from the lorry I looked up at the leadened sky and thought to myself that there was more rain to come.

Chapter Eighteen

What a crappy way to start my two weeks leave. I took shelter in the station waiting room as the rain came belting down so hard it bounced off the floor. I was pretty flush, having just received my leave money so a taxi wasn't out of the question. I checked my watch. Five to five. I decided to wait another five minutes and if was still persisting I'd splash out and get a dry ride home. I stood in the doorway watching the rain for while longer and then went back in the Waiting Room to fetch my bag.

"Mark."

I turned to see Alf walking in. "Can't hang about, I'm still at work." He took my bag. "Come on."

He was in the works flat back lorry parked right up to the station door. As I climbed in he said. "Illegally parked as well."

We set off on the short journey home. "It's been raining since lunchtime," he said. "I popped home for bit of lunch and your mum said if it was still at it come five, would I see if I could I give you a ride home."

I nodded. "Well, I appreciate it, Alf. Ta." I was tempted to ask how things were but decided I'd be better asking my mum.

He dropped me off right outside the door. The rain was easing. "What time do you finish?" I asked.

"Half five."

"See you soon then."

The kettle was on and my favourite biscuits were sat on on the table. I kissed my mum on the cheek.

She asked about the journey home, was I enjoying the RAF, did I have a girlfriend, was I pleased I was able to get to the wedding? one question after another. "Woah! hang on mum," I said laughing. "Never mind about me; what about you?"

"Me?"

"Yes you, mother. You know what I'm asking."

The kettle began to whistle and she set about making the tea. "I should have made a fuss years ago. He's a changed man. Oh, yes, he still falls asleep in front of the tele and he can still be a grumpy old sod at times, but, all in all, it's not going too badly."

I smiled. 'I'm really chuffed for you."

Lenny called round on the Thursday after work. He was still feeling a bit guilty about the beating and I did my best to convince him he wasn't at all to blame. We had a quick chat and arranged to get together the following evening in the pub. As he left he said. "Oh, by the way, Mark, I told Ricky Windsor you'd be home again, and he said he'd like to tag along." He looked at me a bit abashed. "I said it would be okay. I hope you don't mind?"

I shook my head and smiled. "No, no! I like the bloke, you know I do, I just don't wanna end up pissed as a fart again."

My first letter from Cheryl arrived two days later. She told me how much she missed me and how pleasing it was to have had a sensible chat to iron things out.

She went on to tell me how her and Tina had been approached by two boys at a dance in Barry. They had chatted them up and had a dance and at the end of the evening the boys asked if they would be at the dance the next week.

She wrote: '*but you needn't worry Mark, remember, I'm all yours.*'

I was fuming. The thought of her dancing with someone else got me really angry and then, on top of that, hinting she might see him the following weekend. I screwed the letter up and threw it across the room.

Then it dawned on me; it was so obvious. She was trying to get me jealous as a bit of revenge. I smiled to myself, I bet there weren't any boys at all. I retrieved the crumpled letter. "I'm on to your little game," I said to myself and I set about writing a reply.

I opened with the usual stuff, told her I'd been for a drink with a couple of old school friends and then a bit about the weather, all the time working towards the nitty gritty.

I said how nice it was to be all hers' but that didn't mean I owned her. I said she should enjoy herself while I'm away. Dancing isn't a big deal and the lad in question obviously had good taste. I re-read it twice and nodded. Yes, that should call her bluff. Trying to make me jealous was a waste of time. I almost began to believe it myself.

The day before the wedding Ray popped round at lunchtime for a cuppa. Mom made a fresh pot and slid a plate of biscuits in front of him. He snaffled three down his neck before the tea arrived.

"Hey, steady on, ya greedy sod!" I said, "leave some for later. Anyway, I thought you'd had your lunch already?"

"Shut up misery guts," he replied, taking another biscuit. "Or you won't get to be my best man tomorrow."

I stared at him. "Say that again. "

He laughed. "Don't look at me like that. You heard what I said."

"Why?"

"Because Pete Alison, my best man as was, is sick."

I was stunned. "Are you telling me you've only got one mate?"

Ray swiped me on the back of the head. "Shut up you cretin. I've got plenty of mates, what I haven't got is time."

"Tough!" I snapped. "Cause I ain't doing it."

"Mark!" my mum said, pouring the teas. "Don't be so silly I think It's a wonderful idea."

"You do?"

She nodded, "of course. Why not?"

"Mum, the best man has to make a speech."

"Yes, I know, you can do that."

"Okay, I do a speech. How will it go? Let me see." I rubbed my chin in an exaggerated fashion. "Ladies and gentlemen, my brother Ray. Where do I start? How about when we cycled right out to Reculver Towers and Ray thought it really funny to take the chain off my bike and leave me to walk all the way home. No, how about the time we built a rope swing across the stream out in the marshes. Remember that one Ray? The stream full of stinging nettles? How funny was that, when you cut the rope, dumping me in the nettles. Remember Ray? I was in shorts? And what about…."'

"All right, funny guy, give it a rest." He leaned towards me. "You, due to unfortunate circumstances, are my best men. Get it? And you must make a speech and any of that sarcastic shite and you will regret it, believe me."
I looked at my mum and nodded, "You're so right mum," I said dryly. A wonderful idea."

Cheryl's letter arrived Tuesday morning. I snatched it from the doormat and took it up to my bedroom, clearing two stairs at a time. I quickly opened it.
'Dearest Mark,
What you said in your letter about my freedom was quite well timed because those boys did turn up again. They just came and sat with us. A bit of a cheek really. After the dance they insisted on walking us home, but I told the one with me that he couldn't and told him I had a boyfriend, so he was wasting his time.'
I had a little chuckle at that bit.
'*He wanted a goodnight kiss and I said no, but he kept on until I said he could have a quick one. I think he came through the Mark Draper school of kissing because I suddenly felt his hand groping me. I nearly laughed. Anyway, I pushed his hand away, but he tried kissing me again. Do you remember me saying to you about a two-minute rest and then try again? Well this one only waited thirty seconds. I told him to pack it in, in no uncertain*

*terms and I walked away. If that's me enjoying my freedom
I'm not so sure.*

My heart was hammering against my chest in four-four
time. What was going on here? Had I read it all wrong?
Was she suddenly becoming some old scrubber? How
could she let just any Tom, Dick or Harry grope her?
I found my thoughts being pulled in opposite directions. I
was dragged back to the last letter and how I assumed she
was out to make me jealous? Now, this letter, taking it one
step further. I had to be right, she must be trying it on. I
simply couldn't imagine Cheryl kissing a bloke just to
keep him from pestering her. Definitely not. This was her
testing me to see my reaction in the light of her forgiving
me over Nerys.
But what if was all true? What then? What if she had let
some baggy arsed little twat kiss her and grope her like
that? Was I willing to say it's okay, after all it was me
who said enjoy your freedom? Would it then seem to her
that I didn't really care the way I'd said I did? That could
be fatal as far as our relationship was concerned.

My head was a mess. Now I had to compose a best man's
speech pretending that my twat of a brother was a good
bloke and a letter to Cheryl that was fraught with danger
With Ray's speech I was totally stuck. Heaven only knows
what I was going to find to say. It was very tricky.
Cheryl's I'd tackle when I'd had more time to think.

The wedding was at two fifteen and come lunchtime I still
had a blank page in front of me. I started writing a list of
positive sounding things to say like 'he's a good-looking
bloke' and 'he's a fun guy to have around,' but I quickly

abandoned that. It was no use pissing around trying to please him, I picked up my pen and quickly wrote the speech. Sod the consequences.

I hadn't time to start my letter to Cheryl. That was this evening's project.

I was surprised to find I had no nerves. The drumming on stage must have given me confidence. When they called for the best man speech I rose from my chair and made a couple of opening remarks thanking the necessary parties and then I was up and running:

"Those of you who know Ray well will no doubt be aware of his wicked sense of humour."

I ran through the list of nasty tricks he'd played on me over the years saving the cycle trip to Reculver Towers to last. I glanced over at Ray and caught his glare full on. To be fair the speech got a few laughs along the way, so he shouldn't be that pissed off.

I carried on:

"If some off you are thinking Ray has given me a bit of a rough ride I'd just like to say one last thing. That man there, my brother Ray, bought me the best Christmas present I have ever had. A beautiful acoustic guitar. Something that changed my life and I just want to say, in front of everyone here, thank you Ray. That guitar was the most thoughtful gift I've ever received, and I love it."

I made a toast to the happy couple and sat down. I didn't look over at Ray.

No sooner had I finished my speech than the answer to what I would write to Cheryl hit me in the face like a comedy custard pie. I couldn't wait to get home and get it written.

First, I had to face the wrath of Ray. I dodged him for quite a while a but eventually I found myself cornered. "

"Well then, what was that all about?"

Had you forgotten what I said yesterday?"

I shook my head. "No,"

I'd known him for long enough to know when he was angry. I felt pretty safe. "It got a laugh didn't it?" I said smiling."

He clipped me round the ear playfully. "Cheeky little shite."

And that was it.

The function wrapped up a little after nine and I was home by half past and sat on my bed with pen and paper at the ready. I was well aware that I'd been drinking and needed to be careful, although no doubt I'd read it in the morning before I posted it.

I wrote how much I was missing her and was looking forward t seeing her again.

Then I wrote:

'I can't believe the the change that's come over me the last few days. You've made me take a good look at myself and I didn't like what I saw. I can say now that I was really jealous when you told me about the lad kissing you. I was so relieved when you said you didn't want your freedom and I can tell you now, Cheryl, I don't want mine. I just want you.'

I slipped it in the envelope but left it open. I figured I'd best read it again in the morning.

When I awoke it was the first thing on my mind. I quickly re-read it and smiled to myself. That should put an end to all her silly games. No more fictitious breast groping. It was a good letter and, I thought, more than a little bit true.

I posted my letter to Cheryl and calculated that I should get a reply before I went back. I could hardly wait to hear what she would say.
And I was right. I did get a reply before going back. I got it the day before.
I read it once through and then read it again straight away.
I read it a third time pacing round the bedroom:
'Dear Mark,
I was so touched when I read your letter. So much so that you've made this letter that much harder to write.
I wasn't totally honest about the boy in my letters.'
The first time I read that bit I smiled with self satisfaction.
I knew she was making it all up. Now she was admitting it.
She went on: *'Yes, he did pester at first but when he kissed me again I did it freely. I'm so sorry Mark, I really am, but I've fallen for him totally. We see each other every day. I hope you can understand but I can't see you anymore.*
Sorry,
Cheryl.'

First off, I was angry. I paced round the room swearing over and over again. Then I was jealous, the thought of her kissing and cuddling with this new bloke was tearing me apart. Then it dawned on me that all the time she was writing her last letter she was already seeing him. Then I was angry again. All that rubbish about telling him to pack it in was a load of old crap.
I sat on my bed and burst into tears. There was nothing I could do.

231

A short while later I heard my mum coming in with the shopping and went to the bathroom to wash my face. I didn't want to let her see me like this and so I waited until she'd taken her coat off and put the kettle on and I nipped down the stairs, grabbed my jacket from the peg, opened the front shouted that I was off out. As I shut the door behind me I heard her shout. "I'm making a pot of tea." But I was out.

Walking, almost on auto pilot, I went to the phone box on the corner of the street. I was about to ring Ollie when I remembered he wouldn't be home, he'd be with his mystery lady. I groaned and banged my head against the glass, several times. I needed someone to tell me what to do. When I looked up there was an old gent walking his dog and he had stopped to stare at me. I opened the door and asked if he was waiting to use the phone.

He pulled his dog close in to his legs as if worried I might leap out and attack it. "What are you doing in there?" he asked, frowning at me.

I managed a smile. "I'm having a bad day. My girlfriend has just dumped me."

He snorted indignantly. "Putting your head through a glass panel isn't going to do anything except maybe damage a perfectly good telephone box."

I sighed. "I'm very sorry, okay. Now why don't you just carry on walking your dog and I'll go home like a good little boy."

"You know your trouble young man? No manners. National Service, that's what you need."

I laughed. "You think so?"

"A few weeks square bashing. That's what you need. Do you the world of good. Discipline."

I shook my head. "You know sod all. You're not telling me you did your National Service. You're too old to have been called up."

He looked at me, shook his head, and walked away.

Then I thought about it; maybe he had done National Service. Maybe he was called up for the first lot. He was more than likely a first world war veteran. I was in a crappy mood and I was taking it out on a war veteran.

I called out after him. "I'm sorry, sir. I didn't mean to be rude. I apologise."

He turned and looked at me as if unsure if I was still being sarcastic or not.

"That was rude and uncalled for and I just want to say I'm sorry."

He nodded and set off walking his dog again.

I walked back home feeling like a total shit. As I reached the front door I stopped and thought: It wasn't the old man's fault I'd been dumped. I really was a selfish twat, giving him a load of crap like that. I also had to keep it in mind that it's not Ollie's fault or Geordie's or Monkey's or any other bugger's. It was my problem so why take it out on anybody else? It was a sure-fire way to lose friends. I reminded myself about how bad Ollie had felt about hitting poor old Tommo.

I opened the door and my mum called from the kitchen. "Everything okay, son?"

I told her I was fine. "Just going upstairs to pack."

I went into my bedroom and roared my eyes out.

Not surprisingly, I spent the whole journey back to camp thinking of Cheryl. What was I supposed to do? Do I fight to get her back, or should I accept she's gone?

I couldn't keep the subject out of my head. The only sure thing was I didn't want to say anything about it to the others and I didn't want it to show. I had to appear cheerful and problem free.

It sounded easy enough but when I got back in the hut I threw my bag into the storeroom and crashed out on my bed, eyes tight shut, pretending to be going to sleep. I didn't want to have to talk to anybody yet.

"Bloody hell," Andy Braithwaite called out, laughing gently. "It looks as if Draper's been burning candles at both ends

A voice in my head screamed out, "just fuck off and leave me alone," but I just smiled and gave him the 'V' sign.

Chapter Nineteen

When Ollie arrived back I knew he was pleased about something. I was still on my bed pretending to be asleep, but I allowed one eye to open just enough to see who was coming and going. I saw him look over to my bed and smile. "Anyone know how long Sleeping Beauty here has been gonked out?" he asked the room in general.

"At least an hour," Bonner replied. "He crashed the minute he got in."

Ollie nodded. "Right, time he surfaced then."

He looked at me and smiled again. It was that smile that told me he was pleased about something. "In that case I'll awaken Sleeping Beauty with a kiss."

234

He took off his coat and crossed over to my bed. He kicked the iron bed leg. "Wakey, wakey princess"

I opened one eye. "Fuck off Prince Charming, I'm asleep."

He chuckled and plonked himself down on my bed. "Not any more you're not."

"What's got you so perky?" I said opening the other eye.

"Isn't it obvious? Seeing you again. I've missed you."

I sat up. "I'll ask again: what's got you so perky?"

"I suppose I'll have to tell you," he said, in a jokey fashion. "The fact is Draper I've met…" he trailed off mid sentence. He looked at me and frowned. "You been crying?" he asked in a hushed voice.

I sighed. "Not for at least ten minutes."

He groaned. "Oh, shit. What's up?"

I shook my head. "Later."

"Okay, we'll chat later."

"No, it's okay Ollie. You can tell me your news though." I managed a smile. "You might just cheer me up."

He punched my shoulder gently. "Nah, as you said, later."

Ollie was as good as his word, so I waited 'till I felt I could tell him without getting too emotional.

We were sat in the NAAFI sipping a coke the following evening. Outside the wind was blowing a heavy downpour against the window and it had been for over an hour.

"Bloody weather," Ollie grumbled. He had a cigarette dangling from his lip but didn't seem too keen on lighting it.

"Are you gonna light that sometime tonight?"

He took it out and laid it on the table. "I'm trying not to. Think I ought to pack it in."

"Stone me" I said. "What's brought this on?"

"Karen," he smiled, offering no explanation. "She hates me smoking. Says I taste like an old ash tray."

"Ah, right," I said, nodding. "I suppose this Karen is the reason for your cheerful return?"

"Too true. She's lovely."

"You feel like sharing this?"

He picked the cigarette up and lit it. "Tomorrow," he said blowing a flow of smoke down his nostrils.

"Why not now?"

"I'm not in the right frame of mind today."

"Fair enough," I said. "After all, you understood when I said the same to you."

His forehead crumpled. "What?"

"You know. When you asked me about why I'd been crying, and I said later, and you understood. I'm doing the same."

"Have I missed something here?" he said looking perplexed. 'What are you on about?"

"F'fucks sake, Ollie. You and your new love. What did you think?"

He grinned. "Daft sod. Smoking. I was talking about giving up smoking tomorrow. Tonight's not the right time."

I laughed.

"Well at least it's got you laughing."

"Yeah, sorry mate." I took a deep breath. It was time to talk about it. I was ready. "Cheryl's chucked me."

Ollie slumped back in his chair. "Oh, fuckin' hell, Draper. She's dumped ya?" He sighed. "And just when you'd sorted yourselves out."

I grunted. "Or so I thought. I'm sure that, despite what she said, she never really forgave me."

I handed Ollie the letters. He read in silence. When he'd finished he handed them back to me. "And what did you write to her. She keeps referring back to what you wrote to her?"

I filled him in on the whole exchange and he asked for the letters again.

When he'd read them again he sighed heavily. "It was all a bit quick wasn't it?"

"Wasn't it just. I simply never saw it coming."

He shook his head. "I'm so sorry, mate, I really am."

"I'm gutted."

He nodded. "I can see that."

"But when you weigh it up it don't make sense, Ollie. We've hardly been going out together five bloody minutes, you've pointed that out, so how come I'm so miserable?"

"Don't be silly Draper, that's got nothing to do with Cheryl; you're always a miserable sod." He smiled. "No, seriously though, I'll tell you why; it's because you fell for her as soon as you clapped eyes on her. She was special from the off."

"Yeah, I did, didn't I?"

I really felt that just talking about it aloud was making me feel better. Then I asked him about this Karen lass.

She was sixteen and worked in the local cinema near Deptford. Her dad was the projectionist.

"How did you meet?"

"She dropped her shopping getting of the bus and I helped her pick things up. I was just thinking how tasty she looked when she suddenly said she recognised me. She'd been to the same school only the year behind me." He shrugged. "I dunno, somehow we just got chatting. I walked her home and asked if I could see her again and she said yes. As luck would have it the next day was her day off. So," he said beaming, "there you have it. We were going out together. She worked most evenings and so we met every day."

"You sound keen on her."

"You wouldn't chuckle old buddy. You wouldn't bloody chuckle."

"So," I said, when he'd wound it up "What about you know who?"

"That's got to end. We both know that. I was already gearing up for it before but now, meeting Karen, has just made it more certain."

"When? You obviously didn't do it at the weekend when you were with her?"

"No, true. I bottled it again." He lit another cigarette and blew out the match. "But it's going to happen soon. Very bloody soon." He looked slightly sheepish. "I suppose we ought to get Christmas out of the way first."

I found it really amusing reminding Ollie of his remarks about me and Cheryl. This Karen had him working out how many days to go before our next leave, and we we'd only been back five minutes.

He mentioned her umpteen times a day. Just like a lovesick schoolboy.

But then I'd start thinking of Cheryl again, and feel the pain moving in. It was a case of take a deep breath and soldier on.

The weekend arrived, and Ollie was clearly nervous. No thoughts of Karen now I thought.

I watched him getting ready to go out and I had to admit I didn't envy him one little bit; he really had got himself into a mess. All he'd wanted was a bit of uncomplicated sex and suddenly he was looking at a married woman talking about love and all that entails. I was going to ask him if he had any idea what he was going to say to her, but he looked so preoccupied that I decided to keep quiet. I just watched him go.

I went into Barry with Geordie a bit later. Geordie was meeting Avril and I was just killing time.
It was a big mistake. I passed all the places Cheryl and I had frequented together and couldn't help wondering if I might see her there with her new bloke. My mood sank. That was the last thing I wanted to see.
Then the weather decided to make things worse as the wind began to pick up and there was rain in the air. I headed for the bus.

That evening I tried passing the time by reading but I couldn't concentrate. Every time the door open I'd look up to see if it was Ollie.
Then a little after nine Monkey came in and marched swiftly up to my bed. "Mark," he said, sounding excited. "You're never guess who I've just seen."
"No. Who?"
He grinned, "Tina."
I groaned. "Oh, fuck off Monkey. I'm out of that now. You know I am."
His grin widened. "Yes, but *are* you?"
I frowned. "What the friggin' hell are you on about?"
"Tina wants to see you."
I closed my book. "Tina?"
"Yes Tina. As in Tina and Cheryl. She wants to see you. She was watching the Barry bus stop today hoping to catch you. She wants to talk to you."

"About what?"

He sighed heavily. "How the fuck should I know? All she said was, if you decide to say yes she'll be at the monument in Llantwit, tomorrow, around half-one."

I sat up. "Tomorrow?"

He nodded. "Yes."

"Llantwit?"

He threw his arms in the air in an exaggerated fashion. "F'chrissake, have I got to repeat everything? Yes, Tina and yes tomorrow and yes Llantwit." He turned away mumbling to himself.

Now I had a slight problem. Chas had arranged a practice hour in the Band Hut for the Sunday. It was set for three o'clock. We were getting a short programme ready for the cinema gig on Wednesday. I really needed the run through, but I was totally intrigued as to what Tina wanted. I'd have to whip into Llantwit for half-one and see what Tina wanted, and then nip back for rehearsal. I figured it was doable.

Just before lights out Ollie came back but he slumped on top of the bed and lit a cigarette. I knew not to ask about it yet.

As he lay on his bed smoking Colin Masters poked his head in and scanned the room. "Lights out in five Ollie. If you want the washroom you'd better shake a leg."

Ollie raised his hand. "No sweat mate." He stubbed his cigarette out and quickly undressed. As he left the room he glanced over at me. I nodded. "You okay, pal?"

He grinned. "I really haven't got a clue."

I left it until breakfast. "Ollie," I said as we took a seat, "you don't have to a say anything if you don't want to. But I'm all ears if you need me."

He stabbed a rather charred looking sausage with his fork. "I know. You're a good mate."

I gave a short laugh. "Mate? No, you daft Pratt. I'm not a mate, I'm just a nosey bugger. He managed a half-hearted smile. "Tommo and Andy are coming this way, I'll fill you in later."

After breakfast I got washed and changed even though I was far too early.

The walk from camp to Llantwit Major was a good hour but I had plenty of time. Well, getting there I had plenty of time, coming back might be tight. There were very few buses on a Sunday and if I spent any more than fifteen minutes talking to her I'd be very pushed to walk it back in time for a three o'clock rehearsal. My only hope was that she'd get there early

I popped down the hall to see Chas and let him know my plans.

When I got back to the hut Ollie was laid on his bed with his arms behind his head staring absently at his feet. I don't think he even noticed me come in. Eventually he looked up. "How's it going with you?"

"Better than you by the look of it," I replied, walking over to his bed. "You wanna talk about it yet?"

He shrugged. "Nothing much to report really. Whereas you, on the other hand, have."

"Oh, you've heard."

He nodded. "I suppose that's why you're dressed so early?"

I looked at him. "Your avoiding the subject about you know who. You haven't said anything to her again, have you?

"That's where you're wrong smarty pants."

I was intrigued. "Go on then."

He checked there was no one in earshot."

"To put it in a nut shell, I suggested a cooling off period. I suggested we leave it until after Christmas and she said okay."

I raised an eyebrow and smiled. "Just like that?"

"No alright, not quite as simple as that."

"I'm all ears"

"I wondered why you were such an ugly sod, Draper. Now I know." He laughed at his own joke.

I ignored him. "So, who said what?"

"As I said, to put it in a nut shell, I said that we were busy getting our rifle drill up to standard and, at the same time, swatting for our exams. And she said she understood because she would soon be busy getting ready for Christmas."

I shook my head. "Bloody hell, Ollie, as easy as that? You must feel relieved?"

"Well, it wasn't quite that simple. When it came time for me to leave she cracked. She told me she loved me and how I made her life worthwhile an' all that stuff, and I had to promise that I wasn't leaving her and that it was only until after Christmas."

"And you said?"

"Oh, shut up, Draper, you're like an old woman."

"Will do. I've got my answer anyway."

I was lucky with the weather walking to Llantwit. The last few days had been wet and windy but Sunday it was calm with a clear sky revealing a weak winter sunshine.

I made good time and arrived at the monument over ten minutes early. I had only to wait a few minutes before I saw Tina arriving.

She smiled. "You came."

"Of course. I'm naturally curious. I had to check it out. The only snag is I can't stay long."

"That's not a problem. The next bus for me is in twenty minutes and after that it's an hour wait."

"Right then," I said, not knowing what to say. What is it you want to see me about?"

"Well first, I never said a word about you and Nerys. When I said you'd been naughty I meant about you rowing with Cheryl about getting in her bra."

I laughed. "Can't a fella have any secrets?"

"Not with me and Cheryl, no."

I felt a bit flat. I don't know what I expected but this wasn't it.

She looked at me for what seemed ages. Then she cocked her head to one side. "Do you fancy me?"

I was stumped. "Stone me."

"Is that no?"

I had never really taken much notice notice of her before. She was a little shorter than me, and her dyed, blond hair was cut short with a fringe. She wasn't my idea of attractive but, taking her in now, just the two us, she was quite pleasant on the eye.

"No," I said quickly." It doesn't mean that.

"So, do you?"

"Why?"

"Because I fancy you. I always have, since that first day. I was really disappointed when you paired off with Cheryl."

"Oh, yeah, right," I said, frantically treading water. What was she after? "I don't know what to say to that."

"Would you fancy asking me out?" Her pale cheeks flared. "I won't be offended if you say no."

"What about Cheryl?"

"It's nothing to do with her. She didn't want you. She dropped you for a six-foot streak of piss named Bazza. Why I don't know, I can't stand him."

"Don't you think it'll be a bit embarrassing if me and you… well, you know, turn up together?"

"Why? Do you still want her back?"

If I was being honest I'd have to say yes. Yes, I bloody well do but, as it was, I just shrugged. "A bit I suppose." She pulled a fur collar up round her face. The afternoon temperature was dropping quite noticeably. "So?"

I frowned. "Eh?"

Do you want to ask me out?"

I laughed quietly. "Yeah, why not?"

"So, when do I get to see you then? Next weekend?"

I nodded. "All being well."

"And I believe there's a dance after that?"

I nodded. "True. A week Friday."

"You're sure?"

I shrugged. "Yeah, why not. Could be a bit of a giggle." I pushed my hands deeper into my pockets. "Let's see how the weekend goes first."

She checked her watch and quickly kissed me. "See you Saturday then. Barry? Usual time?"

"Yup. Saturday it is."

And she set off to catch her bus.

As I watched her go I remembered I wanted to ask her something. "Tina," I called running up to her. "I meant to ask you; why did you nod towards Avril when I asked who'd shopped me?"

She frowned. "No, I wasn't nodding to her. I thought you'd seen her. Millie, walking toward us."

I shrugged. "Oh, right."

"Why?"

"It doesn't matter."

Her bus rounded the corner.

The walk back to camp gave me plenty of time to think things over. Did I trust Tina? I wasn't sure. My best bet was go along for the ride and see how things unfold while, all the time, keeping my wits about me. I could just see it; Cheryl arriving at the dance with her new bloke and seeing me with Tina. Then it dawned on me. If it was straight up, no tricks, Cheryl's reaction would say it all. Either way I needed to tread carefully.

Wednesday morning, after breakfast, we were sweeping our bed spaces and tidying up as per every morning when Colin Masters came in. He was looking very pleased with himself. "Hey up lads," he called down the room. "It's good news bad news day. The good news is, when we get back from leave I get to wear these." He held up a shiny new set of Sergeant's stripes." We all cheered. There were stories going around all the time about NCO Boys getting too big for their boots and becoming very unpopular, but Colin was a great lad and I think we all felt he deserved it. "Bad news?" Asked Monkey.

Colin sighed heavily. "It's bloody awful actually Monkey." He pushed his stripes in his pocket. "Apparently poor old Chadwick's topped himself."

There was a stunned silence.

"Poor bastard," I said. "Do we know how?"

Colin grimaced. "I know you two got along, Mark, so you might not want the details. He sounds like a very complex guy."

"Balls to that, Masters, how did he die?"

He was found hanging in his dad's garage."

There were a few groans.

"That doesn't mean he was a complex bloke F'chrissake," I snapped. "Hanging is what a lot of suicides do. He wasn't complex he just marched to the beat of a different drum to you and me. Take that bit of it away and he was just a sweet guy."

"Steady on, Mark. Don't take it personally. I said he was complex for a reason."

I realised I was being over protective. "Sorry Colin, but I knew him better than anyone and he wasn't complex, that's all."

'I don't think you knew him as well as you thought, Mark"

"Eh. Why?"

Colin grimaced again. "He was wearing his mother's clothes and make- up."

"And just how do you know that?" I sneered. I was rattled again but I didn't care. "That sort of information isn't just chucked around."

"Go and see Flying Lieutenant Copperfield up in Admin. As you know he's an easy bloke to get hold of."

"Copperfield?"

"Yes, he's also the press officer. Nothing printed in the papers about this place gets by him."

"You mean it made the newspapers?"

"Just Chadwick's local."

I groaned. "Poor old Adrian."

But there was little or no time to dwell on Chadwick, suddenly It was like being back to the bad old days in ITS. Drill practice every day. It was always on the cards so there were no complaints and it wasn't going to be for long, but it was tough going.

We had to march onto the parade ground, do a full rifle drill routine and then suffer an inspection by the new CO before joining the other entries in the march past to salute him, this included the dreaded 'Eyes Right' as we passed the dais. Marching in close formation in a straight line while facing right was not as easy as it looks.

Then we had to march off the square behind the band. It all had to be exact: the timing, the positioning and the drill. Woe betide any boy who fucked up.

Part three: Love, Hate, and all those bits in between.

Chapter twenty

I finished my evening bull duties around nine that evening
and sauntered into the storeroom. I took three books from
my hold-all and lay them on the floor
I was strangely jealous when I heard people discussing
Chadwick as if they knew him. This room was where he
was special. In here we were together, and I felt as if I was
getting to know him.
 I read the titles as I lay them on the floor: 'Brighton
Rock', 'Ministry of Fear', and the book I'd just finished,
'Our Man in Havana'. All great books from Graham
Greene, an author I might never have read had it not been
for Adrian Chadwick.
I found myself thinking about that evening in the
classroom? Would it have mattered if I'd let him have his
way? If I'd given in, would it have changed anything?
Would he then not have been foolish on the train? And I
wondered what he wanted to do with me? Would it have
been that bad? Might I have, maybe, enjoyed it? I shook

myself out of the poderings and left the room. I couldn't change things now even if I wanted to.

Chas had an idea. At his request we arrived at the cinema with ample time to get ready before the doors opened, and quickly set up.

"Are you going to tell us what you're up to?" Jumbo asked impatiently. "Or is it a secret?"

"I'll do better than that. I'll show you." Ollie took us all to the side of the stage behind the curtain. His idea was for us to be out of sight during the time the audience were arriving.

"We're opening with that short instrumental version of Lucile, right?"

We nodded.

"Well, I start that great bent note what I hold for ages, yeah?"

Again, we nodded.

"Well, just to add a bit of show to things, I've worked out a killer of an intro."

Paul groaned. "No rehearsal?"

Chas shook his head. "No need. It's straightforward. Jumbo, you walk on stage and pick up the bass. You play through the intro, okay?"

"What, on my own."

"Yes, yes. That's the bit that gets the audience intrigued. Anyway, as you get to the end of the intro, Mark gets behind the drums and you play through the intro again. Just the two of you. Then same thing with Paul."

"So, the intro goes on forever." I said.

"No, well yes, well in a way. Then I come on and play the the long, haunting, bend and then we launch into the song."

Jumbo laughed. "You can't be serious?"

"Hey, don't knock it 'till we've tried it."

"I think it's a great idea," said Paul. "What d'ya reckon Mark?"

I shrugged. "Might as well give it a whirl."

There wasn't much room for a drum kit and three amps, so walking on without kicking something wasn't going to be that easy. We were supposed to do three numbers before the 'B' film and then four numbers after the 'B' film, before the main film. The amps would stay on the stage during the showing, but the drums had to be hurriedly carted off and on again.

"I haven't seen Carry on Constable," Jumbo said, tuning his bass. "Now I get to see it for free."

My nerves were jangling a bit as usual but, as if reading my thoughts, Chas came over and gave my earlobe a tweak. "Are we all fired up and ready to go?"

"As near as I'll ever be," I answered. I held out my shaking hands. "Is that what you call fired up?"

The doors opened, and the cinema began to fill.

"All tuned up and ready?" Chas called down to Paul and Jumbo. They gave the thumbs up. Chas checked his watch. "Five minutes."

As he spoke Flight Lieutenant Copperfield walked in front of the stage and smiled up at us. "Give us a good show boys. This is a first but I'm hoping not a last." He looked around at the audience. "Full house. Excellent."

The audience was a low hum of conversation when Jumbo stepped out from the curtains but by the time he'd reached his guitar and plugged in there was silence.

I joined him as he finished the first run-through of the intro and we played the intro again just as Chas wanted. Then Paul walked on and plugged in just in time to play through the third intro. It was going like clockwork, even Jumbo was smiling.

Then the big moment; on came Chas. He donned his shiny new Fender, lifted the guitar high in the air and hit the note that would break the spell and start the song.

Nothing.

We watched in amazement as the red-faced guitarist frantically plugged in his guitar lead.

The place erupted with laughter. Chas's face was glowing to match his guitar as he began playing. We quickly got into the flow again and once we'd regrouped and got back on track again the three numbers were perfection and we finished to great applause.

We went outside, and Flight Lieutenant Copperfield joined us. "Keep that up lads and I think we can look at something in the NAAFI perhaps." He wished us luck again and marched off.

"It's amazing," Chas said, watching him go. 'He's as keen as mustard as far as we're concerned."

Paul nodded. "He was pleased with the start." And we all laughed. I felt so sorry for Chas I tweaked his earlobe.

Chas smiled at me. "You gonna be okay with Walk Don't Run in the next set?"

I smiled. "Yeah," I said. "I do believe I am."

I hated winter, it was cold, it was wet, it was dark, and it was endless. By the time we get back from leave we would have been here a whole year. It had been a long, tough journey but, I think it's fair to say, seldom boring.

Ollie was more his old self again. Although he still hadn't managed to get out of his predicament with the mystery woman, being out of it until after Christmas was a good second best. He was constantly writing to Karen and she'd sent him a photo that I'd had to look at. And again, and again.

He was unsure about me and Tina. "You better be careful. This could be a set up of some kind," he said after I'd filled him in about the meeting in Llantwit. "She may have fallen out with Cheryl and wanted to make her jealous, or something like that."

"Do you think I haven't considered that?"

"Oh, right."

I ruffled his hair. "I'm not as green as I'm cabbage looking."

"No, fair enough."

"The thing now is, if Tina genuinely fancies me, then I have to ask, do I fancy her?"

Ollie laughed. "What's fancying her got to do it? Does she go is all you need to know?"

I shook my head. "You have to bring it down to sex, don't you?"

He shrugged. "Of course."

"Well, whatever way you look at it, it could be amusing," I said. "We'll see."

Come the weekend I felt strangely nervous. It was like stepping into the unknown. Andy Braithwaite, Geordie and Tommo were on the bus so if Tina was waiting at the bus stop the whole hut would know about it. Geordie was still seeing Avril and they seemed to be to be hitting it off well enough. Tommo's parents had sent him some birthday money and he was off to Barry to spend it.

My doubts about Tina were triggered when I got off the bus and she wasn't there. I pulled my collar up to my chin and decided I'd give it ten minutes and if she didn't show I'd go for a swift pint and then back to camp.

Ten minutes later, just as I was about to call it a day, I saw her hurrying up the street. "Sorry, Mark," she said, huffing and puffing from her hurried walk. "I had to take my little sister to her friend's house." She paused to catch her breath. "She's sleeping at her house this weekend." She bit her lip. "I bet you're freezing."

I shook my head. "No. I'm not freezing."

"No?"

"No, I'm bloody frozen."

At first, she thought I was serious, it showed in her expression, but then she saw me grinning. "Oh, you bugger," she laughed, and slapped my arm.

We set off walking and she linked her arm in mine.

"Where are we off to?" I asked.

"Nowhere in particular," she said, squeezing my arm. "A nice hot cup of tea somewhere to defrost you, and also to kill some time."

"Kill some time before what?"

"Well, my sister is at her friend's for the weekend and my parents are off to Cardiff for dad's firm's Christmas dinner and dance. They won't be back until very late." She smiled. "I thought we might watch a bit of telly."

"Good lord woman," I said, staring at her in mock horror. "Don't you know my reputation?"

She giggled. "Yes, I do."

As we walked on there was only one thing on my mind.

Her house came as a bit of a surprise. I imagined a nice, cosy two up, two down like Cheryl's sister's but Tina's house was a bit of a palace. "Stone me!" I said. "Just what does your dad do? Rob banks?"

She laughed. "Don't talk silly. Hand me your coat."

"But this place must be worth a bomb." I handed her my coat. "Should I take my shoes off."

Well, it's not essential, but you can if you feel more comfortable."

My stockinged feet sank into the lush hallway carpet. I couldn't stop myself from laughing, it felt so luxurious. The living room was enormous and when I sat on the settee I sank into it. "Your bloody settee is eating me," I joked.

We sat for a while talking about Cheryl. It was interesting hearing things from Tina's side. She was quite angry about Cheryl not being honest in her letters. As I had suspected Cheryl was lying about the meeting with the boys. "I know she said that Bazza joined us uninvited in the dance hall," she said. "But she was quite happy. She fancied him from the start. And all that rubbish about a quick kiss at the bus stop? Ha! They were almost eating each other."

Although it stung me to hear Tina saying these things it also helped me. It seems Cheryl wasn't the nice girl I'd thought she was.

It was getting dark by four and Tina got up and drew the curtains. "Which lights do you prefer?" she asked turning the living room lights on. "This one," she switched to a standard lamp. It gave off a subdued blueish glow." Or this one?" She smiled. "This one I think."

"Oh, yes," I said. "Much better. We'll be able to see the telly better."

"The telly?" She came and sat with me.

"Well isn't that what you said earlier?"

She frowned. 'Yes, I did."

"What do you want to watch then?" If this was a set up, I couldn't see how. She looked genuinely disappointed at the thought of just watching the box. I asked if she had a TV guide and she went to look. As she got to the magazine rack in the corner of the room I burst out laughing.

She turned like a shot. "You sod, Mark Draper." She didn't look too pleased.

"Sorry. But I couldn't resist it."

She came back to the settee. "Are you always like this?" I pulled her to me and kissed her. "No. Sometimes I'm like this," and I kissed her again. She slid her arms round my neck and whispered. "I heard you were a sexy kisser." She bit my neck gently. "And I think I agree."

Somehow, we managed to get laid out on the settee with her on top. We kissed for what seemed ages. Then she looked at me and pouted. "I also heard you were a breast man. What's wrong with mine?"

"Yours?" I smiled, "I'll just check." I unbuttoned her blouse. "From where I'm sat, there's nothing wrong at all." She giggled as I helped her out if her blouse and bra.

When I told myself this Tina lark could turn out to be amusing I never expected it to be *this* amusing.

Afterwards I decided to walk to the bus stop alone while Tina watched TV "There's no point in us both getting frozen," I said to her, collecting my coat. She laughed. "I'm not going to argue."

I kissed her briefly on the lips and I set off back to the bus stop. I had plenty to think about on my walk.

The bus was about to leave when Geordie came running up the street. He waved at the driver who stopped for him. He panted his gratitude to the driver and slumped down next to me. "Phew, that was close."

The conductor smiled as he took his fare. "They keep you lads fit up there." He handed Geordie his ticket. "Just as well, eh?"

Geordie watched him move on down the bus and shook his head. "Every one's a comedian." He unbuttoned his coat. "Bloody women!"

"Oh, like that, eh?"

"Avril wants me to get another blind date for Nerys." He nudged me. "How you fixed, bonny lad?"

"Right now, Geordie," I said, smiling. 'I'm fixed just nicely thank you."

He turned to look at me with a frown. "You pulled another one? You're a jammy bugger, Mark. You really are."

I laughed. "It's not a bad life is it?"

Monday morning, after an hour of square bashing, I got a message pinned to the notice board asking me to report to Flight Lieutenant Copperfield at six o'clock that evening. I shot round to the others and they all had the same message.

"What do you reckon he wants? I asked.

Chas shrugged. "You're guess is as good as mine. We'll just have to wait and see."

We walked down together, trying to guess what it could be for. Eventually Chas said. "You don't think we've got to pack it in, do you?"

We walked on in silence.

The only light on was his office. I was surprised to see he was not in uniform. He waved us into his office.

"Just a couple of minutes of your time if I may. Take a seat." He slid a newspaper across the desk. "The popular music presses top twenty,' he said. He had circled one of the entries. He tapped it with his pen. "Telstar. Have you heard it?"

We all nodded, "yes sir."

Chas frowned at the officer. "We can't do that, sir. It's nearly all keyboard."

"No, no, no. I just want you to tell me why it's the odd one out?"

We thought for a moment. "Well, I suppose being an instrumental," Jumbo began, but Flight Lieutenant Copperfield didn't wait for any more. "Exactly," he said. "The only non-vocal record in the charts."

I think we all saw where this was leading.

"You boys have amazed me with your progress. Every performance sees you moving up a notch. I was especially pleased to see you trying to incorporate a bit of showmanship. Yes, it went rather pear shaped but the idea was good, and you recovered exceptionally well. I'm simply impressed."

He sat back in his chair. "I love my job here. I get a thrill conducting the station band when they play a concert. We play several performances a year for local functions off base. Especially with the Barry and District Men's choir. Naturally we play several march tunes, but we also do arrangements of pop songs. Things people recognise." He lent forward. "We've never had our own pop group. I'm rather proud of you. Now, I know it's not for me to tell you what to play, but what would you think about finding a singer? Play some of the pop songs the audience recognise?"

We looked at each other as if waiting to see what the others three were thinking.

257

"We could advertise on the notice boards," he went on. "In not pushing this it's simply an idea I wanted you to consider."

Chas shrugged. "We don't need to advertise, sir. "Draper sings."

I stared at him in disbelief. "Oh, thank you for that, ex friend. And who's gonna drum?"

He smiled. "You of course."

"Don't talk wet. I can only just play the drums, never mind sing as well."

"You don't need to do anything except a steady snare drum beat until you get confident enough."

I groaned. "How simple you make it sound."

"Boys, boys, not now," the officer sighed. "Go away and talk about it. Perhaps just two songs for the dance Thursday would be a start."

"Thursday?" we all said as one.

"Right, no pressure here then lads," laughed Chas as we wondered back to the hut. "Its a simple task. We just have to come up with two songs for the dance Thursday, which means we've a whole two practice sessions to do it in."

"We don't *have* to," I reminded him. "He didn't make it an order, just a suggestion."

"Yeah, that's true, Mark, but it's obvious he sees us as his little project. He dropped a big enough hint about playing off camp." He looked round at Paul and Jumbo. "What d'ya reckon? Do you think it's worth a try?"

"It's not a problem for me," Jumbo said. "It has to be Mark's decision. He's the poor sod having to do it."

Chas nodded. "I suggest we try it and if it looks like being awkward we give it up straight away. No wasting time on it."

And that was that. Nothing more was said.

I struggled to think of the easiest songs to sing while drumming. I had to forget what Chas wanted it; had to be what I wanted.

Tuesday as we set up in the Band Hut ready to practise, we chatted about anything except the two songs.

Then Chas bent over his amp a fiddled with the controls for a minute or so and without turning asked me what I wanted to do.

"I've chosen two songs that I think aren't complicated. "Traveling light" by Cliff, and Lonnie Donegan's "It takes a Worried Man."

I looked at the other three.

After what seemed an age Chas shrugged. "Not keen on either, but, as we said, you've gotta sing them so it has to be your choice." He lit a cigarette and blew on the march. He was anything but pleased, I could see that "Do you know the words."

I smiled. "I've sung 'em loads of times. Mostly in the bath or in front of the bedroom mirror."

"So, you ready to give it a go?

"I've never sung into a mic before."

Jumbo smiled. "If that's all you're worried about we're laughing."

Chapter twenty one.

Thursday evening came around all too quickly for my liking. Having just about got free of my fear of playing drums on stage I now had to battle with the nerves as a singer. I kept telling myself not to be stupid. I'd sung for an audience before. Okay, maybe it was only the local church hall in a skiffle band, but an audience is still an audience. I'd chosen simple songs and that should help but my throat was still drying up and I couldn't even muster up any spit to swallow. I went to the bar and got a bottle of coke. I downed most of the stuff before I took a breath. What I didn't need was anything else to have to think about. So, when the girls arrived, and Cheryl marched straight up to me wearing a face like thunder, my heart sank. "What a childish sod you turn out to be."

I wasn't ready for this assault. "What?"

"What were you thinking? 'How can I get back at that bitch Cheryl? Oh, I know, I'll date her best friend'?"

It was coming at me force nine. I was simply not ready for it.

"Did you honestly think that was clever? Did you not think how stupid it made you look?"

I was aware of people all around staring. My head was clearing slightly, and I wondered where Tina was.

I pointed to the door. "Everyone's looking. Take this outside, please."

She wheeled away and made for the door. As I set off to follow I saw Tina standing and watching. "I think you should come, don't you?"

As soon as we got outside I jumped in quickly before Cheryl could start ranting again. "Why are you accusing me? It was Tina who asked me."

"Tina and I have been best friends right through school and never had a row and now your trying to set us apart. Some sort of petty revenge just because I dumped you."
I turned to Tina. "Just put her straight, will you?"
Tina looked at the floor and said nothing.
"Tina told me how she bumped into you in Barry and you were so upset and almost crying and how you pleaded with her to go out with her. She was so sorry for you she bought you a cup of tea and let you get it all out of your system before going back to camp."
I stared at Tina. "Oh, silly me. What a mug." Then I thought, okay Cheryl, you say I'm childish then, so I shall be. "In that case I have to ask where she bought this cup of tea?"
Cheryl just frowned.
"She never said about how she took me home then?"
"Don't start that rubbish.'
"Home to her luxurious house with the big settee and plush carpets. I suppose you've sunk into that soft settee many times."
That hit the target. Cheryl glared at her friend. "What?"
But I hadn't finished. "And Tina, just before I go back in, thanks for some great sex. I loved those panties you were wearing." I looked at Cheryl and smiled. Have you seen her panties with all the love hearts? Very pretty."
I left them looking at each in stunned silence.

I smiled to myself as I went to buy another coke. Of course, I hadn't screwed Tina, plenty of fooling around but no full-blown sex, but I figured Tina would have a hell of a job convincing Cheryl. The thing that was puzzling me was why had Tina said anything to Cheryl in the first place. Very strange. Sometimes girls could be weird.

We were just familiarising with the stage equipment when the band's vocalist tapped me on the shoulder. "I gather you're the vocalist?"

I turned. "Ask me after we've done our set."

He smiled. "Oh, like that is it?"

"It certainly is."

"I just wondered if you want echo and reverb or or just dry?"

He saw the blank expression on my face.

"Okay," he said and took the microphone from it's stand. He flicked a switch on the mic and did a check. "One two, one two, testing."

He handed me the mic. "Try it."

I did exactly as he did. He nodded and pressed a switch on the floor. "Try again."

I did as he asked but this time my voice came out of the speakers bathed in the echo effect he was talking about. It was like singing in the wash rooms only ten times sweeter. He took the mic back. "On or off?"

I grinned from ear to ear. "What do you think?"

Once I got started singing I was okay. The main struggle was playing the drums at the same time. Even just playing a straight snare drum, bass drum rhythm took all my concentration. But what made my night was that magic little floor switch. It made me sound so different it took away a good deal of the nerves.

We kicked off with an instrumental and followed it with 'It Takes a Worried Man' and, if I say so myself, apart from a slight hiccup when the two fizzy cokes I'd guzzled down caught me out mid sentence, it was rather good. I looked out at the surprised faces. Nobody had expected us to to do a vocal number. I saw Cheryl and Tina at the back of the

263

hall and they were looking more surprised than anyone. I wondered if they were talking to each other.

We closed with 'Traveling Light' and it went down a storm.

When I told Ollie the details of my conversation with Cheryl and Tina he seemed pleased. "Well played that man," he quipped. "I'd love to have heard what was said when you left them to it?"

I nodded. "Yeah, me too."

"The panties bit was the cruncher." He frowned. "Come to think of it; how did you know about them?"

"I tried to get down there but she pushed me away, but not before I caught a flash."

A couple of weeks before we were to go on leave it started. The first taste of a real winter. The chill, carried in the bitter wind, was fast becoming unbearable. The last drill rehearsals before the break were full-dress with gleaming brass buttons and white webbing, all painstakingly cleaned and polished, hidden below the heavy greatcoats. As it was, the wind blowing over the square was so bitter we had to wear our gloves and chin straps.

Then, on the Friday morning, the snow began. It looked like settling straight off and there were plenty of worried faces around the place. We were packed and ready to go and the thought of getting snowed-in was unthinkable.

The relief when the transport pulled up outside was almost audible. Yes, it was the usual lorries, but for once no one was complaining.

As it turned out the journey home was trouble free and the snow turned sporadic and much lighter.

My mum smiled when I got in. "Home again? Do you lot do any work?"

I kissed her on the cheek. "Now where have I heard that before?"

It was wonderful having the bedroom to myself. I'd forgotten about Ray not being there any more. I had a lie-in just for the hell of it.

Monday, on the first walk of the leave, I bumped into an old schoolmate.

I was walking along the cliff tops, just after lunch, on the way to Birchington, for no other reason than a walk. The snow was trying to get going without actually making it, although the forecast wasn't too promising. There was talk of a Siberian winter.

As I rounded Epple Bay I saw this face coming towards me smiling. "Who's this I see before me?" he said. "Could it be Mark Draper?"

I laughed. "Bloody hell. Gary Latimer. How's tricks?"

We shook hands. "I'm fine," he said. "How's the Airforce treating you?"

"Ah, well, there's a question."

He looked at his watch. "Listen Mark, I can't chat now I've got to pop into my sister's. She's got a problem with her boiler. What about meeting for lunch somewhere?"

I nodded. "How's the café in the square sound. It does sandwiches and stuff?"

He slapped me on the shoulders. "In an hour?"

"Fine with me. See you then."

Gary was the running star at school. He excelled in both sprints and distance and, if my memory was correct, he was never beaten at cross country running. He was very bright and at one time there was talk of him going to university, but I don't know what happened there.

He hurried in the café looking flustered. "Sorry, Mark. Have you been waiting long?"

"Hey, it don't bother me, Gary. I've got all the time in the world."

"Yeah, well, that may well be, but I hate keeping people waiting."

We played catch up: who did what, when and where. He told me that Billy Knox, from our class, had crashed his motorbike and was in a wheelchair. I couldn't stand the bloke but wouldn't wish that on the poor sod.

Then the conversation got rather amusing. I can't say how we got around to it but the subject of music arose.

"I'm in a band," he said. The Cool Cats." He grimaced." Yes, I know, it's a bit corny, but it's great fun."

I laughed, and Gary thought I was laughing at the name. "All right. It isn't that funny."

I shook my head. "No, I'm not laughing at that it's just that I'm in a band. Sky-High."

He sat back in his chair and smiled. "Wow, really? What do you play?"

"Drums."

"No! Well bugger me backwards. So, do I."

"Also, believe it or not," I said. "I'm the vocalist."

"Oh, blimey," he snorted. "Do you actually get bookings?"

"Ha, bloody ha. I'm not that bad."

"No, seriously though, Mark. How long are you home for, 'cause, we're playing at the Twenty-One Club this Thursday."

"Oh, say no more. I'll be there."

We chatted on for almost another hour and then, with a shake of the hand and a promise of being there Thursday, I said goodbye.

There's an old saying my mum always uses that says, 'pride cometh before a fall'. On Thursday evening, in the Twenty-One Club I found out just how true that could be. When The Cool Cats finished their first spot and disappeared back stage I joined them in the dressing room. I'd enjoyed the first spot only I found the vocalist, the bass player, a bit weak. Gary asked what I thought and, as if reading my mind, he said they were looking round for a vocalist. "Dave does a reasonable job, but he isn't keen."
"Gary says you're a vocalist, Mark?" The lad Dave said."
I nodded. "True. Not great but I manage."
"Do you fancy singing something with us?"
"What? Do you want to get thrown off the stage."
"No, seriously," he said.
Gary nodded. "Yeah, come on, Mark."
And so I said okay and after a while we agreed on a Johnny Cash song, Fulsom Prison Blues.
The Cool Cats went back on stage and I went to the bar. I needed a bit of Dutch courage. We'd agreed I'd sing at the end of the second spot.
The beer did the job. After a few pints I felt confident and when they beckoned me to join them I was ready.
After, in the dressing room, they were pleased with the way it went. Gary patted me on the back. "That was excellent, good on ya."
Dave agreed. "Spot on, Mark. Do you fancy doing another one in the last spot?"
After a few suggestions they asked if I knew Shaking All Over?

Why I said I knew the song I can't fathom. I suppose it was too much beer. Well, I don't suppose; I'm sure it was. Why had I got so bloody pissed? Why did I have to be such an arsehole? If ever I wanted to go back in time that was it.

When I woke the following day I felt awful. I knew I'd never ever get over that moment as long as I live. The look of horror on Gary's face when it became clear I didn't know the words, would be etched in my mind forever. I just hoped I didn't bump into him for the rest of my leave. I actually wanted to be back in camp. Once the guys realised I was making a total cow's arse of the song Dave pushed me away from the mic and took over.

With the end of the first week came the snow. The whole country seemed to come to a standstill. And it was cold. After two more days of the wind and snow I received a telegram. I'd never had one before.
"I hope it's not bad news," my mum said as I opened it. "Telegrams invariably are."
"No, mum," I said reading it for the second time. "Not bad news. We can't return to camp until further notice. It's snowed-in by the sound if it. My pay is in the post."
I went out to the phone box and rang Ollie. His mum answered, and I heard her call him. After a couple of minutes, I heard him picking up the receiver. "Hello?"
"Ollie it's me. I assume you've got a telegram?"
He said he had. He sounded down.
"Ollie," I said, "something wrong?"
"No, not wrong, I just got a letter this morning from you know who. She seems eager to talk and I don't like the sound of that. I thought we'd got thing's sorted until after

we get back." He sighed. "I could do without this extension really."

"No, I can imagine."

"Going by the forecast this is gonna be a with us for fair old while. Another fortnight at least."

"What about Karen? How's that going?"

"Oh, bloody hell, Draper, I'm so into this girl it's frightening and that's not helping the situation 'Cause I need to clear up all this other crap and get on with loving Karen."

That gave me a start. "Did you say love?

"I think it must be. She's all I think about. And now this bloody snow is holding things up."

"Let's hope it ain't too long then."

But it was over three weeks before it was decided we should make our way back. Under normal circumstances we would be only a few days from the completion of our first year and the Senior Entry should have graduated by that time. Naturally that was all on hold. I was interested to see how this would unfold.

I rang Ollie to check we were getting the same train from Kings Cross. We both had things to chat about, but the train was pretty full and our compartment was full by the time we left the station and so we just joined in the general discussions.

Once again, the transport waiting to take us up to camp was the three-ton lorries. As we trundled along the now familier road to St Athan, we looked around in amazement at the walls of snow. As far as the eye could see the landscape was a blanket of snow. I'd never seen anything like it before. In one way it was beautiful, in another, quite eerie. Either way, it was Mother Nature at her most awesome. And the forecast said more to come.

Ollie was clearly still worried and said nothing the whole trip up to camp.

Once we were settled in and all unpacked Ollie and me wandered over to the NAAFI. "I tell ya something, my old china, I think I'm paying the price for being a bad boy somewhere in my murky past." He managed a wan smile. "I don't remember being quite that bad though; I really don't."

We bought a coke between us and chalked our name up for a game of darts.

We were stood watching a group of lads playing darts when out of the blue Ollie leant over. "Her name's Gretchen."

"Oh, right," I mumbled. I couldn't think of anything else to say.

After a short while I handed him the coke. "You could be worrying about nothing, my mate. You don't know."

He smiled. "That's why you're a good mate."

"What just 'cause I try and cheer you up?"

"No. Cause sometimes you talk fuckin' daft."

Chapter Twenty Two

When a week Friday was announced for the new Station
Commanders welcome parade we were told that practicing
our rifle drill and marching would be a priority which

didn't go down well at all. We were learning our trades now and, as far as we were concerned that should be more important than drill.

Ollie rang Gretchen at work as soon as he got a chance. She was still insisting they meet to discuss things. He had no problem with meeting her at the weekend but, he warned her, he couldn't guarantee being there. Any sign of snow and we weren't allowed to go off camp because of the possibility of us not getting back.
It was so cold come the weekend that I was happy staying in doing a bit of swatting or reading but Ollie had other plans. "I'd like you to come with me this afternoon," he said.
I frowned. "She won't like that."
"You can come with me to Barry and wait for me in the pub. I can't see me being very long."
"I dunno, Ollie," I said. "The weather is bloody freezing and I ..."
"Fuck of Draper," he snapped. "I'm not asking much. I just want my best mate to keep me company." He ran his fingers through his hair and sighed heavily. "The truth is, Draper, I'm shitting bricks. I have a bad feeling about this and I could use a bit of moral support. F'chrissake I'm not asking for the world."
I felt like a total shit. "Yeah, fair enough, mate. Sorry. Of course, I'll go."

Chas had come in Thursday evening as I was drying my hair. "Copperfield's getting excited about the weather. He's been in touch."
I smiled. "He's excited about the weather? How weird is that."

"What he's thinking is, with more snow on the way soon, we're bound to get snowed in again sometime. That means a lot of bored lads."

"Ah, I get what's coming: the NAAFI?"

"Exactly. So, how are you fixed for Sunday?"

"Okay."

He went for my ear, but I was ready and knocked his hand away. "Will you stop that!" I said. "It's weird."

He smiled. "Just think of a few songs you want to sing, and we can get cracking on a program to keep the troops happy."

"*And* Flight Lieutenant Copperfield."

"Of course. Most important."

He turned to leave but stopped in the doorway. "You do know what Copperfield is hankering after, don't you?"

I frowned. "No, what?"

"He hinted when he told us how much he enjoyed taking the station band out on civilian gigs."

"What, and you think we're destined to be playing for the Barry choir?"

"No," he said. "I think more like hospitals or what-have-you." He winked. "We'll see."

It was touch and go as to whether we'd get away on Saturday. There was a showing of snow as we came back from lunch but luckily by the time we signed out it was looking quite clear.

I was the only one who knew where Ollie's girl worked, and I'd been in a couple of times for a coffee and tried to guess which waitress it was.

Ollie stood in the doorway quickly checking to see if any of the lads were in and, having satisfied himself it was all clear, he nodded to me and went in. I carried on to the pub.

It was less than half an hour later that he came crashing in to the bar blowing into his bare hands and grumbling. The guy behind the bar glared at him. "Next time you come into my pub can you manage it in a more civilised fashion and maybe open the door before you come through it."

"Fair do's, landlord," Ollie said. "My apologies."

I smiled to myself as I recalled a cold day in Cardiff Station buffet and a cheeky young Londoner crashing into the room grumbling.

It was a year ago almost to the day.

He came over with his beer to where I was sat and slumped into his chair. He found his cigarettes and lit up. He didn't look too bright. Gone was the cheeky twinkle in his eye. The face I saw before me now looked drawn and tired.

He took a long swig of beer. "Oh, I needed that. Cheers Draper."

We sat in silence for some time.

"Well?" I asked, eventually.

"Yeah," he said quietly. "What's happening?" He drew on his cigarette and blew the smoke to one side. "Well, Draper, it could be worse. I don't know how, but it could be, I'm sure. The main problem is, as we rather feared, she's pregnant."

He saw the shocked expression on my face. Even though it was always a possibility I was still stunned. "No!"

"Oh yes, and before you ask, it has to be mine."

"Why?"

The reason they have a fruitless marriage is because he can't produce enough of the old baby juice. They'd had all the tests, so it couldn't be his, so it has to be mine."

"Stone me Ollie. Didn't you use a Johnny?"

274

"Of course, I did," he said, but quickly added. "Well, most of the time.

She says she's never going to consider getting rid, so that's out.

Her idea is for her not to say anything to the old man until she can't hide it any more then she'll tell him she's leaving him. She says she can happily wait six months for me to graduate and then we can move in together and she'll get a divorce." He drained his glass and offered to buy another.

I shook my head. "Not for me thanks."

He belched quietly. 'No, you're probably right."

"So, you're getting hitched?"

"No fucking way, Draper. I told her I'd do my best to help out financially, but I had no intention of marrying anyone for a long while yet. Then I got the old, "don't you love me?" shite, and I thought it time to be straight with her. So, I was. Then she was going to all weepy on me in the bloody kitchen with all the staff in and out."

"Kitchen?"

"Yeah, the kitchen in the coffee bar. Anyway, she was just about holding on."

"So?" I asked. "Now what?"

"I don't know what to think. She asked me to give it more time. She wants me to call her Thursday."

I sighed. "Again? You've been down that road before. Does she expect you to change your mind after all you'd said?"

"Oh, Draper, you don't understand her. Yes, she does. She really believes that somehow, I'm gonna give in. She followed me all the way out to the street asking me to think about the fun we have together and asking me not to make my decision so quickly. I told her people were watching but it made no difference."

The last thing she said was that she loved me, and she believed I loved her and she was thrilled to be carrying my baby."

"What ya gonna do?" I asked, finishing my beer.

"I dunno. Ring her Thursday, I suppose. Tell her nothing's changed and wait to get beaten up by her old man in some dark alley I imagine. He's big enough." He stared into his empty glass and went quiet. I left him alone. Suddenly, he put his head in his hands. "Oh Christ, Draper," he groaned. "What the fuck *am* I gonna do?"

I felt guilty Sunday afternoon as we set up in the Band Hut. Normally I'd have hated leaving Ollie like that, but the fact is I was beginning to get fed up with it. He always set off to straighten things out with this Gretchen woman and never seemed to have the balls to do it. Now he has to ring her again, as if that was going to change anything. I certainly wouldn't be holding my breath.

Besides, I was feeling good about my life now. Seeing Cheryl and Tina at the dance had opened my eyes and shown me a Cheryl I didn't recognise. I hadn't just finished with a lovely, kind and caring, young girl. The girl I was putting on a pedestal never existed; I just thought I knew her. The Cheryl I'd just finished with was a spiteful little bitch and I had no regrets at all.

My drumming was improving all the time, my vocals had gone down well at the dance and, at long last, I felt part of the band. Not just part of the band but, now I was the vocalist as well, an important part of the band.

My mum was happier now than she had been for years and we were moving rapidly toward the day when we would no longer be Boy Entrants. Things seemed to be coming together nicely.

I had written down some songs from my skiffle days and a couple of pop songs. Being as 'Fulsom Prison Blues' went down so well with the Cool Cats I included that. I thought it best not to try 'Shaking all Over'.

When everyone was tuned up and ready to go Chas looked at my list. "Oh, Mark. You can't do these old skiffle songs. Nobody plays that shite anymore." He glanced at the list again. "Ah, what's this? Fulsom Prison? That's better. We'll start with that.

He counted it in and off we went. Chas's country finger picking was brilliant, he was in his element.

But, then, half way through the second verse, I noticed jumbo looking at Chas and shaking his head.

They stopped playing. "Mark, your dragging it again," he said.

I nodded. "Fear not," and went into the equipment room and returned with the metronome. I pulled up a chair and positioned the timer where I could see it. "Try again."

We set off again. After a while Jumbo smiled and shouted. "That's better."

We ran through it a couple more times and soon had it working a treat.

It was decided that we'd stick to simple songs that I knew well and Chas, after a bit of pressure from Jumbo, agreed to include 'It Takes a Worried Man' and 'Tom Dooley'. 'Traveling Light' was included being as that went down well at the dance and then, I chose a Marty Wilde number 'Bad Boy'.

By the time we started breaking the gear down we had the makings of a set for an evening entertaining the troops in the NAAFI.

Wednesday morning Sergeant Sharpe set up a blackboard in the freezing cold hanger and ran through the parade plan using the blackboard and chalk markings on the floor.

Sergeant Boy Masters would have us outside the huts and ready by nine-forty where he would run through a quick inspection. Then Corporal Evans would arrive at nine forty-five to march us down to the parade area where we would form up to one side of the hanger.

Then, just before ten, Corporal Evans would hand us over to Sergeant Sharpe who would march us to the front of the hanger where the band will be ready to march us to the inspection dais. Here we would do our rifle drill.

"I appreciate it's not ideal after all the time you've put in on this parade outside, but it's what it is, and we have to make the best of it. So, do me proud, do yourselves proud and let's make it a roaring success."

We replied with a full-throated RIG-A-DIG-DlG!" and then we were marched back to the warmth of the hut.

That lunchtime Ollie got a letter. He looked rather surprised as his name was called out and he looked at me and shrugged. "A letter for me. What about that?" He took it to his bed and opened it. I watched as he read it. First, he frowned. "It's from Karen." Then a hint of a smile. Then a big cheesy grin. He chuckled quietly as he read and came over to my bed. "Here," he said handing me the letter. "Read this." He leaned close to me. "But say nothing. Nothing, okay. Or mate or no mate I'll jump all over you." He was deadly serious.

I nodded. "Okay, hold ya hat on.' I began to read.

I'm so very thrilled to know
Your coming home for sure.

I'm counting hours until you're here
And in my arms once more.

My love for you is like a spell
I'm dizzy but I'm fine
I know it's LOVE it feels so right
I'm thrilled to know your mine.

When you're not here I'm incomplete
You are my very being
You're all I need to make me whole
The thought of you is thrilling.
Hurry home now my love I'm waiting. Xxxxx

I frowned. "What's she on about coming home?" He put
his hand over my mouth. "Say nothing," he hissed.
He signalled me out of the hut and into the corridor.
"I was going to tell you tonight." He shrugged. "I've
applied to buy myself out."
"When?"
"I've already got the green light."
"Well thanks a fuckin' bundle," I moaned. "You said fuck
all about this."
"I had my reason."
"Yeah, you don't think I can be trusted,"
He put his hand on my shoulder. "No, Draper, it's not
that."
"Well, What then?"
"I know you'd try and make me change my mind."
"So, you're running away."
He grunted. "I wouldn't say that, but I suppose you're
right. Look, give me a break here Draper." He half smiled.
"This is special, I'm sure of it. I'm in love and Karen's all

I can think of. I can't let Gretchen fuck this up. It's times like now I need a best mate. Don't let me down."

I was devastated. "I just think you could have told me if no one else," I said sulkily."

He nodded. "I'm sorry."

"Yeah, so am I," I snapped, and I stormed back into the hut.

Thursday evening, Ollie made his way to the phone. As he left the hut he looked back and managed a wan smile. I nodded. I hadn't stayed angry at him for long, he had enough shit to be dealing with without me adding to it. Despite what I'd thought about him not telling me about his discharge, seeing Ollie like this was still heartbreaking. I'd always thought him as damage proof. He was riddled with guilt.

Waiting for his return was awful. It dragged by so slowly. When he eventually came back into the room his face told me things were probably as bad as he'd feared. He flopped onto his bed, looked over at me, and dragged his finger across his throat.

I went over and sat on the foot of his bed. He shrugged. "What can I say? She reckons she's gonna have to tell her old man. I suppose it was always gonna happen, but I've tried not to think about it." He gave me a wan smile. "I guess I'm gonna have to steer clear of dark alleys."

He lay gazing at the ceiling in silence. Then he shook his head slowly. "It's a crappy marriage, but it's still a marriage, and I hate knowing that I was the one who fucked it up."

We sat in silence. There was nothing more to be said.

The hut next morning was a hive of activity. Buttons, that had been polished only the night before were quickly polished again, even though they were hidden. Boots, at least, would be on view

Last minute ironing of trousers was followed by a vigorous session with a clothesbrush. Boys queued to get a last look in the full-length mirror. I was ready in plenty of time which was not the case with Ollie. He seemed totally detached from all the hustle and bustle.

I went over to him. "Do you want anything doing? Trousers need ironing? Boots need a quick polish?"

He shook his head. "Nah, I'm okay cheers."

"If you say so my mate," I said. "But keep your eye on the time."

We formed up outside the huts and Masters gave us a quick inspection.

It was freezing cold and threatening snow.

Nine forty-five came and went. Minutes ticked by and the cold breeze was making light of our heavy greatcoats.

"Come on, come on," said Geordie in a hushed voice.

"This is a bloody good start."

Masters looked at his watch. "Right lads pay attention. He called us to attention.

"Squad, running on the spot. Running on the spot begin."

We were only too pleased. It was a clever idea by Masters and I think we all appreciated it.

Just before ten, Sergeant Sharpe came rushing into view. He looked flustered to say the least. "Right, listen here," he said, somewhat breathless. "We've hit a snag, but we should be okay now. He quickly called us to attention. And then, instead of marching to the hanger we were given the order to double.

We arrived at the side of the hanger, puffing and panting from our exertions and the air above our heads was one, long condensed vapour cloud.

Sergeant Sharpe left us for a moment as he went to consult with the Parade Officer.

As they chatted an RAF Jeep cam careering round the back road, weaving all over the place and finally crashing against the high paving. The door flew open from the impact and the driver poured out. It was Corporal Evans. He was wearing pyjamas under a greatcoat and unlaced boots. He pulled himself to his feet using the Jeep's open door.

There was a stunned silence and then Tommo laughed. "He's as pissed as a fart."

Sergeant Sharpe stared in disbelief. He ran towards the drunken Corporal. "Clive, what the hell are you doing?"

At that moment an RAF Police Redcap came hurtling over the square in a police Jeep. He skidded to a halt and jumped from the vehicle. "Corporal Evans," he called marching briskly towards him. "Stand away from that vehicle please."

The drunken NCO leant into the Jeep and emerged holding a Lee Enfield 303 rifle. The Redcap froze. "Now come on Corporal, he said. "Be sensible." He began walking again, cautiously this time, his eye firmly on the rifle. "Hand me the weapon please."

Corporal Evans raised the rifle and fired a round in the air. The Redcap and Sergeant Sharpe fell to the ground as one.

We remained on parade. A squad of teenage boys staring at a dishevelled drunken man, shuffling towards them carrying a loaded weapon.

Then he saw the object of his attention. "Wilson," he bawled. "I can see you, you bastard. You little shit!" He wiped tears from his cheeks. All eyes. turned to Ollie; faces full of bewilderment.

Then I realised what this was all about.

"Jesus Ollie!" I hissed through clenched teeth. "Not Evans? You daft twat! What the hell were you thinking of?" It was a bitterly cold day and yet a bead of sweat ran down my back.

Corporal Evans stopped "What was it Wilson, not enough girls your age to choose from so you've got to move in on married women?" He raised the rifle and aimed at Ollie. A shot rang out across the square and the air above us crackled as the bullet passed overhead.

An officer ran out of the hanger followed by two Sergeants, but quickly weighing up the situation they disappeared back inside.

"There is one of life's angels left in tatters thanks to you and your filthy lust," the Corporal sneered. "She deserves better than that." He fired again and stumbled slightly from the recoil.

"Run!" a voice yelled out from somewhere behind me. "Run!"

Suddenly there was pandemonium. Boys ran in all directions some heading for the hanger others heading anywhere off the square and others running just anywhere. Geordie tripped on a discarded rifle and fell heavily. I followed Tommo heading for the hanger.

After only a few yards I looked back and to my horror Ollie wasn't with us. He remained, alone, at attention. I called out to him to run but it was clear he was rooted firmly to the spot.

Every fibre of my body screamed for me to keep running away, but the sight of my best friend waiting to be shot was too much to bear. I turned and ran back, shouting to him all the time.

Corporal Evans raised the weapon and fired again. The impact as the bullet hit me was like someone scything me down with a metal bar. I left the floor for a fleeting moment and then crashed down just behind Ollie.

"Are you happy now Wilson? Now that you've torn my world apart?" The Corporal wiped the tears away again. "How do feel now, eh? Now that you've got your little friend shot? Not so pleased with yourself, I imagine. Look at him Wilson, just look at him crying out in pain. And all the time he knows it's your fault."

I reached out for Ollie's trouser leg hoping to pull him out of his trance, but the pain suddenly kicked in and I yelled out in shock. The pain was becoming unbearable, and I found myself looking down at my thigh and moaning. It was torn open and bleeding everywhere.

Ollie," I yelled through gritted teeth. "Think of Karen waiting for you. Run!"

My yell had somehow shaken Ollie out of his trance. He turned and grabbed my hand, trying to get me to my feet, but the pain was so much I just wanted to be left on the ground. I yelled for him to stop but he kept pulling. Somehow, he got me up on one knee, but before he could do any more the rifle in Corporal Evans' hand jumped wildly and Ollie spun round with blood gushing from his shoulder. He crashed on top of me. I called out in pain and pushed him away. To my amazement he pulled himself up on to his knees and reached out for me.

"How are we doing Wilson?" The Corporal jeered. "How's it feel? Not the big ace now eh?"

Ollie knelt clutching his shoulder for a moment and then tried to get me up again. Realising it was hopeless he looked at me and gave me a resigned smile. "Sorry Mark."

"This is for Gretchen." Corporal Evans was sobbing as he spoke. "This is for all the times you've taken advantage of my wife and then sat in your hut bragging to everybody about what it was like. Am I wrong Wilson?" He fired off another round, the noise making my whole being being jump. "You think it makes you better than me? You talking about Gretchen? *My* Gretchen," he yelled, sending out a spray of spittle. "You think she prefers a little shit like you to me?" Eh? Is that what you think? You're a coward, Wilson. A dirty little coward picking on…." his voice trailed off and he wiped a long stream of snot away with the back of his hand.

"You've totally ruined the life of a caring, loving woman." His face contorted with rage. "You've wrecked *my* life, you cocky little bastard," he snarled. "You won't be ruining any more lives."

He took aim and fired.

Ollie's head jerked wildly one side and shattered everywhere. I seemed to forget my pain for a brief moment as I found myself staring at the mess that had been my friend. The back of his head was just a hole.

Then I realised the gun was aimed straight me. "Don't think for one moment that I don't know you were his big buddy. You knew all about this Draper," he growled.

I brushed my fingers down my cheek and stared at the bits of Ollie. I can't remember exactly what I felt as I looked down at the sticky, grey mess, my pain was far too fierce. Then I waited for the bullet.

One moment the Corporal was squeezing the trigger, the next he was sent flying sideways and crashed to the ground with Bonner on top of him. I watched in amazement as the big Irishman wrestled the powerful NCO to the ground and struggled to get the rifle from his grip. He held him down hard on the ground and kicked the butt of the gun several times until it spun free from the Corporal's grip.
He grunted loudly as he tried to hold him down. The NCO was thrashing about wildly underneath Bonner and trying to reach the rifle. I yelled out to Bonner as the Corporal's hand got near. Bonner gave one more mighty effort and kicked the weapon again.
There was a loud report as the weapon fired again, then silence.
The first thing to be heard was a strange gurgling sound and I looked over to see the Corporal with blood pumping from his throat. I watched Bonner get slowly to his feet and then the pain was too much, and I began drifting in and out of a faint. The last thing I remember was thinking about all the hard work we'd put in rehearsing the band, now wasted.

Epilogue

RAF Binbrook. I'd come from a windswept Welsh valley to an even windier North Lincolnshire hilltop.

Apart from the normal Arrivals forms, I'd been handed a note by the Station Adjutant. I was summoned to the Station Commander's office and I decided that should be my first port of call.

I walked along the shiny corridor to the CO's office. On the left-hand side of the door was a name slot with the title: Group Captain G D Morrison. I knocked and was called in.

The Station Commander was a total caricature of the RAF type, with a thick moustache, waxed and rolled at the ends and sucking on a, seemingly, empty pipe.

I put my arrival slips on his desk. "L A C Draper sir. I was told to report to you on arrival."

"Draper, ah yes, of course. Take a seat Draper." His cut glass accent matched perfectly with his appearance.

He sat back in his chair with his fingertips together and pursed his lips. "I see you were given the choice of a free discharge or finish your schooling at Saint Athan."

I nodded. "Yes sir."

"Well I'm pleased you decided to stay with us. I suppose it was a bit strange joining a totally different bunch of chaps so near to graduating?"

"Very much so, sir, yes. The biggest problem came watching the lads from the band graduating. We had so many plans."

"Band?" He frowned. "Ah, right, of course, Flight Lieutenant Copperfield's pop group."

"Yes sir. We were just getting going when …." I couldn't think of a how to put it.

There was a silence and he got up from his desk and stared out of the window. "And the injury? How's that now? I gather you weren't too long hospitalised?"

"Not long at all sir. It was the physiotherapy that took forever."

"I see. Well, the reason I've asked you to report to me is to give you an assurance with regard to your unusual circumstance. You probably aren't aware of this, but the name Mark Draper is well known here. You're in danger of being something of a celebrity for a while.

I understand you've had a hard time dealing with the loss of a good friend, and I have been fully briefed regarding the circumstances of that unfortunate day. And so Draper, that's why I'm a little concerned. I don't want this awful experience to mar your chances of settling down to a normal life here on the squadron. But I have no doubt that the first few days or so are going to be a anything but normal."

He stood. "That is why I say to you now, if you have any problems at all, no matter how trivial, my door is always open. So, all that remains is to welcome you to Binbrook and hope you enjoy life here with us."

He offered his hand and smiled. "You'll be just fine. I'm sure if it."

When I left the Admin Offices a Canberra was coming in to land and I stopped and watched.

"Not a pretty plane is it?"

"Pardon."

Walking up to me was a young airman around my age.

"The Canberra. Ugly old thing." He glanced down at the Arrivals Chits in my hand. "So, you just arriving then?"

"S'right."

"Posted to the Canberras?"

I nodded. "Yup."

He held out his hand. "Welcome aboard. I'm Larry Travis."

I shook his hand. "Mark. Mark Draper."

His eyes lit up. "Mark Draper as in the graduation day shooting?"

I nodded.

"Wow, I heard a rumour you we were posted here."

"You did?"

289

He beamed. "Yeah. You're a bit of a legend. That's all everyone talked about last winter. You and a bloke called Bonner. Hero's under fire. You're gonna have to tell us all about it."

"Yeah, well, I suppose so."

As Larry Travis went his own way I felt a sense of gloom. I inhaled heavily and shook my head, the last thing I wanted now was to talk about Ollie. I missed the old lad so much.

I made my way to my last port of call, in the Station Warrant Officer's office, then crossed the parade ground. I tried not to think about that day, but it was almost impossible. I stopped and looked around me. It was a cold, empty square with no features apart from the usual flagpole and dais; no ghosts to be seen here, but all the same, a shiver ran through me and I heard Ollie's last words: "Sorry Mark." The one time he called me by my first name.

I needed to get off the square and I set off walking briskly. I absentmindedly brushed my cheek with my fingers. It seems there was a ghost after all.

Printed in Poland
by Amazon Fulfillment
Poland Sp. z o.o., Wrocław